Readers love the Sylvan stories by JAN IRVING

Sylvan

"*Sylvan* is a sweet, realistic story of the burdens we carry and how love can lighten them... I really enjoyed the slow pace of the relationship in Sylvan, and the likeable, and believable, characters."

—Joyfully Reviewed

Luke

"The characters drew me in immediately and I didn't want the tale to end... The plot moves well, rife with emotion and plot twists. I couldn't put it down."

—Whipped Cream Reviews

"This is a sweet tale of two men who help each other when they need it most... a great book to introduce a person to m/m fiction."

—The Romance Studio

"*Luke* is almost an 'innocent' novella, it has the feeling of an old fashioned serial romance with the added bonus of the modern gay romance twist."

—Elisa's Ramblings

Nathaniel

Night Owl Reviews Top Pick

"Nathaniel and Aaron's story is both sweet and sexy. It's the perfect antidote for a cold winter's night or if you need a perfect pick-me-up."

—Night Owl Reviews

"*Nathaniel* is a sweet story of finding love when and where you least expect it. Ms. Irving penned a great story that you will want to read again and again."

—TRS Reviews

By Jan Irving

Mask
Mastering Toby • Sahara Blue
The Pleasure Slave
The Summer Gardener
Sylvan • Luke • Nathaniel • Sylvan (Author Anthology)
Wishing on a Blue Star (Dreamspinner Anthology)
Wylde • Born to Be Wylde

Published by Dreamspinner Press
www.dreamspinnerpress.com

Sylvan

Jan Irving

REAMSPINNER
PRESS

Published by

DREAMSPINNER PRESS

5032 Capital Circle SW, Suite 2, PMB# 279, Tallahassee, FL 32305-7886 USA
www.dreamspinnerpress.com

Sylvan
© 2016 Jan Irving.

Cover Art
© 2016 DWS Photography.
cerberuspic@gmail.com
Cover design by Paul Richmond.
Cover content is for illustrative purposes only and any person depicted on the cover is a model.

ISBN: 978-1-63477-602-8
Digital ISBN: 978-1-63477-603-5
Library of Congress Control Number: 2016911386
Published August 2016
v. 1.0

Printed in the United States of America
∞
This paper meets the requirements of
ANSI/NISO Z39.48-1992 (Permanence of Paper).

For Nana and Aunt Poppy and a wonderful weekend at the lakeside.
And for my mom, who taught me about unconditional love
and also brought me to Sylvan.

Table of Contents

Sylvan

The best portion of a good man's life is the little, nameless, unremembered acts of kindness and love.
—William Wordsworth

Prologue

HEART POUNDING, Mal Harrison stood outside Coach Mather's office door. He licked his lips, looking at Mather's secretary. She flicked him a grim look, and his gut twisted.

He'd just finished his latest swim meet, and although he was being mentally tough and fighting off negative thoughts—something every athlete who made it to the Olympics had to learn how to do—the frustration he'd been living with was rising like smoke from a growing fire. He trained hard, very hard. He was focused. So why had he come in third again?

He went over the event in his head, seeing his turns were still his weakness despite the way he worked out over and over again to improve them. Maybe Coach Mather wanted to cover that with him again? Mal swallowed thickly, hoping that was the case.

After a moment Mather's secretary nodded to him stiffly. "You can go in, Mr. Harrison."

Mal nodded, taking a deep breath the way he did before an event with stiff competition. He reminded himself of everything he'd accomplished in some very tough years. Everything he'd sacrificed. How discreet he tried to be about how hard he partied when he wasn't working out all the time—he knew it stemmed from his frustration. And finally he reminded himself in the duffel in his hotel room was an Olympic gold medal for the backstroke.

But that didn't stop him from smoothing his still-water-slick hair back from his face before he reached for the doorknob; something told him when he walked over this threshold again, everything would be different.

COACH MATHER leaned back from his desk, his steel-gray gaze on Mal. He ran a hand over his jaw and then cleared his throat, saying the words Mal dreaded: "You're off the team, Harrison. I'm… sorry."

Mal's face stiffened like a pale, sweating mask as he held the coach's uncompromising gaze.

6

He knew this was it. He was officially washed up at age twenty-three. He wouldn't be competing for Olympic gold in two years in the butterfly and backstroke events.

"Coach, if it's about coming in third today...." Mal leaned forward. He held on to his dignity with his fingernails, taking another deep gulp of air and fighting tears. He couldn't stop pushing now, even knowing it was useless.

"It's about coming in third for almost a year, Mal," Coach Mather said flatly. "I'm really sorry, son. You push hard—maybe too hard. Lately I don't feel like you have the passion for it anymore, so believe it or not, this may be the best thing for you—a fresh start. What will you do now?"

Mal swallowed, fighting the need to throw up. He rubbed his stomach through his T-shirt, feeling sweat prickle his underarms and his upper lip.

"Go home, I guess," he said, his voice echoing dully in the coach's office. "Hey, good news is at least I don't have to shave my body hair anymore," he quipped weakly.

A second too late, he asked himself why he'd said something that inane. Fighting the swell of emotions that felt like seawater right up to his neck, Mal stared blankly at the wall as the coach gave him a few suggestions on what he might do next. Teach, for one. He was an invaluable asset—just not to his team.

Or he could start a business. A sporting store or club. A lot of former athletes did that. Or there was always school.

He had the rest of his life to figure it out. He was really a lucky man, not a washed-up ex-swimmer.

Right, lucky.

And the words echoed mockingly because Mal felt completely blank: *the rest of his life.*

ALONE IN his room later, Mal sat on the bed, a page from his grandmother Nan's latest letter in his hand. He squeezed his eyes shut for a moment, not wanting to cry. He'd have to call her. He'd let her down.

But when he looked at her letter again, he reread something she'd written: "More and more you don't sound happy to me, Mal. Are you sure this is truly what you want to do? I have a feeling if you just came home, you'd find what it is you are looking for...."

Nan had pressed him to think about the bigger picture of his life more than once, but Mal had blown her off. He shifted so he was sitting with his back to the headboard of his bed, looking out at the cold, winking lights of New York City that never seemed to go out.

At least he could still go back to Nan and to Sylvan, the little farm town he was so desperate to escape as a teen.

He lifted the gold medal out of his duffel, fingering the disc as he remembered winning it at a very young age. Maybe he wasn't as successful as his other teammates, but he had this.

After a moment he reached for his phone. Nan had always accepted him. She knew who he was, and unlike him, she didn't struggle with the fact he was gay. He knew she'd take this in stride also, welcome him home. Back under her roof and with her loving support, he'd somehow figure out what to do.

The line rang a long time, and then Jed Morris, Nan's nearest neighbor, answered. Weird, Mal thought. Why was he—?

"Mal, that you?" Jed asked, though he had surely recognized Mal's voice.

"Yeah, is everything all right? I want to speak to Nan," Mal said, his belly knotting up again, though this time, he wasn't sure why.

"Mal." Jed's voice was heavy. "Son, I have some bad news...."

THE TRUCK driver who gave him a ride let Mal off on an unpaved road. Mal got out, stiff from sitting for so long, and banged on the cab in thanks, then watched the rig pick up speed, leaving him. He felt very small standing in the shadow of the bleached wooden grain elevators. They towered like sentinels over the yellow-and-green-striped fields that stretched out like a carpet all the way to the purple foothills.

He put his duffel over his shoulder and pushed back his black hair from his eyes before he started walking. He was probably two miles away from Sylvan Lake and Nan's cottage by the water.

Wearing jeans so worn they were white and a pair of his old cowboy boots he'd dug out of his storage locker, Mal walked past some fenced-in grazing cows. A curious calf trotted close, watching his shadow as it passed by at a laconic pace.

The hot July sun, the huge bowl sky—everything was home, even the choking dust that rose in the wake of a car that passed him, going much too fast on the country road.

Just ahead Mal saw someone dart into the center of the road, and the speeding vehicle swerved, music blaring.

8

"Shit!" Mal dropped his duffel and sprinted ahead, seeing with disgust the unknown driver hadn't even stopped, just picked up more speed. Couldn't be from around here, that was for damn sure.

He knelt next to an old man with gray hair in his eyes who had fallen in the center of the road, panting. His elbows and hands were raw and scraped from the tumble he'd taken to avoid the car. When Mal's shadow fell on him, blocking the hot yellow ball of sun, he blinked up at Mal through dazed eyes.

"Hey, mister," Mal said gently. He reached out and took the elderly man's arm. "Are you all right? You might want to move off the road."

"Road?" the man asked, looking around, obviously confused. Had he hit his head somehow? "You tricked me, didn't you?"

Mal shook his head, helping the old boy climb to his feet and then guiding him to the sandy side of the road. "No, I didn't trick you. Uh, are you alone out here, mister?"

"I don't know...." The man sounded abruptly frightened, and Mal's throat tightened in sympathy. Lately everything hurt. Everything got to him where he lived.

"Don't worry, I'll help you," he said.

"Oh, here's Leif!" The elderly man pointed to a tall man running toward them on the dirt road, his hair flashing silver. As he got closer, Mal could see it was silver-blond, not gray. He must have been about six four, wearing a blue work shirt plastered to a muscled chest, and jeans as well as work boots. He was also deeply tanned, with crow's feet at the corner of his pale eyes.

"Papa!" he huffed, taking the older man's arm and pulling him away from Mal. "What are you doing? You said you'd wait for me in the truck."

Mal stuck his hands in his pockets, caught by the interplay between the pair. "He nearly got run over," he told the stranger.

Cool-gray eyes pinned Mal with a look, and Mal felt his chest constrict. Whoa.

"You nearly hit my papa?" the man growled.

Mal put up his hands. "No, sir, I helped pick him up off the center of the road. He's scraped up some."

"Oh, Papa." The younger man put his arm around his father, examining his bleeding hands.

"Leif, let's go now," the elderly man urged. "You know I don't like you talking to strangers."

"Yes, Papa, I know," Leif replied, shoving his hair back. He gave Mal a searching look, hesitating a moment as their gazes locked a little too long. Finally he muttered, "Thanks."

Leif's voice dismissed him despite the high-octane look they exchanged. Mal shook his head, sure he must have imagined the weird chemistry. He put his hands on his hips and watched as the two men walked down a long driveway until they disappeared under a strip of arching birch trees.

"You're welcome," Mal said wryly before heading back to retrieve his duffel. It was a long walk into town, so he'd better get on with it.

Chapter One

"GREAT. I was right about you. You're cute," a rough voice growled in disgust.

Mal choked, and half the lake seemed to come up. His head was pounding—not an unfamiliar feeling, unfortunately, over the past few nights—and he was chilled, his swimsuit sticking to his soaking body. He heaved again, the water lodged in his throat bringing that primal fear: *Can't breathe, can't breathe*.... But then someone gripped his neck with a warm, callused hand and stroked his hair where it was plastered to his neck.

"Easy," the voice coached. "Take it easy, and it'll pass."

"Where am I?" Mal instinctively asked. "Dreaming?" Catching a glimpse of those eyes that had haunted him since his dusty roadside arrival, Mal had to wonder.

"Did you hit your head?" The voice was impatient now.

"No." Okay, not a dream. Mal blinked, taking a moment to absorb his surroundings. He'd been swimming... and drinking... and here he was in a boat with the Viking he had met the same day he hit town.

Sylvan Lake was serene, the light on the water seeming to have a poignant feeling to Mal, or maybe he just felt that way while out here in the middle of the lake, in the middle of the night.

How often had he looked at that light with his Nan? They'd walk the beach, especially after a storm, and gather driftwood and shells to line up on the windowsills of the cottage. As she got older, she didn't come for that walk as often, so Mal drifted the night alone.

Like tonight. Only he hadn't planned to half kill himself.

As the spasms eased, Mal was able to take in more details: he was dripping water on the bottom of a worn wooden dinghy. The hand touching him felt warm while he shivered. After he finished puking up lake water, a woolen lumberjack's coat was wrapped around his back while the dinghy rocked back and forth in reaction, but it was a sturdy craft, like its owner, so it didn't tip.

He blinked his wet eyelashes and looked up finally, his cheeks heating in humiliation. But then his eyes widened. "It's you," he said. "And you're definitely not cute." What the man was, was handsome. And then he wanted to take it back. How could he say something so dumb? He wanted to groan. Coach Mather had told him again and again to watch his mouth. The silver-blond Viking Mal had fantasized about since he'd returned to Sylvan raised a brow. "No, I'm not cute," he said coldly, his gray eyes suddenly the color of lake ice, where Mal had sworn at first glimpse they seemed like July moonlight, gentle on Sylvan Lake's easy, rippling water.

Mal swallowed. "Shit, I'm sorry." He was crying, shuddering, pathetic. He hoped his rescuer would assume it was the lake water running down his cheeks as he wrapped his arms around himself.

"No worries; it's nothing I haven't heard before. So, beauty, where do I row you?"

Mal took a deep breath. He guessed he had no choice but to go home to Nan's. Only it wasn't Nan's anymore. The cabin belonged to him alone now. "Nan Carter's place," he directed. Beauty…. He guessed the man was alluding to *Beauty and the Beast*. Great, his stupid comment had probably offended the guy.

Leif raised his pale-ash brows at Mal's words. They were as silvery as his hair, Mal noticed, and they suited his large-boned Nordic appearance. He was a Viking dressed in jeans and a blue T-shirt, leaning forward so his massive muscled chest rested against propped-up oars.

"So since you pulled me out of the lake, do you want to share your full name?" Mal asked lightly, trying to drum up some of the charm he was known for in some circles. "Your father called you Leif."

"Just Leif," he said, looking at Mal like he was a piece of lake debris he'd picked up in his dinghy. Apparently Mal's charm wasn't scoring any points. But after his comment about his rescuer not being cute….

"Oh." Mal blinked, making a sudden connection. "You're the carpenter who moved into the Driscol place on the other side of the lake."

Leif gave a cautious nod. His skin was deeply tanned, so it appeared dusky under the moonlight, highlighting those squint lines beside his gray eyes Mal personally found rugged and appealing, as if Leif spent a lot of time out of doors.

"I remember you now. You're the kid who is an Olympic swimmer."

"I'm not a kid," Mal noted, irritated. Leif looked to be about thirty. He wasn't *that* much older than Mal's twenty-three, even if his face and eyes seemed to possess a wealth of sad experience. "And I'm also not on the team. Not anymore." It still hurt to say it, but not as much as being in Nan's cabin for the first time in more than a year without her in it. It drove him into her cooking brandy, and then, in an even stupider move, into the water. He was lucky Leif had fished him out, or he probably would have drowned.

"Too bad," Leif said. He didn't look remotely sympathetic.

So much for the chemistry that had seemed to brew between them previously. What was the guy's problem? It was as if he didn't want Mal anywhere near him.

Mal's jaw hardened, and he turned away, facing the bow as Leif rowed them serenely and with unhurried strokes toward Nan's pier.

WHAT WAS Leif supposed to say to someone like Mal? He didn't know, so of course he insulted him. But how could he help it when Mal made it clear how he didn't find Leif attractive? Of course it was for the best, Leif told himself firmly.

Yet Leif couldn't help but admire Mal as his oars stretched, dripping musically, the late-night wind hushing over the foaming water of their passage.

He tried to get out and go rowing every night so he could escape the cabin he shared with his father. Sometimes he just sat idle in the dinghy, oars suspended, the big prairie moon over the lake, the planted willows dripping leaves into the water, and he felt a peace he needed after a long day's work... and taking care of Papa.

He sighed since he'd have liked to linger in taking Mal home. He'd like to stare at Mal's midnight hair, drying now, and catch his striking blue eyes under heavy lids.

Mal Harrison had a sensual face like a merman, and like a sea creature, Leif had pulled him from the water. In some strange way, Leif felt as if that made Mal his.

What would it be like, to possess a merman? Leif was aware there were Norse tales of creatures from the sea who could be tricked into living among humans, but only at a price... and always, always they found their way back to the ocean, abandoning anyone fool enough to love them.

His papa told him such tales when he was very young. He'd always wanted to rewrite them for a more practical—and therefore satisfactory—ending. Not a "happy" ending, because that was trite. Just more satisfactory.

He thought if he ever possessed a merman of his own, he'd damned well find a way to lure the creature back to him.

It was late, and he was tired. That was the only reason for his fanciful thoughts. But he enjoyed the view of Mal's muscular back, his rounded athlete's arms. Mal had made it clear he found Leif unappealing, but there wasn't any harm in looking at what he could never touch.

WHEN THEY approached the sagging dock, Mal flushed at its obvious deterioration. He knew from rumors in the small town of Sylvan, a summer resort and year-round farm town, Leif had to be Leif Gunnar of Gunnar Construction, a local company that specialized in repairing and maintaining a lot of the older cottages that surrounded the lakeside here, as well as some of the farmhouses and barns in the area.

"I… uh, didn't get back last fall," Mal said, shrugging, shoulders tight. "So the dock stayed out all winter."

The shallow lake froze every season, so the older docks had to be dismantled and stored in a boathouse over the winter so the ice didn't distort and crack the dock fixings. Nan always managed it on her own, wearing a swimsuit in the late-fall lake, detaching each part of the dock piece by piece and dragging it up the beach.

"I offered to do it for her," Leif surprised Mal by admitting. "But even though she was almost ninety, your grandmother was a stubborn woman. She said she'd do it herself."

Mal nodded, feeling regret pang him. "I was training, as usual." And partying, which was something he'd turned to more and more, dissatisfaction eating at his gut, though he had no clue why. Whatever the reason, Mal knew it contributed to making years of work crumble like the wood of this dock. "I… should have come home."

He took the lumberjack jacket off, immediately shivering as he handed it silently to Leif, but the big man only shook his shaggy silver-blond head. "Keep it for now. Leave it for me in the diner in town. I'll get it there."

"Thanks," Mal said, taking back the warm wool. He took a minute to hold Leif's gaze, seeing something there in the steady look he sensed on their first meeting: attraction. "Do you want to come in for cocoa?" Cocoa was something the old-time cottagers drank at night in place of coffee, since most were up with the dawn. Mal had never thought about it before, but maybe it had to do with how the cabins were originally built by farm families in the area. He grew up drinking Nan's milky cocoa, kept warm in vintage 1960s green mugs over the woodstove.

Leif sat back, oars resting in the water as he considered. "I have to get back…."

Mal gave a one-sided shrug as he hid his disappointment. "Sure."

14

"I hadn't heard you were planning on staying at Nan's place for the summer," Leif commented.

"I... just ended up hanging around," Mal admitted. "I don't have anywhere else to be right now."

"Rough staying here since your grandmother passed away?"

Mal's throat tightened. Why was it that here, at the only home he'd ever known, people seemed able to arrive so easily at the heart of things? He nodded.

"I wouldn't mind coming up for a bit," Leif said, and Mal knew it was because Leif had guessed this was not an easy homecoming for him—as if he needed another clue after dragging Mal's sodden, half-baked ass out of the middle of the lake.

"Okay." The dock wobbled a little, but Mal had found the middle was fairly sturdy. He crawled up from the dinghy and then took Leif's tossed rope, securing his boat. Leif followed him, the deck wobbling even more precariously at the man's greater weight. When he stood up, he loomed over Mal. Leif put his hand on the small of Mal's back as they gingerly made their way to the beach and the path through the wild roses to the old highway that bisected people's waterfront properties on this part of the lake. They both paused, but there was no traffic, so they hurried across.

That hand on his back burned through the lumberjack's coat.

Abruptly Mal wanted to take Leif into his body, pull him into the trees, and fuck with him like a captive with his untamed Viking.... Sheesh! He told himself to be patient. Leif had accepted his invitation. Mal would get what he wanted.

MAL GAVE him a strange, sizzling look that made Leif warm up as they walked past the bunkhouse Leif had constructed for Nan at the back of her property a few years ago. She'd hoped Mal would come home and bring some of his friends for the summer, but it never happened that Leif had heard. Now Mal was probably feeling the regret of not coming home more often.

The cottage was charming, maybe built around the 1920s. There was still an outhouse in the hedge-screened front yard. They walked up creaking front stairs, and Mal opened the screen door, inviting Leif inside.

He switched on the lights, and nothing happened.

"Fuck."

"No worries," Leif said, used to older cottages. The wiring sometimes suffered from being old and having weathered a lot of storms. "Have you got a lamp?"

It was dark and close inside the kitchen. He listened as Mal opened a drawer, rooting around, and then a moment later, lit an oil lamp. The light was even more flattering on Mal's sleepy features than the moonlight had been, and that was saying something.

Leif opened the vintage fridge and pulled out some milk while Mal pulled out a tin of old-fashioned cocoa and some sugar to sweeten it. Two green mugs in hand, he moved with Mal into the dining room, where the woodstove sat. Mal opened it up and put a match to the newspaper balled inside, along with slivers of kindling and a chunk of fresh log.

Leif knew he had to get home soon, but even as he saw it was almost 4:00 a.m., he wanted to stay and watch Mal make him cocoa. That was the real treat.

Mal's hair was as dark as the wings on a crow, and silky looking. Leif could imagine feathering it through his big, callused fingers. Mal's eyes were a startling, brilliant blue in contrast.

But before they could drink their warming cocoa, Mal surprised him. He discarded the jacket Leif had lent him and hooked a thumb under his swimming trunks, tugging them down and off in one heart-pounding movement.

The moonlight and soft glow of the lamp were very revealing, as was Mal's body. He stared into Leif's eyes, and then he climbed on Leif's lap, and Leif found himself grabbing hold of lake-water-cooled ass.

"What are you doing...?"

"Come on...," Mal whispered in Leif's ear before he nipped it.

Leif was panting, and he betrayed himself for a moment, smoothing his hands down Mal's firm skin, but then he took a deep breath and gently lifted Mal off his lap and stood up. He was conscious the moonlight must be revealing his own condition as well.

"I have to go now," he said.

"What?" Mal laughed.

"Home. I have to go home. Papa might wake up, miss me—"

Mal shook his head, moving forward like the siren Leif had pulled from the water, winding his arms around Leif's neck. He rubbed his hardness wantonly against Leif, making him burn.

"Leif, really? You need to go home to your papa? I've heard some excuses, but...."

"It's not an excuse." Something in his tone must have hit Mal. He stopped his distracting play with Leif's earlobe.

"It won't take long, baby."

"You said I wasn't cute," Leif said, disengaging Mal's arms.

"Who cares what I said?" Mal said. He had his hands on his hips now, blue eyes narrowed and flashing annoyance. "Look, you like what you see. Let's just—"

"That's not how it's done," Leif said primly, picking up his jacket. He tried not to look at Mal.

"Not how it's done?" Mal's voice rose in disbelief. "What the fuck are you talking about? Do you need some fricking roses before you get it on? Dinner? Christ, we're men!"

"Good night," Leif said, opening the screen door. He clattered down the three steps, looking over his shoulder once to glimpse frustration in Mal's eyes. "I'm sorry for your loss," he called.

Chapter Two

MAL WOKE up with a pounding head. He squinted at the sunshine coming in through the patterned curtains in the great room… which meant he'd slept in one of the rocking chairs by the stone fireplace.

He scrubbed his jaw, yawning, but then memories of last night flashed like a movie in front of his eyes, and he groaned. "Geez, Harrison," he scolded himself.

First he got drunk and went swimming alone, which was pretty much the stupidest thing he could do, and then he made a play for the Viking who fished him out of the water. The guy hadn't even been hot… or had he? Mal remembered the way Leif held his gaze. He swallowed, feeling sweat break out on his upper lip.

Since he had nothing better to do, no one to talk to, Mal spent a few minutes staring at bits of dust drifting in the sunlight. No, Leif was the definition of manly-man handsome, but his silver-blond hair looked like it would feel nice to the touch. And he had a gentle air about him that Mal had found attractive. It made Mal want to scratch his back and make him wild….

He shook his head. Clearly all those years in the big, bad city had changed Mal since it was obvious from his prim refusal last night that Leif expected… what? Flowers and chocolates before they fucked?

Mal made a frustrated sound. He'd wanted sex. He'd wanted to get it on and burn away the too-quiet atmosphere of this empty cabin. He wanted to forget he was alone now, that he had no one.

He dropped his head back and scratched his unshaven jaw, putting his bare feet up on Nan's coffee table, something she would have tsked at him for doing. He wished she were around to do it.

Well, what now? It was the question he had been ducking since he had no answers. He'd spent most of his life training for the gold, but that was over now, possibly because he'd lost his drive somehow. So he'd basically fucked up the first part of his life.

What now?

LEIF TOOK a sip of the sweet tea Mrs. Watson had made, sitting down in the wooden garden chair outside the cabin he'd rebuilt with his father—now two stories with lots of windows. He liked to look at it, a log cabin with stone chimneys that towered over the roof, made by a special Italian mason back in the 1950s. Leif had had to bring in an expert to help shore up the old stonework when he remodeled their home, restoring and winterizing it.

His papa was toying with his food, clearly still unhappy with him. "I didn't know where you were," Leif's papa fretted, lips downturned. "I didn't mean to cause trouble."

Tension made Leif's shoulders tight, so he rolled his neck. He had to get back to the Anderson place soon and make sure progress was happening with the trades he had working there today, the plumber and the electrician. They were taking out a lot of the old wiring and working on new pipes to the cottage so it could be used in the wintertime.

"No, I know that, Papa. It's fine."

"The firefighters didn't mind coming around," Papa noted. "I made them tea and gave them some of Mrs. Watson's cakes."

Leif bit his lip since he knew the volunteers, all locals who had properties around the lake, were good sports. They all knew Leif's father wasn't all there, so they looked out for the old man. Before his illness the older man also had a lot of friends in Sylvan. Still, it was embarrassing to come back from his unsettling encounter with the gorgeous Mal Harrison to a bunch of guys sitting on his front lawn since his papa was afraid he'd gone swimming and drowned.

What to do? Give up his night rowing? But it was one of the few times he had to himself. Or maybe it was time to find someone to move in— possibly Mrs. Watson, who was calm and capable—so someone was always on hand when unexpected anxiety struck his father.

He didn't like that idea either. It had always been him and his father living together, and despite the heavier and heavier burden lately, they got along tolerably. Leif didn't know if he wanted anyone else under their roof. It would mean his papa would never again be the man he was.

But he wouldn't, Leif knew, and there wasn't a damned thing he could do about it.

He rubbed his chin, unsure how much longer he could leave Papa alone at all, even when he went to work.

Leif sighed. The biggest problem wasn't work. What he didn't have anymore was time to himself when he wasn't working a job. It made it hard to, say, drive past a certain new resident's cabin and ask if he'd like to go with Leif to the diner for meatloaf.

"What do you do out there, Leif?" Papa asked him again, eating some apple crisp made by Mrs. Watson.

How to explain that when he went rowing, he looked up at the stars and wondered if he'd always be alone? It sounded pretty lame. But mostly he just liked letting the little boat coast over the water, rowing past other cottages, familiar patches of wetland, even the local mission church, which had beautiful windows that were lit up the nights they held choir practice.

And then there was last night, the night he pulled the man of his dreams from the water. Mal Harrison. Electric blue eyes, black inky hair. Muscular but slim, built for speed like running and swimming. He had a bit of a reputation as a bad boy, but....

Leif could have stared at Mal all night, as entranced as he was by the view from the water as he went rowing. Mal was mouthy, tough... sad. Probably that's why last night happened. Heat burned Leif's cheeks as he thought of Mal's unsubtle offer. He'd wanted.... Oh, the feel of Mal on his lap!

Leif closed his eyes, willing himself to forget Mal's body against his own. He'd already relived it in the shower, twice, and had been late to his first job this morning.

"I just like a little time on my own, Papa," he admitted, hoping his father would be reasonable. Sometimes it worked....

"Well, I *don't*," Leif's father countered querulously. "I don't like it when you go anywhere!"

And Leif pushed aside his own dessert, his appetite gone.

A TOWEL wrapped around him from a dip in the lake, which had been a substitute for a morning shower, Mal took a deep breath as he confronted Nan's closed bedroom door.

Normally he'd sleep in the rooms off the great room, but there was some kind of leak in the roof, so he'd had to strip away and toss all the bedding, leaving the old-fashioned bare-spring mattresses.

Since he'd come back, finding his old truck still parked in the sand driveway and bringing his duffel inside, he hadn't been ready to open this door. Maybe he still wasn't right then. Maybe there was more cooking brandy....

Hesitating, Mal relived seeing Leif's startled gray eyes when he rebuffed Mal's offer the night before. Shit, look where drinking got him. He had to try to get a handle on his life, whatever it was now that he was back here in Sylvan. Resolved, he put his hand on the knob and opened the door.

Apple-green curtains sewn by Nan's wrinkled hands rippled at the open window, letting in warm sunshine. The bed was made, spotted with more fresh green, and the round table with its matching tablecloth displayed pictures of Mal. Like him, she hadn't had anyone else since Mal's parents were long gone after dumping Mal on her doorstep when he was two years old. There'd just been the two of them.

Grief caught Mal's throat and tears stung his eyes as he walked over to her rocking chair and sat in it, rocking, looking out at the empty patch of grass and hedge beyond her window.

"I wish you were here," he whispered.

LEIF BLINKED in surprise as Mal Harrison drove up in his battered vehicle, blue eyes fixed on Leif's face through the windshield, dark hair windblown from the open window. Leif had been walking out to his work SUV, getting ready to head back to the job, but now he paused, waiting, his heart pounding.

He cleared his throat, conscious that behind him his father and Mrs. Watson were still sitting in the garden and had a clear view of his visitor.

Mal climbed out of his truck, closing the door and running the palms of his hands over the back of his jeans, as if they were damp. Was he nervous? He had been so astonishingly cocky the night before.

He saw the memory of what had happened between them move in Mal's eyes, but then Mal was standing next to him, a hand on Leif's Toyota Highlander.

"Hey," he said.

"Hey back," Leif replied.

Mal ran a finger over the dust on Leif's dark-blue SUV. For some reason the movement struck Leif as coy, as if Mal were touching *him*, and he swallowed thickly, reddening.

"So I have a leak in my cabin," Mal said, looking up to meet Leif's quizzical gaze. "It's over the loft, and I'm worried if I leave it, it's going to get a hell of a lot worse."

"Yes?" Did Mal want to hire him? And what would it be like to work for Mal, to be around him and the temptation he offered? Would he offer himself again?

Feeling himself sweating in the hot July sunshine, Leif cleared his throat again.

"I can't afford to get someone to do all the work, and… I also don't really have any kind of job." Mal laughed without humor, flushing as he kicked up some of the sandy dust with his cowboy boots. "I thought maybe… I could learn how to fix it myself if someone with experience were to point me in the right direction."

So he did want Leif's help. But since this wasn't Mal sitting on his lap, all cool, bare, silky skin, Leif felt a bit more confident. This is what he did, after all. "I could come by and give you an estimate on what you need to do," he said. "Maybe after I finish work today."

Mal nodded, swallowing, as if he really were nervous. "I, uh, was also wondering if you had any openings. You know, for someone to help out with your crew?"

Leif shook his head. "I usually deal with experienced tradespeople. I had an apprentice for a while, but he went to work in the city."

Mal nodded, his gaze falling. "Yeah, I figured." He shrugged.

"But…." Leif took a deep breath, considering his words carefully as usual, and shit, Mal probably thought he was such a country hick. "I could probably use someone for odd jobs."

Mal looked up, and his eyes were the color of the sky when it began to lighten at dawn. "Yeah?"

"You'll need proper work boots and gloves," Leif outlined. "But you can find what you need at the general store in town."

"Yeah, I guess they cater to the working man," Mal joked.

"That's what you find out here, yes," Leif said lightly. He wondered how long Mal would stick around this time. From what Nan let drop, he liked to party in the city. Sylvan might as well be the dark side of the moon, if that was Mal's thing.

"I like a working man," Mal said, his tone a little flirtatious, but then he seemed to realize what he'd said, and he flushed. "Sorry," he added, moving his gaze toward Leif's father and Mrs. Watson, sitting in Leif's garden. They were watching the pair talking with interest.

"I will come by your place around four," Leif promised.

Mal nodded, stepping back from Leif's SUV and putting his hands in his pockets as he watched Leif climb inside. "Okay, thanks."

Chapter Three

TRYING TO demonstrate he knew something of the unwritten rules of cottage hospitality when hosting a visitor, Mal put out a plate of cheese and crackers and two glasses of Ribena juice—he figured it probably wouldn't be a good idea to offer beer after Leif had fished him out of the lake.

He wanted to make a good fourth impression on his new boss. And... he wanted to understand what Leif meant when he stated Mal's come-on was not "how it was done." How did the Viking get it on? Mal found himself more than a little curious about that.

He paced by Nan's window out into the garden, and so saw a strange sight—a cowboy got out of his truck with a baby in his arms, and then put the baby down on the grass across the road before taking a horse out. He walked the horse back and forth in the field adjacent to Mal's cottage while talking to the baby.

Feeling rather charmed, Mal watched until the cowboy spotted his audience and then ducked his head self-consciously before putting his horse back in a trailer that had seen better days and taking the baby with him back into the cab of the truck.

For some reason the little vignette relaxed Mal. He might be alone right now, but he had known family. He had been loved. He had that memory to take with him going forward, to give him strength.

Nan, like that unknown cowboy, was willing to do anything to keep him, even raising a boy she knew she would not live to see much beyond his twenties. She'd made up for that with the quality of her love, making every day count.

And from observing Leif, he knew the other man also honored love, honored his family.

Maybe he'd find something he'd lost, coming back to Sylvan. Something not found in flashing lights and alcohol and what his stats were that day at a swim meet.

Mal sighed. If only he knew who he was without all that.

LEIF HAD a few misgivings as he slammed the driver's side door in Mal's driveway. He rubbed the back of his neck, still stiff from his unproductive conversation with Papa and the work he'd supervised and participated in—the drywall guy hadn't shown up, so Leif had ended up installing some sheets once the wiring and new foam insulation were properly finished. He'd have to do some more plastering and sanding to prep it for paint, but hopefully his man would show on the job tomorrow so he could simply help out with the painting.

He hesitated in Mal's yard, taking in the outhouse in one discreet corner of the front yard. It looked like Nan never installed running water to the house. Probably Mal had to walk with a bucket over to the shared well at the dusty crossroads.

Mal was looking at him from one of the dining-room windows off the kitchen. Mal gave a hesitant wave, biting his full bottom lip. He was still the enticing siren Leif had pulled from the lake, but somehow Leif had to resist him.

He didn't have time in his life for a merman, no matter how much he wished it might be different.

"HEY, THANKS for coming," Mal greeted him as he pushed open the screen door.

Leif nodded politely, his throat tight as he entered the cabin, conscious of the kitchen and dining room where Mal had stripped off his clothing and offered himself. Would he ever forget that gut-wrenching sight? In the shower he'd replayed it over and over again, the touch of Mal's skin, his solid weight on Leif's lap, his breath against Leif's lips.

Mal gestured to the food and beverages waiting, and used to this familiar ritual, Leif smiled in thanks and sat down on one of the painted benches that ran along one side of the dining table. It was covered with one of those plastic tablecloths with flower prints so it was easy to wipe up. Leif recognized it as Nan's touch. The whole cottage still seemed so much like it had when she had served him cake and coffee that he expected to see her.

If he could feel her presence, it couldn't be easy for Mal, her grandson. Leif studied him, seeing the shadows under his eyes despite the rosiness of a new tan. He wasn't sleeping well.

"It's not wine," Mal said, giving a self-conscious little laugh, as if he were aware Leif might think he was drinking again. "It's juice."

Leif lifted the glass to his lips, taking a sip. "Nice," he said, thanking his host. He was ill at ease, but he wanted to help Mal relax. How did he do that?

Mal shrugged, a rueful look in his eyes. "I can be civilized sometimes. Nan did try."

"You're lucky you had her," Leif said, sincere. Despite all the work he knew needed to be done in this cottage, it was a home full of the memory of living and love. He could feel it and see it in all the country knickknacks and quirky framed needlepoint works hanging in the room. Off to one side was a vintage sewing machine, some pieces of fabric slotted to the side as if Nan were still working on a project.

"I didn't treat her as well as I should have," Mal reflected, his face darkening. "I avoided coming home the last two years."

"Avoided?" Leif raised his brows, not hiding his curiosity about this man he found dangerously enticing.

Mal grimaced. "She knew I was gay. I almost think she knew before I did… and I think she worried for me since she didn't want me to have a hard time, but when I first joined the team, I tried—I didn't want to be who I am. I slept around with a lot of women."

"Oh. Yes, I'd heard that you had a reputation as a party boy."

"I bet the whole town heard." Mal shook his head. "I didn't want to face that, that I might have shamed her. And… after a while, I wasn't sleeping around with women, but with all the hot men I could find. Kind of… bingeing."

"Mmmm."

Mal skewered Leif with a look. "I doubt you know what I mean."

"No, I don't," Leif agreed, coloring.

"I didn't think so. You seem kind of… innocent." Now Leif could feel Mal's curiosity about him. "Despite the fact you're older than I am."

Leif took a sip of his juice, giving himself a moment. "I believe in romance."

"Romance," Mal repeated, saying the word as if he found it a foreign concept, but then from his experience, it must be. "Really."

Leif looked at him with dignity. He would not be made to be ashamed of what he wanted, what he was waiting for, or who he was. "Yes."

Mal gave an odd-sounding laugh. "So that's why you pushed me away? Because I, uh, jumped the gun?"

"It would probably not have been very nice," Leif said primly. He felt heat rising in his cheeks anew.

"Oh, I disagree," Mal said with another laugh, but he looked a little pissed off as well, as if Leif had trod on his pride. "It would have been very 'nice.' Know what I would have done?"

Leif swallowed thickly.

"Dropped down on my knees, opened your jeans, and sucked your cock. And I give un-bee-lieveable head."

Leif lifted a hand. "White flag."

Mal's eyes softened. "You're very old-fashioned, huh?"

Leif nodded, feeling a bit relieved Mal was turning down the heat. He was only human. "I really want to meet one special person, someone who will be with me the rest of my life. But you were... very hot, Mal. I've thought about little else," he found himself admitting as he dropped his gaze to the plate of cheese and crackers.

"I'm glad it wasn't because I smelled bad or something."

Mal looked appeased, which made Leif a little sorry for him. Was his skill in giving head all he felt he had to offer someone? But he kept that thought to himself as he bit into a cracker.

"Does your father know you're gay?" Mal asked, helping himself to some cheddar.

Leif shook his head. "It never really came up before my father fell ill, and now I'm afraid it would confuse him, so I don't talk about it. Besides, I don't have a boyfriend."

"*Yet*," Mal said. And then he looked as if he wasn't sure what he meant by that provocative word. He cleared his throat. "So do you want to see my roof? I think it's how the bats are getting in."

Leif relaxed, feeling the sweat on the back of his neck from sitting so close to bewildering and gorgeous Mal. "They do that," he said.

THEY BROUGHT in a ladder from the open storage place below the cottage. It was kind of a shed that ran half the length, built into the slope. Thin wooden boards separated it from the outside, so it would not provide any insulation in the harsh winter months, but then, this was strictly a summer cabin, Leif noted. Mal's grandmother must have spent most of the winter close to her fireplace and woodstove, just like in the old days. Leif remembered the times he'd come by to shovel out her driveway. He and his team did it for a lot of the seniors in the area in case they needed emergency services. But he didn't mention this to Mal now since he knew it would only make him feel worse about his absence from Nan's life.

Mal spotted him under the ladder after they maneuvered it up the stairs to the patio off the great room, through the narrow door, and then past the curtained gap that led to the small sleeping loft and two bedroom spaces. Once up on the ladder, Leif touched the rift he could see easily. Blue sky actually shone inside the space through the holes.

"Looks like a storm maybe took off some of the roofing," he noted. "The wood underneath isn't very sturdy. You're lucky you didn't wind up with a heap of melting snow in here. Must have been one of the spring windstorms."

Mal nodded. "Storms out here sound like the end of the world. I remember," he said with feeling. "Sometimes Nan and I would put pillows in the windows so they wouldn't shatter, and one year all the boats out on the lake wound up in the trees."

"Yep." Leif hesitated on the ladder, mulling over what had to be bad news to the new cottager. "Mal, you really should replace the whole roof, and that's not something an amateur is going to have much luck with. You could maybe help out, but to do a job like this…."

"Nan saved for years, so I have a nest egg, but I want to be careful with it," Mal said. "It's all I have." He moved back as Leif climbed down the ladder. The two of them were standing very close together now, but Mal did not move back. Instead he lifted his chin, holding Leif's eyes. "I'd like to make some improvements, bring running water in, build a shower, and make it possible to live here year-round in comfort."

"Year-round?" Leif was startled. "Don't you plan on going back to the city life?"

Mal furrowed his brows. "No. What for?"

"Uh, I just assumed…."

"For more threesomes?" Mal poked. "Been there, done that. Times a hundred."

Leif rubbed the back of his neck, blushing. "I didn't mean to offend you."

"I bet the whole town thinks I'm just… a party boy. After all I fucked up my chance to make the cut again for the Olympics."

"I think people were disappointed you didn't make it that far. It would have been something for folks around here," Leif corrected gently. "But you already won a gold medal, which is something most people never attain." Mal was so defensive, but it was obvious it hurt him to be seen in a bad light. He was far more vulnerable than Leif had expected of someone who had spent years away in the heart of everything.

"I fucked up somehow, maybe pushed myself too hard." Mal sighed. "I can't take it back."

"We all make mistakes. And even when we don't, we still have to live with some things that are hard." Leif thought of his papa. The love was always there. He hadn't stopped loving his father when he was diagnosed with Alzheimer's.

Mal studied Leif with shadowed eyes, as if he could see what he was thinking. They both had shit. "So what do I do about my roof?"

Leif backed away slightly since he was so close to Mal he was afraid he might reach and touch the tangled black hair, feel the cool silk in his fingers. "I can give you an estimate after I give it a thorough look, and then bring in my roof guy. We can discuss options—what kind of roof you want to put in, though I recommend you bite the bullet and get the best grade you can. It'll save you money in the long run to do it right."

Mal nodded. "Okay. It seems logical to start with that. Looks like I got a lot of work to do on this place, huh?"

"Some folks opt to tear down these cottages," Leif admitted reluctantly. "Because building new from the ground up is easier with renovations and winterizing. Cheaper too."

"No way. This is… Nan's place. It's all I have of her," Mal said, his voice tight. "All I have of someone who actually loved me." He gave a rusty laugh. "So you say I can help out?"

"If you want to work with my crew, you could schedule working on the roof in the late afternoon. It's light long enough this time of year, and it might cut you a break with the roofing guy if he could squeeze it in after other jobs."

"Okay, sounds good," Mal said. "I even want to eventually do something with the storage space under the cottage. Maybe build a staircase down there and turn it into some kind of useable space, like a studio."

Leif blinked. "Studio?"

"Um." Mal ran nervous fingers over the side of the wooden ladder. "I like to paint."

"Oh." Leif could see Mal was still a little defensive. Shit, he was prickly. Well, fortunately Leif was a pretty patient guy. He had to be. "It's kind of dark down there for that kind of thing."

"Hadn't thought of that," Mal said.

"I'll think on it," Leif promised. "Maybe I can come up with some kind of solution for you, like extending the space into an atrium. If you had a glass roof over some of the space, it would bring in more light."

Mal curled his lips, the bottom one all the fuller with the half smile. He was enticing without making any effort. "Thanks, that is a cool idea." He shifted his hips so he was again a little closer to Leif. "So how about dinner sometime?"

Chapter Four

LEIF WAS sipping a beer on his dock hours later. It was past midnight, but he couldn't sleep. Rocking gently beside him, as if encouraging him to go out over the lake, his dinghy bumped amiably in moorage.

But he didn't feel right tonight leaving Papa. He was afraid of a repeat of the night before, and this time the firefighting volunteers would probably not be as understanding, not that he could blame them.

More, he wasn't sure he was ready for another unsettling encounter with Mal Harrison. He'd made a few monosyllabic noises after his offer of dinner sometime and got the hell out of there. His last sight of Mal was his disappointed blue eyes through Leif's windshield as he beat a hasty retreat. But he couldn't be for real, could he?

The truth was Leif found himself more and more drawn to Mal, to the loneliness and loss he could relate to, to the vulnerability that lurked under the cocky façade. But he was an unsuitable man. He had scoffed at the idea of romance.

On top of all the other painful shit in his life, Leif was afraid of getting hurt.

His phone buzzed with an incoming text. Leif checked it automatically, finding a message from Dr. Morgan Gallagher about coming over sometime soon for an assessment of restoring his outbuildings. Yes! That was a job Leif really wanted. Plus Morgan had made no secret of his orientation. He was mature and sophisticated, and Leif's age.

And Leif had an idea the lonely doctor was also interested.

He was far more suitable than Mal.

Leif was taking another sip of his beer when a dark seal's head popped up right next to the dock. He almost lost his grip on the can, but then the seal transformed into a selkie instead. It was Mal Harrison, out for another late-night swim.

He grinned up at Leif, his teeth white against the darkness of his face. "Hey," he gasped. "I hope I didn't scare you."

You always scare me, Leif thought, but he only shook his head reprovingly at the imp. "You snuck up on me deliberately."

"Maybe." Mal reached up to climb on the dock, and Leif took his arms, lifting him easily.

Mal's eyes widened at this display of strength. "Wow."

Leif flushed, self-conscious. "I am a working man."

"Are you ever," Mal said, that coy appreciation in his blue eyes. He took Leif's beer and sipped. "Nice after the swim. Warms you up."

"Hmmmm." Leif hoped Mal hadn't been drinking again.

Mal seemed to read his thought. "Nope, no drinking tonight. I have to be up early for my new boss man." His tone took on a silky quality on the last two words.

Leif cleared his throat. "You must be able to hold your breath for a long time. I didn't see you until you were right under the dock."

Mal's eyes danced, as if he refused to take anything seriously. His hair was slicked back from his face, droplets from the lake running down his sleek brown form. His nipples were pointed from the slight breeze. Leif tried not to stare and imagine them in his mouth.

"Holding my breath is useful for swimming… and giving a good BJ," Mal noted.

"Mal." Leif looked away. He took a deep drink of his beer. "I am easy. Please don't."

"Hey," Mal called softly.

Leif looked at him reluctantly, finding him beautiful under the moonlight in his sodden swimming trunks, his body glistening with moisture, his eyelashes clumped together, his lips parted, cheeks flushed. He looked like he'd had a bout of energetic sex, not mere swimming.

"I'm sorry. I forget sometimes that you're pretty innocent."

"By choice," Leif grumped. He wasn't pathetic. If he wanted to play around, he would.

"Right," Mal nodded, studying Leif's face. "Want to come in?"

"In?" Leif repeated suspiciously.

"The water!" Mal kicked out his dangling feet, making a gentle splash.

"I don't have on swimming trunks," Leif began.

"So what? I skinny-dip when I'm near my place," Mal admitted, waggling his dark brows.

"I won't do that!" Leif shook his head. "It's late."

"You go out rowing late. Come on, the water feels incredible." Mal slipped back into it in a smooth movement, looking up at Leif.

31

Leif hesitated since some wild part of him wanted to follow Mal into the water. When was the last time he'd done something purely for fun? Except the rowing he did, and that was always alone.

He listened to the pounding of the blood in his veins, holding Mal's bright blue eyes, and next thing he knew, his hands were on the buttons of his overshirt. He peeled it off first and then his T-shirt, blushing when Mal whistled from below. Self-conscious now, he shucked off his leather sandals and jeans, leaving his boxers.

"Teddy bears?" Mal's voice was gently amused.

"It was a joke last Christmas," Leif said. "But they are serviceable, so...."

"Very practical," Mal agreed, approving the bear-patterned boxers. "Come on."

Leif walked back down the dock to where it was shallower and carefully dropped in, hissing a little since the water felt chilly to his warm skin.

Mal waited, treading water.

Leif decided to get it over with and flopped forward, laughing at the sudden dunking. He grew accustomed to the water quickly, and it *was* very nice, like satin against his skin. Grinning shyly now, he swam to Mal.

"Not bad. I thought you'd take forever, dipping in a leg and then an arm." Mal quirked a brow.

"I usually do," Leif admitted. "But tonight I'm being reckless."

"Sexy and reckless—sounds good."

Leif blinked, eye level with Mal in the water. "Sexy?"

"Are you kidding? You have muscles on muscles." Mal's voice was a little tight. "No wonder you can lift me so easily. It's hot."

MAL WAS feeling some smugness over getting Leif to come in the water. When Leif lit out so quickly after Mal's dinner invitation, it hurt. Stupid, but that's what Mal experienced. And geez, it was just dinner in the hick diner in town—a place that served pancakes practically 24-7—but it felt like a big deal when Leif drove away and Mal was left alone in his quiet cottage again.

He filled in the time with walking to the well to get fresh water in the bucket to wash his dishes and make some coffee, and then he made a quick supper out of the spaghetti and canned sauces he found in Nan's pantry. There was nothing fresh like salad or bread, so he'd have to do some grocery shopping.

Then after dinner he went in the water for his daily long swim, which surprised him by feeling so good—maybe because without the pressure of training, he could actually remember how terrific it felt. He headed like a homing pigeon for the opposite side of the lake, the side where Leif lived. He hoped he'd intercept him rowing, but lucked out when he spotted him on his pier.

"When I first saw you, I thought of a merman," Leif admitted now. His gray eyes were soft in the starlight, fixed on Mal's face. "And now you've lured me into your world."

Mal nodded. "It is my world. I always loved swimming and sailing and all that shit here at the lake every summer. This is where it all began for me."

"Full circle, then," Leif noted. "Maybe you needed to return to a simpler place."

Mal chewed his lip. "Yeah. I think maybe I might find some stuff I've been missing and put together the puzzle that is me."

"Where do you want to swim?" Leif broke the heaviness of the moment, and Mal felt gratitude. He wasn't usually a deep thinker, and all this time alone was giving him too much time to examine his past actions. Right then he just wanted to have a little fun.

"Let's head to the marsh two cabins over and then come back," Mal said. He wasn't sure how often Leif swam, so he decided to take it easy on him.

But Leif kept up with him, his longer, muscled arms and legs powerful. It felt great to move through the water with someone, like sharing a secret. They didn't talk, but they occasionally smiled at each other.

At the marsh Leif pointed, and Mal watched a Canada goose swim through the reeds with some dark fuzzy babies following in her wake. Mal and Leif treaded water, hearing the frogs nearer to the beach croaking softly. Above them the stars were scattered in a bright pattern, so many more than it was ever possible to make out in the cities where Mal had lived the past few years. And at water level, there were lights dotting the circumference of the lake where people were still up. Mal caught the smell of woodsmoke.

Finally they headed back. Mal's calves and arms were a little heavy since he hadn't done such long-distance swimming in a while, and there was a resistance to real water you didn't find in a pool. He knew he'd have to take a break before heading back to Nan's cottage.

Leif seemed to pick up on this, and when they exited the water next to his dock, he said, "I think you better relax and warm up a little. I can drive you home."

Mal said, "I was a little surprised you weren't out rowing. I thought we'd just pass each other tonight or something like the cliché of two ships in the night."

Leif flushed under the moonlight, as if pleased at the idea Mal had sought him out. "No, I didn't want to leave my papa. He's a little unpredictable and can get really agitated if I'm not close to the house at night."

"Shit, I'm sorry," Mal said, feeling bad. Had it been okay to lure Leif away? And yet the other man had seemed as if he wanted to go swimming with Mal. "Don't worry about driving me home."

"You're shivering," Leif scolded, eyes narrowed on Mal's huddled figure.

"I'm just not used to that much distance." Mal shrugged. He tried to stop, but his body shuddered spasmodically every now and then.

Leif leaned over the pier and into his dinghy and hefted out a big plaid blanket. "Put that on around your shoulders."

"You're shivering a little too," Mal pointed out.

"The breeze has picked up." Leif pointed to the beach. "I'll make a little beach fire."

Mal was content to follow after Leif, watching as he put some driftwood and kindling into a ring of stones as Mal settled on the beach. His suit felt clammy, so he pulled it off under the blanket, shaking it out and hanging it over a leaning willow branch. He saw Leif's quick glance and knew he'd noticed.

In a few moments, Leif had a small crackling fire started. Mal stared at it, not knowing what to say. It was late. They both needed to get some sleep, and yet it seemed that, like him, Leif was loath to let the evening end.

"Come under the blanket. There's plenty of room for us to sit side by side," Mal encouraged. He could see Leif was still a little chilled.

Leif obediently edged closer and put a tentative bit of wool over his legs. He swept Mal a sideways glance.

Mal gave an impatient sound and tossed more blanket his way so they were both snugly under it.

34

They sat without speaking, staring at the blue-and-gold lick of the flames, sparks rising every now and then as the fire spat out some bit of wood. Then Mal felt abruptly sleepy, his body heavy from all the exercise and fresh air, so he leaned back on his elbows and then pillowed his head on a bit of driftwood.

Chapter Five

JUST BEFORE dawn Mal woke up, his back stiff and his prick also stiff and interested. He was curled safe in Leif's arms. "Mmmm," he commented, thinking he didn't care that sand had dried in his hair or they'd barely gotten any sleep. In fact, they hadn't even gotten it on yet, but this was… nice.

Leif blinked at him, and Mal said, "Did you sleep at all?"

"A little. I kept watching for Papa."

Mal had heard in town about Leif's dad and the problems he gave his son. He sighed, thinking of his Nan. "We weep for ourselves," he quoted softly.

Leif stared at him, and in that humming moment, as birds made busy in the trees, waking up, there was a moment of total understanding. Mal couldn't help but cup Leif's cheek and press his lips gently against him. A first kiss…. He hadn't even kissed him when he shucked his clothes and offered himself that first night. Now….

Licking, tasting, gentle, like the water lapping lazy onto the beach.

Leif trembled, making restless movements against Mal's back with his big hands, as if he didn't know what to do.

And Mal pulled back. "I don't want to hurt you," he whispered. Innocent. This man was innocent like no one Mal had ever been with. He could taste it in Leif's kiss, feel it when he looked into his serious eyes.

He was going deep with him, deeper under the water than he'd ever gone. Mal realized he'd stuck to the surface, to the shallows, in his professional and personal life.

Being with Leif would demand more of him.

"I don't want to get hurt either," Leif croaked. Then he cleared his throat and smiled. "I have to get up."

Mal cocked a brow.

"I mean up up, not…." Leif blushed since Mal's nude body was pressed against his own answering hunger.

Mal sighed in surrender. "All right." He rolled away and then reached for his swimming trunks, hissing since they were still a little damp against his aroused body as he tugged them on.

"What are you doing?" Leif asked, standing up and stretching his large body. Oh, he had muscles on muscles, as Mal noted previously. Mmm-mmm. Mal wanted to trace them with his tongue.

Instead he splashed into the shallows, hoping to cool off. "Heading home."

"I can drive you," Leif offered faintly.

"Go see to your papa," Mal said. He understood Leif's need to do that. If Nan were alive, he'd want to take care of her too. "I'll see you at work, boss man." He put some sugar in the last two words, just to make Leif blush again.

He was delighted when it worked.

HIS FIRST day on the job wasn't exactly easy for Mal, it turned out.

First he got home and barely had time to eat half of one of Nan's frozen diet cakes he found in the freezer—which tasted a bit like highway gravel after a hard frost—since he was out of anything for breakfast. He'd forgotten again to go grocery shopping.

Then he realized he had no idea where today's job was. He ate an icy brownie and stared out at his front yard, trying to think how to handle that. He didn't exactly want to call Leif and come off like a moron his first day.

So he called Marty Swenson, who knew everything happening in the small town, and soon found out the work was on the old Small property. Okay, he just had to get there in time.

He dressed in an old T-shirt and jeans and put on his new work boots, which right away started rubbing a blister on the back of his left heel. Then he got in his truck and headed over, thinking maybe… had he forgotten something?

But once he arrived, the guys working there greeted him in an easygoing manner, and he waited until Leif had a moment from talking to his electrician before finding out what he'd be assigned to do that day.

He didn't expect the big *thump* his pulse gave when he saw his Viking again, even though he'd just seen him an hour before.

"Wheelbarrow's out back," Leif said. "The guys pulled down a lot of old walls, so all that debris needs to go to the dumpster in the driveway. You brought heavy gloves, right? You need them to protect your hands from old nails and stuff."

Mal nodded. Okay, so he was on cleanup duty. Well, he could handle that.

Leif studied him sharply for a moment and in a lower tone asked, "You okay?" Meaning he knew how late Mal had been up since he'd been there.

"Fine," Mal said, though he did feel a little wasted. But he was used to sucking it up after partying, and it wasn't that hot. Yet.

THE JULY day climbed steadily in temperature into something that made Mal wish he could sit in the shade and sip a cool drink, or spend it submerged in the shallow water next to the beach.

Instead he collected debris from the half-torn-down old cabin, piling it into a wheelbarrow and making trip after trip. Pretty soon sweat dripped from his face, and his upper arms and back were burning, not to mention the fucking blister, which had grown and cloned itself on his other heel.

Lunch was called, and then Mal realized what he'd forgotten. He didn't have so much as a soda, but that was okay. He was so tired he flaked out under a birch tree, letting his head fall back as he just breathed for a while.

"Cheddar-and-apple sandwich?" Leif's voice broke his exhausted stupor.

"Um?" Mal blinked, looking up at his new boss. Leif had spent most of the day talking to his guys or on the phone. Mal caught brief glimpses while he hauled load after load.

"You need to eat. And drink up. Don't you have a water bottle?" Leif scolded. "Shit, Mal…."

Mal flushed since as an athlete he normally always carried things like snacks and water. He knew he could bleed energy and crash if he didn't eat up and keep hydrated when necessary, but today he'd completely forgotten about lunch.

"Here. Bottled water, cheddar sandwich, and a danish."

"That's *your* lunch, Leif," Mal protested, though his stomach growled. He felt a little shaky with hunger.

Leif towered over Mal, his hands on his hips. He definitely wasn't looking unsure of himself now. He was the boss. "I'm going home to check on Papa. I'll grab something there. Eat up." He turned to walk back to his SUV and then paused. "And good job today."

Mal managed a tired smile as he reached for the food, deciding to be practical. Besides, even though he knew Leif was just doing his job, he felt kind of looked after. He guessed it was corny, but he liked the feeling.

"Thanks."

MAL FELT almost too tired to stagger to his truck and drive home when three o'clock finally arrived and it was time to stop for the day. Every part of his body hurt despite the good shape he'd thought he was in. He felt drained, and his head thumped dully from his early bout of near dehydration.

Leif walked over to the driver's side of his truck and Mal rolled down his window, feeling the effort in his sore wrists and forearms. Geez, he was in a pretty pathetic state.

"I was going to drop by with my roofing guy at your place in an hour," Leif said. His forehead creased. "But, Mal, you look…."

Mal shook his head, not wanting to seem like some kind of loser in Leif's eyes. He knew his reputation as a party boy, and he wanted to show him there was more to him. Or maybe remind himself. He was so beat he wasn't sure.

"I'll be okay. I'd like to move forward."

Leif chewed his lip. "Okay, then. See you in an hour."

MAL TOOK some soap and headed down to the lake. He had to do something with the laundry that was accumulating, had to go into town to do his grocery shopping and use the Laundromat. Man, he really wanted to get some machines hooked up in the cabin too. And he couldn't exactly bathe in the lake in the middle of December.

December…. Was he really thinking of staying here that long? He'd moved around quite a bit over the past few years, calling nowhere home. Except in his heart, *this* place was always home. Now after coming back, he recognized that was because Nan was here. Could he make a life in Sylvan without her?

The water cooled him off, and he felt a little better, though his body had an all-over ache, like he was coming down with the flu. On stiff legs he headed back to his cabin, rubbing his hair dry with a towel. Just in time since Leif pulled up seconds before a stranger with sandy hair and smiling blue eyes, who got out of his own truck and shook Leif's hand. Leif introduced him to Mal as John Moreton, the roofing guy.

Leif added, "We'll need the ladder again for the outside of the cottage."

Mal nodded, and despite how warm he was feeling, he tried to push it aside, leading the way down the slope to the storage space under the cabin. He watched the other two men pull out the ladder, so tired that he was content to just let it play out. He had enough money to cover fixing the roof and maybe some of the changes he wanted to make. And hopefully he'd figure out what he was going to do with his life now that being on the swim team was over. For now the job with Leif's company should keep him in groceries.

"John will go up on the roof and poke around. Why don't you go inside and take it easy?" Leif looked concerned, and Mal was so bushed that all he did was nod. Yeah, he really needed to put his feet up.

As MAL was halfway up the slope to go back inside Nan's cottage, a car screeched to a halt in his sand pit of a driveway. Brown-haired and lanky Joey Delany and slightly tubby and red-haired Martin Jacobs climbed out of an old Toyota Camry. Both men were former friends of Mal's, guys he used to spend time with in Sylvan.

Mal flashed back to what it was like when he was younger, impatient to see the world and living with a secret—that he preferred men. He'd experimented with both Joey and Martin.

"Hey, Mal, we heard you were here!" Joey greeted him with a hug and an appreciative wink, as if it hadn't been years since he'd seen him.

With mixed emotions, Mal sighed, rubbing the back of his neck. What now? He wasn't in the mood to see these guys. Maybe it was just that he felt like he was coming down with something. But he wasn't sure if they were people he'd want to hang with now. Did he have anything in common with them anymore?

Still, he had to laugh at himself. Since when did he care about that? Usually he just went where the action was.

Belatedly he noticed the atmosphere had grown charged and his two former friends were looking beyond his shoulder. He also looked back and spotted Leif glaring at the newcomers. Terrific. Now what? But he couldn't help but appreciate the view. Leif looked like Thor with his shirt off. No, even better than Thor because he was accessible and not a Nordic god on the silver screen.

"Yeah, I needed a place to take it easy for a while," he said, hoping the guys would take the hint. He wasn't sure if he wanted to see them again or not, so he was going to put it off for now. "Matter of fact, I just put in a long day's work, so I was going to crash."

"You, crash?" Martin scoffed. "Come on, why don't you come back to my place? We can put on some steaks, some music...."

Yeah, and Mal knew where this would go. His cheeks heated as Leif moved up beside him quietly and gave him a comprehensive look. He'd obviously guessed correctly these were some of the guys Mal had been with—at the same time.

After an awkward pause while Mal tiredly groped for words, Leif put in softly, "He said he was tired. You should respect him if you're his friends."

Mal's eyes widened in surprise. He didn't expect Leif to stand beside him like this. It had a subtle feeling of staking territory.

"Who is this?" Joey asked, raising his eyebrows at Leif.

Mal opened his mouth, but Leif beat him to it again. "I'm a friend of Mal's."

"Uh-huh. But not a boyfriend, so...." Joey smirked at Mal. "You can bring your friend if you want. There's plenty to go around."

"I don't share," Leif said in an undertone only Mal could hear.

Mal glanced at him, saw the tension in his stance. He was glowering at both men now, really resembling Thor. Mal half expected him to smack them down with a giant hammer, but then Leif gave Mal a look, and Mal saw vulnerability in his gray eyes. He was probably expecting Mal to head off to the party, dumping any chance with Leif.

The hell of it was, just a month ago, Mal would have done that. He'd have regretted it, but he would have made the wrong turn.

Mal took a deep breath. He was so tired, and his head was thumping. He felt really shitty, worse than he should after a day's work. "I don't feel like it," he said honestly. "But thanks, guys."

Martin shrugged. "Invitation is open for the rest of the week." Joey followed him back to the car while Leif crossed his arms.

Once they pulled away, Mal sagged down on the stairs, not sure he had the energy to head inside. Leif again gave him a frowning glance, but John called to him from the roof, and he disappeared around the side of the cottage.

Mal rubbed his forehead, which was sweating. His hands were swollen and kind of pink-colored. He realized he had to have come down with something, maybe from the chill while he slept in Leif's arms that morning.

He dozed while he waited for the two men to return. Eventually they did, and John said he'd write up his findings and get back to Leif and Mal. Leif saw him off and then walked back to where Mal was still flaked out on the wooden steps.

"You're not well!" Leif sounded pissed. "Shit, Mal, don't try to deny it."

"Nope," Mal admitted. "I'm sorry, I don't know if I'll be able to make it to work tomorrow—"

"Never mind." Leif put an arm around his shoulders and helped him inside. "Where are you sleeping?"

"On the floor, mostly," Mal admitted, feeling oddly buoyant, as if Leif had again lifted him from the water. He probably wouldn't have admitted his odd sleeping arrangement if he weren't so wasted.

Leif guided him gently into Nan's room, to her nicely made bed with clean sheets and a lightweight summer comforter with green ivy and pansies on it. The bedding felt like heaven against Mal's hot skin.

"I can't sleep here," he mumbled.

"Yes, you can," Leif contradicted him, glowering now at Mal. "I'm sure Nan would insist on it. Stay there and I'll bring you some dinner."

"You don't have to." Mal wanted to bury his head in the pillow and drift. He wasn't even hungry, like it would be too much effort to eat.

"I want to take care of you, Mal," Leif said. He reached out and stroked the damp hair off Mal's forehead. His palm felt good, cool against Mal's sweaty skin. Leif cleared his throat. "I guess you would have gone off with your friends if you weren't so sick."

"I don't know," Mal croaked. "God, I hope not."

Leif tightened his mouth, but his eyes remained concerned on Mal's face. "I'll go into town and get you some soup and juice." He climbed to his feet and opened the door to Nan's bedroom.

"Leif," Mal called him, sitting up in bed. Heat washed through him at the movement so he sagged back a second later. "I don't want to hurt you."

Leif shook his head. "Don't be an asshole. Rest and I'll be back soon."

For some reason Leif's response left Mal smiling.

Chapter Six

MAL WOKE when Leif told him softly to sit up. He blinked hot, gritty eyes at Leif, wanting to be left alone to sleep, but that didn't seem to be an option from the determined look on Leif's face.

He moved up in the bed, Leif adjusting the pillows so he could eat the soup he'd brought in a take-out dish.

"It's minestrone from the diner," Leif said. "And I bought you some apple juice. Not sure if you like that, but it's all they had on hand today."

"Thanks," Mal rasped. He wasn't sure how he felt right now. Only Nan ever took care of him when he was sick. This was…. He liked it. "You seem to be a real caregiver."

"Lots of practice with Papa." Leif sighed, sitting back to watch Mal spoon in a little soup.

"I'm not used to…." Mal shrugged.

"You've never had a boyfriend?" Leif prodded, looking interested.

Mal felt that stretchy discomfort again, like he felt when the guys showed up. He wasn't the man he had been since he really let himself down. So who was he now? Someone who could be a boyfriend? He had no idea. He wanted new things in his life, but he didn't know how to get there.

"No," he said. "In some ways it would have been easier to go out tonight. Fall into a pattern, you know?"

Leif's eyes were bleak for a moment. "It's what I expected you to do." He shrugged. "Even though you are sick, you dope."

"Staying here isn't so bad," Mal said, smiling a little. "I get you to take care of me."

Leif chewed his lip, pushing his silver-blond hair out of his solemn gray eyes. "I can't stay."

"No, of course not."

"I want to, but…."

"Your father. I *do* understand," Mal said. He reached out and brushed his hot, sausage-feeling fingers against Leif's cool ones. "I'm used to going it alone, anyway."

Leif got up from the chair next to the bed and paced restlessly through Nan's bedroom. His expression was tight and unhappy.

Mal said, extra gently, "It must be hard."

Leif gave a rueful laugh. "I never know what to expect, except lately if he's under any kind of pressure, like to make a decision, he overcompensates. Big-time."

"I heard about the volunteer firefighters on your front lawn."

"Yeah." Leif flushed. "That was the same night I met you."

"Well, now you won't forget it." Mal pushed away the last of his soup in a sleepy gesture. Leif poured him some apple juice and left the jug on the table next to the bed.

"I wouldn't forget," Leif said. He put his hands in his pockets. "I'll come by in the morning to see how you are."

MAL HAD hot fever dreams, so hot he twisted on the bed, dreaming of paddling a canoe through a rocky stream—it seemed no matter how hard he put his back into it, he could get nowhere.

He finally woke in the morning, feeling dispirited. The dream seemed so much like his life now. What was he doing? He had never wanted to work construction. But it was a job, he guessed, while he figured out what to do. He had to pay the bills if he wanted to keep the cottage, and that was the only thing he *was* certain of.

And then there was Leif. Mal wasn't sure what was happening between them. He worried about hurting him since Mal wasn't sure who he was anymore. And Mal had never really dated anyone. What he had going with Leif felt kind of… old-fashioned, like the town of Sylvan itself, sleepy and warm and unhurried.

He closed his eyes, too drained to worry about it, and next thing he knew, he heard the door creak open and Leif call out, boots stomping as he walked through the kitchen and dining room to Nan's bedroom.

"Hey," Leif said. He reached out and touched Mal's forehead. "Wow, still pretty warm."

"Yeah," Mal croaked. He liked Leif's hand on him, cool and caring. He wondered what it would be like if Leif slept with him all night.

"I'll get some ice to put in the apple juice," Leif said, heading back into the kitchen. Mal heard him break some cubes out of the ice tray for the juice. When he returned, Mal took a sip, enjoying the chilly treat.

"I guess you haven't had breakfast?" Leif sat on the corner of Nan's double bed and opened a familiar paper bag, pulling out hot sandwiches. "I had to leave early so I'd have time to drop by. I haven't eaten either."

"I don't want to screw up your day," Mal said. He bit into the steaming breakfast. Heaven. His appetite was back. Best of all was watching Leif watch him, gilt hair in his eyes, big and muscled, and seemingly crushed on Mal. It was nice. Good for his ego, yes, but nice to have someone.

"You could never screw up my day," Leif said. He cleared his throat. "So I have an estimate for you on the roof."

"Great. When can your guy get started?" Mal asked.

Leif put his sandwich down. "It's a big commitment financially. You really are planning to live here?"

"Year-round if I can figure out what to do with myself," Mal said.

"There's the university not so far from here," Leif pointed out. "It's a bit of a drive, but you might want to explore some options there."

Mal's eyes widened. He hadn't thought of that at all, going back to school. "Maybe… fine arts," he admitted shyly.

"Sounds good."

"Sounds like I'd still need a job, you mean." Mal smiled. "But it's okay. I decided to take it slow, figuring out what I'm supposed to do next."

"I wish I could have stayed over last night," Leif said.

Mal nodded. "I was wondering what it would be like to wake up with you."

"I have never stayed over at someone's house." Leif put away their paper trash in the bag. "And it's unlikely I will have the time for a… romantic commitment any time soon."

"You look a little down," Mal noted.

Leif rubbed his chin. "I don't know how to have any kind of life with Papa, and I'm not sure he'd accept anyone helping us. And I want him to be the man he was so I can tell him who I am, and that at this stage of my life… I ache to be with someone. Sometimes I even think that one night when I'm not alone will be enough."

Mal reached out and cupped Leif's cheek. "No, that's not who you are."

"If you offered yourself to me again, Mal, I would not be able to resist you," Leif admitted. "But then you'd go off with your friends, and I'd feel…."

Mal took a deep breath. "Let's just put a roof over the cottage. Nothing has happened. I haven't hurt you." *Yet.* Mal didn't trust himself not to do that, and it made him afraid. He'd screwed up two good things in his life:

losing a lot of time with Nan he wished he could make up now and his shot at Olympic gold. "We have the summer."

Leif also took a deep breath. "Summer is a good time here," he agreed. "So will you keep the same footprint of the cottage as it stands now?"

"I think so. I'd just like to work a few things into the existing space. I was also fantasizing about a washer and dryer in the storage room downstairs."

"That's a lot to do before winter comes in and freezes the ground," Leif said. "You'd have to have that space properly insulated so that the pipes don't freeze."

"Yep, I know. Probably I won't get it all done this year, so I'll have to do more next spring."

"Next spring." Leif looked a little heartened.

"I figure there will be plenty more nights for me to swim over to your place and fall asleep on some driftwood." Mal stroked the back of Leif's hand with his fingers. Leif's hand trembled beneath his.

"But this time I'd have enough blankets to keep you warm."

Mal whispered against Leif's ear, "You don't need blankets to keep me warm."

Chapter Seven

MAL HEALED slowly over the next week. The virus was surprisingly strong, so he felt wrung out, but the first morning he woke up with the roofing team taking down his old roof, shingle by shingle, he got into his swimming trunks and bathrobe to go outside and see the work. And if he were honest with himself, he was hoping to see Leif, whom he hadn't seen in days.

"Hey, Mal," John Moreton called down from the roof. "Sorry if we woke you. Leif said you were under the weather."

"No, I'm totally happy you're here," Mal said. "I've been really worried about the water coming in."

"That could cause some problems," John agreed. "But we'll take care of it. We're taking down that part of the roof now."

"I, uh, thought Leif might be by," Mal asked, feeling shy for some reason. Geez, Sylvan small-town life must be rubbing off on him. He wasn't sure Leif would like it known they were interested in each other.

John shook his head. "I think he's probably spending all his free time at home. You know his dad."

"Yeah," Mal said. "I know." He shrugged. "Well, I'll let you get back to work."

As he walked down the slope and then back up to the raised highway on his way to the lake to swim and get washed off, Mal was thinking about Leif. He'd really like to see him again. At this rate he'd have to be on the job again before he got a glimpse of Leif, but he wasn't quite ready for that, still shaky as he was from the flu.

The water felt cool and wonderful as he swam out, seeing sparrows dipping down to take a drink, feeling the serenity he always experienced here at the lake. He wondered what it would be like in wintertime to go ice-skating on this same surface or to maybe rent a snowmobile. One thing was for sure: even if they got to the pipes this summer to winterize them, probably the walls and windows would be letting in a lot of the cold. It would take some time before he got the place snug.

Once he finished his swim, he decided to go into town and do something about the mound of laundry he had and finally pick up some food. He'd been living on Nan's canned soups, and he wanted something fresh.

Leif still wasn't at his cottage when he returned, and it made Mal feel a bit down. He wanted to see him and see himself through his eyes. He didn't feel so bad about himself then. He felt like he might have some kind of future. So Mal added one more thing to his list. Maybe he'd swim over to Leif's dock as soon as he was up to it again.

LEIF THREW pebbles into the lake water from his dock, watching as ripples radiated out. He sighed, drawing up his knee while he dangled the other one. It had been a hell of a week. He managed to ask John Moreton a couple of times in as casual a manner as possible how Mal was doing, but he hadn't had the time to get out there. He was doing an emergency fix on an old farmhouse a new client had purchased, which was on the verge of falling down. And his papa…. He was more demanding than ever, as if he sensed Leif's attention was elsewhere.

Finally he decided it was better to leave it. By now Mal had probably moved on, was visiting those party-minded friends. It wasn't as if they'd really done anything, though Leif thought about it all the time, imagining kissing Mal, imagining covering him.

When a familiar wet-seal head popped up next to the pier, Leif didn't jump this time. Instead his heart started pounding. Mal smiled at him and reached up, and Leif knelt, braced himself, and pulled the slighter man easily from the water. He stood over Leif, dripping, his body tanned, his nipples pointed, his swimming trunks tight around his body so that Leif wanted to drag his lips against the outline of Mal's sex.

"You look like you want to eat me." Mal's voice was caressing as he reached out and tangled a damp, cool hand in Leif's hair.

Leif bent close and pressed his face against Mal's thigh. He couldn't be offhand about this. He felt alive again for the first time in days. He parted his lips and tasted lake water and Mal. Mal laughed at the warm tongue touching him.

"Leif," Mal said. He knelt beside Leif, and Leif noticed belatedly Mal had a plastic bag tied around one shoulder. "It's something I wanted to treat you to," Mal continued. "Since I know you can't come out with me to dinner."

"Not lately," Leif rasped, unhappiness weighing him down like rocks pulled up from the lakebed. But then Mal stroked his cheek, and he felt a hundred times better, like he'd been catapulted out of his depression.

"I need a beach fire," Mal directed. "Then you get your treat."

"*You're* my treat," Leif countered. This time he wouldn't hold back or be so damned shy. This time he would kiss and touch Mal and make love to him the way he'd dreamed of doing.

MAL SEATED a metal pot on the coals of their discreet beach fire. He could feel Leif's eyes on him, and it made him feel sexy, made a pulse beat in his throat, his inner thighs, and his cock. Anticipation simmered between them even as the water heated.

To draw out the moment, since it looked like Leif had moped around as much as Mal the past few days, Mal busied himself with more of the supplies he'd brought over in plastic containers: Japanese green tea powder, a bamboo teaspoon, a scoop, and two tea bowls. He placed green tea into each cup and then opened a biscuit box, offering Leif a sweet.

Leif raised his eyebrows. "This is different." He took the cookie and bit into it.

"I hope so," Mal said, looking pleased at Leif's curiosity. "It's matcha tea. I wanted to bring you something I'd experienced while traveling in Japan."

Leif watched as Mal used the scoop to pour out water into a black, lumpy-looking tea bowl. He then used a whisk and, when the tea was foamy, passed it to Leif with a slight bow.

"Taste. It might seem a little bitter."

Leif's silver brows met as he sipped. "Tastes a bit like coffee."

"Yeah, it has a kind of… authority. It's not a mild tea," Mal agreed. He mixed his own and took a biscuit for himself, and then shifted so he was rubbing shoulders with Leif.

Leif's heart started pounding again at the contact. He'd told Mal he was easy. Should he say something? Should he just kiss Mal?

They both sipped, the firelight reflected in the water that hushed onto the beach in the wee hours. Leif's gaze fell to Mal's lips. As if he also felt the tension between them, Mal put aside his tea cup as Leif's hit the sand with a dull thud. Leif took Mal's mouth, making a sound of need, climbing on top of him.

"*Leif.*" Mal pushed up so his cock rubbed wantonly against Leif. Leif was like a silver warrior gilded in the moonlight, and Mal had the fantasy he was a captive of Thor, claimed by him. His muscles, his bigger body—he felt wonderful crushed into the sand. Mal pictured Leif pounding into him as Mal dug his heels into his ass….

Leif moved his hands over Mal's hips, holding on tight as he thrust his tongue inside Mal's mouth, hungry, fevered. He was shaking. "Oh God, Mal."

Mal raised one leg and netted his man closer, like the merman Leif sometimes called him.

"Mal…." They rolled, and Leif peppered kisses against Mal's neck, smoothing his hands over Mal's damp swimming trunks, and then he tugged them down, as if now too impatient to experience the real thing, and his hands were full of Mal's ass.

Mal was partially under Leif's larger body, his eyes half-closed, a sexy gleam in his eyes. His body was sleek as wet marble from the water, and he looked so perfect to Leif. Ever since Leif had first pulled Mal from the lake, since Mal had stripped and sat on his lap, Leif had jerked off thinking of him.

Leif felt something rising up inside him, a pent-up feeling like bitter lava gripping him by the throat. He'd gone years without touching someone. "I'm going to—" Oh God. No, he couldn't embarrass himself this way!

Mal's wide blue eyes seemed to read Leif's distress. "Shhh, it's okay," he murmured. "Leif, take it easy. Don't be scared."

But it wasn't okay! Leif thrust against Mal, his muscles knotting painfully, reaching down with his trembling hand, tugging aside his own swimming trunks. He shot on Mal's stomach while Mal clenched his hands on his shoulders. Oh shit. What was that? It wasn't even sex! He hadn't made love to Mal the way he did in his fantasies. He just—

"It's all right," Mal said again, his voice stern, as if he were trying to reach Leif.

Leif sat up, turning away so Mal couldn't see his face. "No," he whispered. "No, it's not."

MAL PUT his arms around Leif from behind. He ached for him, even as he was shaken himself. He hadn't been innocent sexually for a long time. He tried to remember how it felt to he'd know what to say.

There was a terrible vulnerability to Leif right now. Mal knew if he said the wrong thing, he'd hurt him.

"Will you please just fucking go?" Leif demanded, sounding like he was fighting tears. "I'm sure you'd get a much better performance from your friends."

"Leif? Leif, where are you?" a voice called from the property above them.

Leif jerked his head up. "Shit," he swore. "It only needed this!"

Mal dropped his hands as Leif pulled violently away from him.

"Leif?" A frail figure staggered into view on the grass. Leif's father's eyes were fixed on Leif as if he were the only compass to offer direction. "Leif, I was afraid you drowned…. I woke up and you weren't in the house!"

Leif snatched a towel to cover himself and tugged up his swimming trunks. "No, I was just spending some time on the beach… talking. It's okay, Papa."

"Talking to *who?*" Leif's father sounded angry, suspicious, as he peered down toward Mal.

Leif didn't even glance at Mal as he hissed, "Get dressed! And put out the fire, will you?"

Words jammed up in his throat in the wake of the unfinished encounter, and Mal watched Leif jump up to the grass where his father was. Leif took his father's elbow gently. "Come on. Let's head back into the house."

"But who were you talking to?" The older man still sounded peevish.

"No one," Leif said flatly. "No one."

On the beach Mal reached for the towel Leif had abandoned. He stared at it numbly as he heard the door of Leif's cottage slam behind him and his father. After a second he remembered why he'd wanted the towel and used it to scrub off his stomach.

He sat with his heels in the sand, his lips bruised from Leif's kisses. He could still taste him, could still feel the way he was shaking when he—

"You're experienced, Harrison," he scolded himself aloud. "This is no big deal."

He upended the pot of water, which still simmered like a magic potion, over the tiny circle of flame Leif had made. The dying fire hissed and steam rose. Mal found one tea bowl half-buried in seaweed and shifting back and forth with the waves as they hit the beach. The other was cracked, so Mal carefully gathered the shards, worried someone might step on them.

51

He arranged them very precisely in the plastic bag with the tin of tea as the lights in the cottage above went out. He took the whisk, the spoon, and all the other shit he'd brought with him to impress and delight Leif.

His first real date.

Chapter Eight

A FEW days later, Mal stiffened as a tall figure walked toward his campsite, gravel from the riverside crunching under cowboy boots, silvery hair catching the dim light. He stood up from the fire, sparks rising between him and his surprising visitor.

"Leif," he said, swallowing dryly. "What are you doing out here?"

"Out here" was Charlie LaFountaine's ranch, several miles from Sylvan. Leif was certainly the last person he thought he'd see.

"You didn't come to work for the rest of the week. I was worried," Leif said, dropping his gaze. He put his hands in his pockets. "I, uh, thought you might be visiting those friends of yours."

Mal shoved his hair out of his eyes. "I couldn't go back to work." But he didn't deny Leif's idea of Mal playing around with old friends. Maybe he should keep his options open after what happened between him and Leif.

Leif gave a drawn-out sigh. "No, of course not. Not after the way I acted."

Mal shrugged, not looking for any more hurt. He was still raw from their last encounter, from the cold way Leif dismissed him. He'd tried to tell himself he was the experienced one and it was no big deal, but the rock in his gut said differently.

What a joke, how he worried he'd hurt Leif, when it was he himself who felt raw.

"That cocoa on the fire?" Leif asked, giving Mal a mild look.

"Yeah, want some?" Mal found himself automatically reaching for the metal pot even as he asked himself why he was being so accommodating. But after a few days alone, maybe he was ready to listen to another perspective. He poured a mug for Leif, who looked tired. His eyes were bloodshot.

"Thanks. Mind if I sit with you?"

Again Mal shrugged, uneasy but willing to listen.

Gripping his mug of cocoa, Leif sat on a log near the fire. Mal sat down opposite him on another log, watching as Leif sipped his drink. After a moment Leif cleared his throat. "I'm sorry for how I treated you," he said.

"It's okay," Mal said, not wanting to talk about it. He'd come here to forget it.

"It's *not* okay." Leif's eyes were fixed on Mal's face. "I was angry."

"I got that sense," Mal agreed, somewhat wryly.

Leif gave a humorless laugh, putting aside his hot drink. "Not just at you…. At everything. At my life!"

Now Mal thought he had a thread of understanding. "I can certainly understand that."

"I'm angry because I want someone in my life, and my papa makes that almost impossible. And I'm angry he's not the man he was. And I'm angry at *you* because you are everything…." Leif's voice cracked, and he swallowed, taking a deep breath. "Everything I want, Mal," he finished simply. "And I'm not sure you want to make any kind of… commitment, but now I'm not sure I care. I just… want you. I can't sleep for wanting you."

Mal took a deep breath before reaching out and pouring himself a mug of cocoa to give himself a moment.

"Uh, why are you out here, anyway?" Leif asked, as if wanting to find an easier bridge to cross.

"Charlie LaFountaine's a distant relative of mine. He let me come here to do some camping and hunt for fossils by the riverbank. It's something I used to do as a kid." As he explained, Mal felt a wave of what he'd experienced on the dusty road when he had first met Leif. He was conscious of Leif's pale eyes fixed on his face and the answering constriction in his own chest, as if they were somehow connected.

Leif's brow crinkled. "He's a Blackfoot, isn't he? I've seen him around in town. So does this explain that gorgeous black hair I love to touch?"

Mal flushed. Leif was certainly making his feelings crystal clear. "Yeah, probably. I guess I just needed to do something to return to an easier time, you know?"

Leif nodded, gray eyes burning with understanding. "You lost your way of life, and then your grandmother."

Mal decided to be frank. "Not just that. You *hurt* me, Leif. I sure as hell never expected that."

Leif put aside his cocoa. "I never expected I'd have the power to do that." He took a deep breath. "Mal, does that mean you could really care about me?"

Mal hesitated, still not sure who he was becoming, what his place was. But as he looked at Leif, he realized he knew one thing: he wanted to be with him somehow. "I already do," he rasped.

Leif got to his feet and walked to Mal's side, kneeling beside him and reaching up to stroke the hair he'd teased him about. "After my lousy performance, I'd understand if—"

"Shhhhh." Mal outlined Leif's lips with a finger. Leif took the finger in his mouth and sucked it, definitely warming Mal up despite the unseasonably chilly night air. "I told you that didn't matter to me. But Leif, what about your dad?"

Leif leaned his forehead against Mal's. "I asked Mrs. Watson to stay overnight. I realized that I do need some help. That I can take better care of him only if I take care of *myself* first…. And yeah, still working on the guilt I feel about that, but it's the truth. What's also the truth is I… deserve some time with my boyfriend."

Mal found himself smiling.

THE WIND had picked up, making the plastic of Mal's tent shudder inward in unpredictable intervals, but Mal lit the lamp inside calmly and pulled off his down jacket and then his T-shirt.

Leif was crouched opposite him, and as Mal watched, he removed his lumberjack coat and then unbuttoned his blue work shirt. They were both silent, locking eyes again.

Leif reached out and playfully tugged off Mal's cowboy boots one at a time, and then Mal did the same for him. In socks and jeans, they met in the middle of Mal's sleeping bag.

Mal whispered, "We'll take it slow."

Leif gulped. "I hope that's possible for me."

And Mal smiled again. "We have all night. Just try to relax." He knew Leif was inexperienced and shamed over what happened between them previously, but now they were totally alone, without the nagging fear of being interrupted. They had a sleeping bag to themselves.

LEIF GOT up the courage to ask for what he wanted. "Can you… that is, do you mind taking off the rest of your clothes and sitting on my lap again?" He licked his lips, color rising in his cheeks.

Mal laughed. "So you've thought of that night, huh?"

"Oh yeah. Just every five minutes or so since I met you. I have cameo-Mal on the brain. You on the roadside the day you rescued Papa. You when I pulled you from the lake—after you finished bringing up lake water. Your…

um, rear end in my hands when you sat on my lap." Leif listed the memories as he watched Mal removing his socks and then his jeans. His heart was pounding.

Mal walked over to him on his knees and then climbed on his lap. His eyes were serious for a moment. "I didn't bring anything out here, so it might limit our options."

"I *did*," Leif breathed. "Oh yeah." His hands again were full of Mal's round ass. He squeezed, feeling Mal's erection rubbing against him as Mal put his arms around Leif and nuzzled their lips together.

Mal reached down and cupped Leif's cock through his jeans. "Wow, I'd almost forgotten. What big feet you have!"

Leif snickered. "Don't you take anything seriously?"

"Turns out maybe I do," Mal said.

Afraid to hope Mal might mean him, Leif skated for more solid ground. "This is nice." He was breathless as he let Mal open his jeans and play with what he found inside. "*Mal!*" He fell back, but Mal remained on top of him, legs open on either side of Leif's hips. Just what was he going to do?

"Where are your supplies?" Mal asked, equally breathless. His eyes were brilliant blue in the light from the lamp, and his hair tumbled from Leif's hands onto his forehead in messy lover's peaks.

"Front pocket. I bought, uh, a travel pack."

"Very appropriate." Mal touched on other territory as he dug out lube and condoms, leaving Leif feeling both helpless and hard.

"Mal, I can't—"

"It's okay. I'll take care of you." Mal stretched forward and then reached behind his body. Leif recognized he was preparing himself. God, that was hot!

"Uhhhhh." Leif wasn't capable of words when Mal put the condom on him. He huffed, leaning back on his elbows, eyes wide as he watched Mal take his penis and then slowly impale himself on it, face flushed, lips parted. "Holy shit, look at you take it!" Mal laughed and Leif felt it *everywhere.* "I never thought…. Oh man, it was worth waiting for you," Leif continued.

Mal swallowed. "No one's ever said that. That I'd be worth it."

"Well, you are." Leif worked his hands on Mal's hips, his thighs. "What do I do, Mal? I want to make it good for you, as good as…."

"Now who's insecure? Just lie there, gorgeous." Mal ran his hands over Leif's muscular arms, as if enjoying the shape and texture. He rose and fell as slowly and inevitably as the waves that hit the beach at Sylvan.

The tent shuddered inward again, and a cold puff of air touched Leif's skin, but he was enraptured by the play of feelings on Mal's face. Mal had taken him inside. He was enjoying it, enjoying riding Leif. Leif had never seen anything as sexy in his life. Leif's balls were drawn up tight against his body, and he worried he'd come too fast, but then he didn't worry because how could he lose this feeling?

"How's your first time?" Mal asked him softly. Leif looked embarrassed. "It's okay. I guessed."

"I fooled around some but never.... If I'd known it was *this* good, I could never have said no to you for so long," Leif admitted. Suddenly he had to grip Mal's hips, crushing him closer so he was grinding down against Leif's bigger body.

"Oh, so full...," Mal gasped.

Watching Mal's pleasure, Leif had another idea. He tentatively took hold of Mal's cock, milking it in time with Mal's movements on him until their sweaty dance strained. Mal groaned as Leif gripped his hips. He was barely able to let him move because he had to stay inside, had to stay deep inside him.

They pressed together, eyes locked, hands meshed tight. "I wanted this the moment I set eyes on you," Mal whispered. "I wanted you in me, on me."

"Shit, Mal!" Leif's hands were almost bruising Mal's skin. He loved the feeling of his prick buried inside him, but he was so close now! "I can't—"

"Feel so fucking good." Mal smiled a feline smile.

Leif felt as if the top of his head blew off. His toes curled, he thrust his hips up, and his body went rigid.

Awareness returned as breath panted moist against his skin, Mal collapsed on Leif's body. Despite his pleasant apathy, Leif had to ask, "You...?"

"Oh yeah." Mal sounded content. "Can't you feel it on your stomach? Sticky."

"Whatever." Leif was also content now. Mal had come. He'd pleasured Mal. It made him feel like Superman. Well, a sleepy version. "I wish I could come in you for real."

"One day," Mal surprised him by promising in a drowsy voice. "I think maybe one day we'll have that kind of commitment."

THE TENT was constantly rippling now from the rising wind. Leif frowned at it, thinking the summer storm was picking up speed.

Mal had gone outside and heated some water, and they'd used a towel to get cleaned up. Now he was lying in Leif's arms in the sleeping bag, his bare shoulders and the back of his neck exposed to Leif's exploration.

"What kind of fossils did you find?" he finally asked.

"Um, ammolite. It's a kind of prehistoric snail." Mal sat up and reached into his knapsack, handing a chunk of rock to Leif. "The Blackfoot believe it has healing powers."

Leif examined it, seeing the iridescent red and green and blue spirals embedded in muddy rock. "That's fantastic." He made to hand it back to Mal, but Mal covered his hand. "Keep it," he said.

"Did it help you heal a little?" Leif asked, and he saw Mal's face soften at the question.

"Yeah, maybe. Or it could have been being out here on my own, grieving for Nan and just... giving myself some time, you know? I did a ceremony for her, said good-bye in my own way. It's crazy, but I felt her. I think she stayed with me every night, watching over me."

Leif nodded. "I'm glad," he said solemnly.

Chapter Nine

A CRACK of thunder right overhead woke both Mal and Leif. The tent was caving inward from the force of the wind.

"Shit!" Mal exclaimed, scrabbling to light the lantern. He found it overturned and grabbed his flashlight instead. It was icy cold inside the tent. Leif was shoving on his jeans. "Always sounds like the end of the world, storms out here."

"I know. Papa's really terrified of them now," Leif said, and Mal understood why he was frantically searching for his clothing.

"Your shirt's here!" He cannoned it toward Leif while reaching for his own chilly clothing. "Fuck, it feels like winter and not the middle of July!"

Another gust took out one of the tent pegs so the back of the tent deflated and flapped like a frantic rag in the wind. Mal recognized then this was one of the really bad summer storms that struck from time to time.

Dressed in record time, they barreled out of the tent. "Where's your SUV?" he yelled above the wind.

"In Charlie's driveway, about a quarter of a mile from here." Leif gestured the direction, down the slope and by the river that was now triple its size, shooting past its gravel banks. "You better bring anything you don't want to lose!" he warned.

Mal ducked into the tent and grabbed his knapsack and chucked the fossil he'd offered Leif into it. "I can leave the rest," he called. "Let's get you home and make sure your dad is okay."

As they skidded their way down the rise under furious charcoal clouds, Mal's tent suddenly flew by, lifted free by the force of the wind.

They ran then despite the uneven ground. Mal felt increasing dread over Leif's father, picking it up from him. He said a prayer to his grandmother, asking her to watch over the older man.

Mal buckled up as soon as he climbed into the passenger side of Leif's SUV. Leif checked his smartphone but then shook his head. No messages, which could be good or bad. Mal knew they really needed to get to Leif's cottage to be sure.

Mud and rock spat out from tires and the vehicle jolted forward, and rain hit the windscreen with such force it was hard to make out the unpaved road.

Lightning forked a mile ahead.

"Shit, I hope he's all right!" Leif said.

The SUV skidded to a stop on a mound of sand in Mal's driveway.

"What?" Mal looked at Leif. "This isn't your place!"

"It was on my way." Leif gestured toward Nan's cottage. "Mal, the windows are broken. You need to—"

"What I need," Mal managed evenly as he glared at his lover, "is to make sure your dad is okay. This is just four walls and a roof without Nan in it."

Leif reversed the SUV back onto the road, and Leif muttered, "Brace yourself, okay? I know I'm a cliché and all, falling for the first guy I really slept with, but... I love you."

MRS. WATSON sprinted to the driver door, not waiting until Leif could get out to hear her, a rain hat plastered to her gray hair as she gestured frantically.

Leif and Mal leaped from the SUV, sliding on the mud, lightning capturing the moment like a flashbulb going off.

Mrs. Watson snagged Leif's arm. "I tried to stop him, but he had one of his notions, and there was no talking him out of it—he was sure you'd gone on the lake, so he took the rowboat to look for you!"

"Oh God." Leif's face was a tight mask as he looked toward Sylvan Lake, which was crashing above the stones he'd piled to separate the beach from the grass. The rain coming down was leaving pits in the earth, cutting down visibility.

"Do you have a powerboat?" Mal yelled.

Leif nodded, pointing to the boathouse just above the beach. "But it's on tracks—"

"We'll take it out."

"Mrs. Watson, go on back to the house and stay away from the windows!" Leif escorted her part of the way despite his urgent need to search for his father.

"Lived here all my life, haven't I?" But her eyes were full of fear. "Leif, be careful!"

IT WAS a nightmare getting the little powerboat out of the boathouse. The water had risen to the level of the double doors, so Mal had to pry them open while Leif manned the boat, using the battery-powered track to inch it down.

Water crashed against the craft so it wrenched free of the rail with a screech, but then Mal was there, swimming, muscling it so it drifted free.

Wheel in one hand, Leif looked over his shoulder to navigate. Painted wood towered high in the water—

"Mal!"

"*Uh!*" Mal grunted as a section of Leif's dock struck his back. His head disappeared.

Leif abandoned the wheel, trying not to fall out of the boat as the propeller lifted high in the air and then thudded into the surf. "*Mal!*"

"*Here!*" A hand gripped the side, water washing onto the deck as the craft wallowed, but it didn't matter because Leif tugged Mal aboard and they slid to the bottom of the boat, panting, holding on to each other.

"Oh fuck!"

"I'm all right!" Mal shouted despite blood running down his forehead. He had stripped down to his briefs, so he was also shivering.

Leif took a deep breath and managed to make his feet. He staggered to the steering wheel and gripped it, gunning the engine to pull them away from the shore while Mal flipped on the powerful light on the bow.

"Let's find your old man!" Mal leaned forward, knuckles white as the boat took a pounding.

CANADA GEESE dived deeper into the reeds as the powerful searchlight spotlighted them, high above their usual nesting ground. Mal's face was focused, but Leif felt despair rising like the storm. They'd been out there a long time.

They passed the Kilpatrick cottage and the old sawmill on the farthest part of the lake. Beyond were the rocks that surrounded the old mission....

"*There!*" Mal yelled, pointing.

Heart in his throat, Leif saw the upturned dinghy. *Oh, no. God no. Papa!*

"He's holding on to the side. I can see his hand!" Mal rubbed his arms and then shook his hands.

"Mal, I can't be sure I can reach you if you go in—" Leif couldn't see Papa's hand gripping the dinghy. Was he really alive?

"Toss me a rope when I reach him!" Mal dived clean, arrowing powerfully through the turbulent water.

The engine sputtered and died, and the powerboat drifted away from the dinghy.

ONE OF the things he'd thought about during his time alone was whether he had wasted those years he competed, but now Mal had a purpose again. His body was strong and sure in the water as he cut through the waves toward the dinghy.

In a flash of lightning, he saw a pale, frightened face and a frail hand curled around the dinghy's tether.

He swallowed more water before he took hold of that hand, looking into eyes the same color of his lover's. "I got you!" he rasped.

Leif's father complained, "Not so tight, boy!"

Mal's arms were getting leaden, holding tight to Leif's father. It was too rough to break for shore. He'd make it, but not Leif's papa. But if they stayed out here much longer….

Water slapped his face, and he choked, but he lifted Leif's father higher against the upturned dinghy.

Leif, come on!

And then he heard Leif shouting and the roar of a laboring engine.

The powerboat was almost on top of them, and then the rope hit Mal's arm, and somehow, even with his numb arms and screaming back, he held tight to Leif's father as he grabbed for the line.

Leif was a dark figure, shouting again, but Mal still couldn't hear him, and then the line snapped taut and they were yanked through the water. Choking, Mal gripped the old man, and Leif was—Shit, he was heading straight for shore to beach his boat!

Mal heard the snap of the craft's spine as it struck and the engine cut off. But in the fork of lightning from above them, he glimpsed Leif pulling the rope, hand over hand, pulling Mal and his father to the beach, to safety.

"YOU DID go out!" Papa accused him as soon as Leif dragged him up on the beach.

Leif laughed, except there were tears stinging his eyes as he crushed his father close. *Oh God, Papa….*

He met Mal's eyes, seeing perfect understanding.

"Who is that man?" Papa demanded, pulling away to give Mal a confused look. "He was in the water with me."

"He's my boyfriend, Papa," Leif said.

"Oh." The older man looked around the dark beach, wrapping his arms around himself. "We have a long walk."

Mal made to trail after them as they climbed onto the grass that ran by the familiar strip of highway, but Leif waited until he caught up.

Finally Mal said, "My place is closest." He looked at Leif's father, who was shivering under Leif's arm but was doggedly walking forward. "I have cocoa."

LEIF'S FATHER slept in Nan's room, wrapped in her summer quilt as Leif and Mal sat in the rocking chairs by the fire in the great room.

"Two broken windows," Leif noted. "And some of the old roof looks like it's in the trees now."

Mal nodded, taking a sip of his cocoa. "Save John the job of removing it, I guess," he joked. "There are more trees down in the back."

The thunder had softened to a rumble, not unlike a herd of cows moving off. The storm was passing.

"I'm thankful," Leif said, echoing Mal's feeling perfectly.

He took a deep breath and reached for Leif's hand, squeezing it. Leif answered by pulling him down to the coiled rag rug in front of the fire. Encompassed in his muscular arms, Mal let himself rest against him.

"You didn't hesitate to get to him. I don't know what to say."

"I'm just grateful I could help."

"You're a gift, Mal. Never think less of yourself."

Mal ducked his head, face reddening. Staring at the fire, he said, "You know, I think I agree with you. I have a gold medal, but tonight I did something to really be proud about."

They were both quiet for a while until Leif continued softly, "Sometimes you can't help but think it would be easier to live without the burden. You wish for the past. But I think Papa was more accepting of who I am now than he would have been before."

"He's in a better place. A place without prejudice, without preconceptions that are man-made chains. It may be he has more to teach you now in this new relationship you're entering," Mal said.

"I don't know how I'm going to see you... you know, from day to day," Leif fretted a little. "Just because I love you, shit doesn't disappear."

"Why don't we just take it day to day?" Mal suggested, feeling serene as he remembered his last letter from his Nan. She'd said he'd find what he was looking for here in Sylvan, and it wasn't all the answers to the questions he'd been asking himself, or even a career. It was more basic than that.

He reached up and adjusted the plaster bandage on his forehead, which Leif insisted he wear though the gash wasn't so bad. "Because I don't know what I want to do or how I'll make a living beyond this summer. But I do know I want you," he said, repeating the words Leif had given him earlier. "More than want you, if I'm honest, and if you'll take a risk on me."

And he saw in Leif's eyes he understood him perfectly.

"I took a risk the day I fished you out of the water. You saved my life tonight, Mal. Saved my heart and my conscience."

Mal got to his feet, putting his arm around his lover. "Let's see if your papa wants some cocoa."

Epilogue

Eight Months Later….

MAL LAID a card over Jenner's cards, narrowing one eye at the older man. "Sure you wanted that one?"

Jenner blinked, and Mal knew he'd lost the train of thought to follow the game. But he had managed through most of it. The nurse Leif hired had told them mind games, card games would help keep Jenner's mind active and alive, so Mal and Leif played cards and word games with him daily. Mal called it "working out" Jenner's mind.

"Is Leif here?" Jenner asked, a trace of anxiety creeping into his voice.

"He got a call to do some work on a leak," Mal said, not for the first time. "How about we go into my new studio and I'll show you my latest assignment?" He helped the older man up, going into Nan's kitchen and snagging some cookies and the tea that was still warm. He could see Jenner was flagging, but Jenner wouldn't rest until Leif was back.

Mal and Leif were managing to balance things. Mal didn't mind taking care of Leif's father when Leif got called away or just needed some time to himself, like when he went to the home show in a bigger town recently to see the lineup of new improvement products coming on to the market. And Mal, as a part-time fine arts student, was busy with classes part of the day when he wasn't working with Leif's team. He'd found a real pleasure in doing restoration furniture and paint finishes. It was becoming a side business that gave him both pleasure and pride, as well as all the extra cash he needed during his ongoing renovation of Nan's cottage.

And taking care of Jenner served another purpose for Mal—he felt as if, in some small way, he made up for not being there for Nan the last years. He couldn't go back in time and change that, but he could play a significant role in Jenner's life, making it easier for Leif as well.

He and Jenner walked down the new stairs they'd cut into the living room leading to the atrium/studio they just finished roughing in. Sawdust still lay in piles, and the windows were in but as yet their surrounds were unpainted. Mal would get to it when he had time.

"This is fine work," Jenner said, running a hand over the drywall.

"Your son helped me."

"Leif is a good worker." Jenner nodded. "He is a good friend to have."

Jenner thought of Mal and Leif as good friends. It was easier to leave it that way in the older man's mind, so Mal kept his own room in Leif's house, though in Nan's cottage, they shared the bed whenever they could both get a night to themselves. Those were rare and treasured occasions.

Mal was even thinking that when Nan's place was finished... well, maybe he could walk without a net. He could put the place up for rent and move in with Leif and Jenner. Not that he'd told Leif yet, though Leif had hinted he could turn the unused attic of his cottage into a fine studio with skylights.

That was a project for their future.

And it was amazing to know there would be one.

Mal had his sea legs now—he knew who he was—a budding artist, perhaps a teacher. A part-time caregiver. A significant other.

He was showing off the paint choices he'd made to Jenner when Leif knocked on the french door to the studio. He was soaking wet.

Jenner scolded him, just as if he were a boy. Leif gave Mal a rueful smile. "Found the leak."

"I see you did." Mal laughed. He snuck in a kiss, which warmed for a moment to passion before they broke apart reluctantly.

"Leif, I am proud of the work you've done in Nan's cottage," Jenner said unexpectedly. Unexpectedly since he had to be reminded from time to time of the project. "You are wonderful. *Wonderful*."

Leif's eyes filled. He ducked his head, swallowing. From what he'd told Mal, his father had been quiet and never demonstrative. Now with his illness, he said things out of the blue that sometimes rocked Leif's world. A gift Leif had never imagined would come from his illness.

"I had a good teacher, Papa."

Mal hugged Jenner, unable to help himself.

"And you are a good boy, Mal. I know your grandmother, you know. She's very proud of you."

"Thanks, Jenner," Mal said, not reminding the older man his Nan had passed. He decided he liked Jenner's world, without judgment, and without the loss of beloved people.

"I think you should take a shower, Leif. You are leaving water on Mal's new floor."

Leif laughed, and with his arm around both Jenner and Mal, they walked up the stairs so he could do that.

Afterword

I WROTE *Sylvan* originally to remember my happy summers at the cottage with my own Nan. Mal's cabin is a twin for hers, and the storm I wrote about is something I experienced more than once. They were truly frightening events on the prairie.

The other reason I wrote *Sylvan* was my mother had been diagnosed with dementia. I know many readers are going to unfortunately relate to this reality. At the time I felt a lot like Leif, that all I wanted was my real mom back. Now, seven years later, I've been blessed in seeing another side to this "disease." My mother out of the blue sometimes said very insightful things, very loving things. Things that rocked my world and changed the way I see myself. Because for a while she was pure spirit, as close to source as you can be and still be on our planet, I was amazed by her insight. When she said to the nurses, "You are wonderful," you couldn't help but be touched by the love she shared. She saw the real person, the whole person. How amazing an example of love is that?

I'm so glad I got a chance to revisit *Sylvan* and give Leif the gift of the insight I have had on the other side of this disease. Even though she passed just recently, I am lucky for the time I had with her and all the love she shared during her illness.

I also got to add in brief cameos of both Luke (the unknown cowboy Mal sees giving his horse a walk with a baby in tow) and Morgan Gallagher, the doctor who'd be a more "suitable" mate for Leif. Luke and Morgan are featured in the next story, *Luke*.

Luke

For Willa Okati

No one can see their reflection in running water. It is only in still water that we can see.
—Taoist Proverb

Chapter One

MORGAN GALLAGHER was waiting on a patient, Tom Hershey. Tom's wife, Ellen, passed away a week ago, and Morgan was worried about the elderly man, who had a bad heart. It was late, and Morgan rolled his shoulders, feeling the stiffness of his 3:00 a.m. morning. He'd had to go over to the Bronson Ranch and stitch up one of the cowhands, who had been in a brawl Saturday night.

Yawning, Morgan let his gaze move with familiar disinterest through Sylvan's old mission church. He liked the new windows folks had chipped in for, especially the one dedicated to Luke the Healer; for someone who took care of others, the man's face looked appropriately tired to Morgan's eyes. As he waited for Tom to finish chatting with Reverend Doyle, his gaze passed on and collided—*bam!*—with hazel eyes brimming with unshed tears.

Morgan's breath hitched, and his heartbeat picked up, even as the stranger looked away, his fawn-colored hair flattened from wearing the cowboy hat that rested on the pale wooden pew. But what Morgan also noticed along with the eyes were the man's tanned hands, which clenched the wooden seat in front of him.

He was tall and thin—maybe a bit too thin to Morgan's critical eye. He possessed the muscular upper body of a man who worked hard out of doors, typical in their Western town. In his bleached jeans' pocket, Morgan saw leather work gloves sticking out.

Throat tight as he remembered the look in those beautiful eyes, the blues and greens reminding Morgan of labradorite, he moved forward, feeling compelled to offer his help to the stranger.

But just then Reverend Doyle took his arm, startling Morgan. He didn't catch what the man said, but then Tom was there, and Morgan shoved aside the unsettling connection he'd experienced with the man sitting in the pew. He wanted to make sure Tom was taking his medicine, getting plenty of rest, and maybe he'd suggest Tom join the local senior's bridge club so he wouldn't feel so alone.

By the time Morgan satisfied himself he'd done right by Tom, his gaze went automatically to the blond pew where he'd spotted the cowhand.

It was empty. The man was gone.

LUKE WALKER shoved his hair off his forehead and replaced his hat as he exited the small mission by the lakeside of Sylvan. He didn't know why he'd gone in there, since God knew how long it was since he'd been in a church, but he was so tired and he'd hoped maybe he might find… something. Inspiration. Hope.

Instead he sat there, fighting tears, and met the compassionate blue eyes of a lean stranger wearing a blue work shirt and jeans, but not quite looking like a man who worked out of doors. He'd had the feeling the man read everything in his face, so he'd ducked away as soon as his attention was elsewhere.

He shook his head as he retraced his steps back to his truck and horse trailer. He had found nothing in the church to help him in practical terms. His meager savings were almost gone, and he couldn't find work because of Jessica. His last job involved leaving civilization far behind, taking people on trail rides deep into a national park, and he had loved it, but it wasn't something he could do now.

Right, take a baby into the wilderness. But hell, he considered it, late at night when she wouldn't, just wouldn't stop crying till he thought he'd break and start crying himself.

Last night he did just that. Went to the window of the cheap motel, hearing a couple fighting and then fucking in the room next door. He looked at that innocent baby and felt shame.

Shame this was all he could offer her. She was covered with a handmade crochet blanket, and her hair had a couple of pink ribbons in it. He'd mangled the knot on one of them so it kept sagging on her forehead.

Her face was pink, and so was one little foot she kept dancing up, jiggling in the air restlessly.

He reckoned maybe she got that from him. He was footloose, always had been. Always eager to hit the trail.

When the moonlight hit her and a coyote howled close by, she started to howl.

And Luke, desperate, crazy from lack of sleep and worry, howled too, mimicking a coyote.

He stopped midhowl, sure he'd scared the baby to death. She went all quiet, staring at him.

Then she made a gurgling sound, one chubby fist in her mouth.

She was smiling at him.

God, he knelt by the bed, tears running down his face.

In the room beside him, he could hear the mean, sweaty sounds of sex. On his own he always ignored that shit.

But he wasn't alone anymore.

That was the problem.

Now as he walked to his truck from the church, the dark voice inside him whispered maybe it was time to give her up. That he'd never counted on this. That this was not what he wanted.

But as he got closer to his old vehicle, he caught her thin cry, and the sound seemed to wrap around his guts. He unlocked the passenger door, feeling immediately guilty for leaving her, even for the few minutes he snatched thinking she was safely asleep.

She wasn't asleep now. Her blue eyes were open as he raised his newborn baby girl high into his arms, rocking her gently. He thought she liked that, but hell, what did he know?

"Jessie," he whispered. "Jessie girl."

She made a fretful sound, and on instinct, since he'd lived in fear the two weeks he had her, Luke touched her forehead. She felt much warmer than she did when he went in the church. Did she have a fever?

MORGAN EXITED the church, still musing on the mysterious stranger he'd glimpsed. His eyes had been so tormented. Maybe he should ask Reverend Doyle if he knew him.

He grimaced because he was aware his attention was also caught by basic attraction. He couldn't help it; cowboys with sandy hair and rangy, muscular builds were always his thing, ever since he'd read *Shane*. Maybe that was what propelled him to come out West once he finished his residency in a Boston hospital: the hot, romantic dream of a cowboy of his own.

It didn't happen, of course, so instead what compelled him to stay was that people in the outlying farms and ranches around the Sylvan area really needed a doctor. He knew he'd saved lives and helped people in this town, so it did make up a little for having little life outside his work.

A baby's cry made him look toward a tree-shadowed part of the cracked asphalt parking lot, and there he was, the tall, sandy-haired man of mystery wearing his cowboy hat… and holding a baby.

The man's face was tight as he looked over at Morgan, who had hesitated by his SUV. "Is everything all right?" Morgan called gently.

"I don't… shit, I don't know!" the stranger rasped. His beautiful eyes were frightened. He was holding the baby all wrong.

Morgan unlocked his vehicle and pulled out his bag before striding over to the stranger. He held those hazel eyes calmly, trying to impart silent reassurance.

"You a doctor, mister?" the man asked him.

"Yes," Morgan said. "I'm Dr. Morgan Gallagher. I have a clinic at a homestead I own about a mile from here."

"Luke Walker." Luke watched anxiously as Morgan studied the baby's face.

"What seems to be the problem?" Morgan asked gently.

"I think she's running a fever," Luke said. He flushed. "I'm not sure I can pay you. I was going to try the emergency clinic in Glenda Falls, since they take charity patients."

"That's a long way from here. I'm sure we can work something out," Morgan offered. No way could he send off a possibly sick child when he might be able to help. "We'd probably be better to head to my clinic, however, so I can examine her."

Luke bunched his jaw. "I'd be obliged, only if there is some way to pay you back, I'd rather work for it."

Morgan nodded, understanding pride. "I'm sure I can find something. Follow me back to my clinic," he said briskly.

LUKE FOLLOWED Morgan's SUV down an unpaved track with birch trees bending over the road, some in danger of falling over and blocking it. Didn't Morgan know to remove them if they were too weighed down by winter snows? Otherwise, they could be a real pain in the ass.

They passed some outbuildings made of logs, some with saplings spurting up from the roofs, the fall meadows surrounding them dotted with late purple coneflowers, blue asters, and wild roses already swollen with reddish hips. A few early fallen leaves rolled from under the passage of the vehicle ahead of him like scattered gold coins.

Luke pulled up outside a log farmhouse with a green roof opposite a dilapidated barn and a corral that had been left to rot and fall down in sections. He couldn't help but shake his head at the decay. Maybe the doctor didn't care, but this was good land and it was a shame.

For a moment, looking at his daughter, who was sleeping again from the movement of the truck, he wondered why it was he instantly felt trust in a stranger. But something about Dr. Morgan Gallagher touched him. His blue eyes were full of genuine concern, and there had been a strange… feeling Luke experienced from the first moment he saw Morgan in the church.

"WELL, IT'S not a fever," Morgan said finally after he'd carefully examined Jessica, pulling the stethoscope from his ears.

Luke's shoulders slumped, and he let out a deep breath. "Shit," he whispered.

"How long have you been taking care of your daughter?" Morgan probed, seeing familiar new-parent exhaustion in Luke's eyes… and something more—a trace of the despair he'd glimpsed in the mission.

"Two weeks," Luke said. "You sure she's okay? She was so hot."

"She was warm from sleeping and the stuff she was wearing. See? She's cooler to the touch now. Newborns can't regulate their temperature as efficiently as older children. So she's three months?"

"Yes, sir, just a day over." Luke scrubbed his face, his fingers rasping against his growing beard. "She's so small. I've been around when calves and horses been born. They come out bigger."

"And her mother?" Morgan continued to probe gently. He knew there was a story here, and probably not a very happy one.

"Zelda Mancuso. She, uh, was a waitress in a road house I met in a town about a hundred miles from here."

"She didn't want the baby?" Morgan guessed.

"No," Luke said with a sigh. "She told me she just wasn't cut out to be a parent. Then she took off and left Jessie with me."

"That's rough," Morgan said. He watched Luke caress Jessie's cheek, seeing love and pain in his hazel eyes. The man had to be overwhelmed by the sudden crushing responsibility of a new baby. "I imagine you've felt that way too."

Luke swallowed but didn't speak. Instead he shrugged before reaching into the heavy baby's bag he'd brought into Morgan's clinic for a fresh diaper.

"When was the last time you had a good night's sleep?" Morgan asked gently.

Luke had the baby covered now, obviously having a lot of experience changing diapers. Morgan had to like him for that alone. And the way those big, callused hands were extra gentle on the baby. He powdered her bum and sealed the diaper before giving a rusty laugh.

"You know, I can't remember. It seems like a blur of terror, the past two weeks. I don't think I'm cut out to be a father."

"I think anyone feels that way at first," Morgan said. "But if you can eat right and get some rest, it would be better for both you and Jessie." He hesitated to take Luke to task for leaving the baby alone in his truck earlier…. Maybe he'd get a chance to bring it up another time. Luke was out of his depth, and making him feel worse wouldn't be constructive for him or Jessie.

Luke tightened his lips, and Morgan could bet he'd been living on caffeine and fast food. "I can't seem to find a job right now, but I've worked all my life, Doc—"

"Call me Morgan," Morgan found himself offering. "Jessie is my patient, not you." For some reason Morgan wanted to hear his name on Luke's lips. He shoved some of his shaggy brown hair out of his eyes and went to wash his hands in the small sink.

"I'm good for it, though," Luke continued.

"I'm not worried about that, Luke," Morgan reassured him. As he dried his hands with a paper towel, Morgan was struck by a sudden, slightly insane inspiration. He knew he was tired and he should think on it, but he had a feeling Luke and Jessie might head back on the road soon if he didn't act. "Luke, you have the look of a working man."

Having finished with Jessie, Luke looked over at Morgan. "Yes, Doc," he said. "I never had any trouble finding a job before."

"Before you had a newborn, you mean." Morgan twitched his lips in sympathy.

Luke nodded, rubbing the back of his neck. "It does complicate things."

"I have a housekeeper, Luke," Morgan said. "Gena Gardenia Anderson." His lips pulled into a smile at the way Luke widened his eyes at the unusual name. "Her mother was kind of a hippy, but Gena is very responsible, the oldest daughter from a family of six kids. She could probably watch over Jessie if you would consent to stay on and do some work for me."

Luke's beautiful hazel eyes widened. "You're offering me a job?"

"Well, yes," Morgan said. "I'm still a bit of a greenhorn, I admit, and this place is falling down, which seems a shame. Sometimes I think it might be nice to keep some horses and improve my riding. I occasionally rent one for an afternoon from a stable on the other side of town when I can catch the time."

Luke shook his head. "You couldn't keep them now, unless you wanted them to wander off."

Morgan nodded in rueful agreement. "Plus I admit I wouldn't know how to take care of them, nor would I have the time, with my unpredictable doctor's hours. I figured you would since you have a horse trailer."

"Yeah, it's for my gelding, Sable, a Rocky Mountain Horse." Luke cleared his throat. "He's first class on trail rides. I, uh, was going to put him up for sale."

"I don't know if the barn is fit for him, but you're welcome to stable him here tonight if you want to think on this," Morgan said. "I really do need you. If I'd had time, I would have hired someone months ago, so it looks like it might have been my lucky night."

Luke held Morgan's eyes, and again Morgan experienced that flash of connection he'd felt in the church. He tried to shove it aside. He merely wanted to help Luke. It was obvious he was straight. Somehow Morgan was going to have to keep his liking of the tall, rangy body and Luke's steady hazel eyes to himself.

"You'd be doing me a favor," Luke rasped, looking down at his daughter.

Morgan wanted to ask if Luke had been tempted to give up his child, but some subjects were too painful to share with a stranger.

"Why don't you see if you can make use of one of the stalls in the barn for your horse. I can watch Jessie while you do that." *Luke, let me help you.*

"The barn might do for my horse, but where would Jessie and I stay?" Luke shook his head. "Your outbuildings look like they need some work."

Morgan blinked, not having thought it out yet. "There is a guest room in the loft if you don't mind your bedroom being open to the great room from below."

"No, I don't care, as long as you don't mind that Jessie has yet to sleep through the night." Luke gave a rueful laugh. "And here I thought going in that mission was a waste of time." He looked at Morgan. "I asked for help."

Morgan suppressed the urge to reach out and touch the back of Luke's hand. "I want to help you," he said.

Chapter Two

IT GOT cold in the barn. The autumn night air stung Luke's cheeks as he led Sable carefully out of the trailer. His horse looked like some exercise would do him good; Luke felt bad because, until he wound up with an infant daughter to care for, Sable had been his family, the only constant in his life as he wandered from ranch to ranch. He'd ached over the need to sell him but was beginning to feel that it probably would be the best thing for his horse. But now… well, now maybe he had more options, though he was afraid to hope.

Was Morgan for real, or was Luke just letting his growing desperation and his exhaustion do his thinking? He sighed since usually he had a good sense of people. When he thought of that first look they'd exchanged in the mission, he felt as if Morgan had wanted to reach out.

The barn had more holes than upright walls, but one corner seemed a likely place to house his horse. Luke first raked out the stall, disturbing a family of mice that made his horse stamp his hooves.

"You're much bigger than they are," Luke teased him. "So cut that out."

Once the stall was cleaned out, he gave Sable a quick brushing and settled him in with a fresh feedbag for the night. He latched the stall door closed and gave his horse a last look.

"I wonder what you'd make of Morgan, boy?" he mused. Wiping his sweaty forehead, Luke considered Morgan's gentle manner. He was good with Jessie, handling her more expertly than Luke did, if he were honest with himself. And he knew more about what to expect from a baby. Luke only had some time at the library, surfing the net and trying to find out all he could.

Despite the shoddy state of his outbuildings and land, the doctor appeared to be in good shape, Luke noted as he left the barn. Luke also liked his warm blue gaze and brown hair. He didn't seem a flashy man, but capable.

MORGAN WAS sitting in a rocking chair in his kitchen with Jessie in his arms when the screen door creaked and Luke walked in. His face was rosy from the chill in the air. He wiped his boots off on the mat by the door, looking a little hesitant.

"Leave them on, if you like," Morgan said. "It's just old hardwood floors with bound rugs. Nothing fancy."

Luke relaxed, nodding. He went to the kitchen sink and washed his hands, and while he dried them, his hazel eyes softened on his daughter's face. "You forget sometimes that she can seem like an angel."

"Um. I imagine around 4:00 a.m. when she won't go to sleep," Morgan noted.

Luke smiled shyly. "Yeah. You're really good with her."

"It's been a while since I've been spoiled with this much time with a healthy baby," Morgan said, carefully passing Jessie into Luke's arms. He studied him for a moment, watching as he settled Jessie against him. "She maybe has your chin."

"You think so?" Luke asked. His face briefly glowed. "I'm probably a little punchy."

"You need some rest, and she seems down for the count now she's been fed and burped." Morgan pointed the way for his new houseguest into the great room. It was a large space with a wooden stove in the center and a fireplace made of river rock. Homemade log furniture was placed as islands of seating groups anchored with rag rugs.

"This is... nice," Luke noted, looking immediately at ease with Morgan's home.

"I do get bats in here sometimes." Morgan felt he had to warn. "I have to get someone to take a look at the roof."

"I'll go up tomorrow, if you have a ladder," Luke offered. "I'm not a carpenter, but I'm pretty handy."

"I have a shed with all kinds of woodworking supplies left over from the woman who built this homestead."

"A woman? She did a damn good job."

"Better than I have, I know." Seeing the weariness in Luke's eyes, Morgan cut short the tour. "My room is through there." He pointed to a door cut of logs at the far end of the room. "There's another guest room right under the staircase, and then the loft is yours...."

Morgan led the way up the stairs, grazing a hand over a mobile made by the former resident out of Sylvan beach wood and seashells. At the top of the stairs, the loft stretched out the rest of the length of the cabin, a double-sized bed made of homespun logs under a window.

But it was the cradle that made Luke pause, also made by hand with tall spindles. "Oh man," he whispered.

"It was just here," Morgan said. "More of that luck, I guess. You can move it close to the bed if you want. And here, you want me to hold her while you get settled? I don't have baby bedding, but you can probably improvise tonight with some of the blankets and sheets. They're all new and freshly washed."

Luke handed Jessie back to Morgan, and Morgan paced back and forth with her while Luke sorted through the pile of bedding at the end of his bed, rigging something up for Jessie.

"She may mess up this bedding," Luke warned.

"That's what the washing machine is for." Morgan wasn't too worried. He liked holding Jessie for Luke while watching him. Luke looked to be in about his midtwenties, about ten years younger than Morgan, and yet his tanned face was weathered by harsh experience. Man, he was appealing. And Morgan had to keep that thought to himself.

Instead he concentrated on Jessie, but before he knew it, Luke was done, the cradle moved up so it was within touching distance of the bed.

"I'll leave the light on downstairs so if you need to heat up some formula, you can find your way to the kitchen easily."

"She will wake up sometime. And then she'll wake you up," Luke said, still looking uncertain over Morgan's proposed arrangement.

"I'm a doctor, so I don't always sleep through the night. I should warn you that if I get a call, I might have to go somewhere or help someone in my clinic."

Luke sat on the bed with Jessie, his fawn hair rumpled, blond stubble on his lower jaw and chin. His blue work shirt was slightly open, revealing a tanned throat and the wisp of soft brown-blond hair on his chest. Morgan swallowed, flashing to what it would be like to put his hand there, feel Luke's heart beating, touch his warm, healthy skin.

He cleared his throat. "Well… good night."

"Yeah, good night, Doc," Luke called. "And… thanks."

MORGAN LIT a fire in the great room since he felt too wound up to sleep. He didn't think the dancing light or the slight crackle of wood burning would disturb Jessie or Luke.

He settled into a wooden chair and wished he hadn't given up smoking. He could use something now to soothe himself from thinking so much he found it impossible to rest.

Above he caught the creak of wood, and then a tall, man-shaped shadow moved around. It was Luke taking off his shirt.

Morgan's breath caught in his throat as he watched the shadow above, knowing he should look away. The soft sound of metal—Luke opening his belt?—and finally the groan of the mattress as Luke climbed into bed.

Whoa. Morgan's heart was pounding, and he felt even further away from sleep than before. As he watched the log consumed by licking gold flame, he decided he'd have to tell Luke he was gay. Not because anything would happen between them, but because… he wanted Luke to know. He'd have to if he were going to stay under Morgan's roof.

As his head fell back on the chair and he watched the play of light through half-closed eyes, Morgan wondered if that would drive Luke away.

He hoped not since despite his inconvenient attraction to Luke, which he *would* keep under wraps, he sincerely wanted to help him and Jessie.

LUKE WOKE up when sunlight warmed the top of his head through the window. He blinked a moment, not sure where he was, but that was a familiar feeling for a wanderer like him.

Then he sat up, panicked, and looked over at Jess.

The baby was sleeping, one palm near her head like a little pale open heart.

Luke's pulse settled down, staring at her. He couldn't remember the last time she slept this long. Maybe the constant travel from motel to motel upset her, though Luke had no choice.

Or maybe the energy those places carried was responsible. Luke couldn't afford anything but the dregs, rooms that smelled of sex and cigarettes and desperation. Jessie's mother was a great believer in energy and vibes. She would have said Jessie was sensitive. His kid certainly was, more so than Luke. He'd never cared where he slept or even who he fucked.

"I have coffee on," Morgan called from the stairs in a very soft voice, obviously not wanting to wake Jessie.

Luke carefully got up, pulling on his jeans over boxers, and then, barefooted and barechested, and shivering a little from the slight chill, he walked over to the top of the stairs.

Morgan's blue eyes widened when he saw him, and he immediately looked away. "I can bring it up so you can stay with Jessie."

"What time is it?" Luke asked, shoving his bed hair out of his eyes.

"After nine." Morgan looked a little smug when he met Luke's gaze again briefly. "She slept well, mmmm?"

"Better than she has since I got her," Luke confessed with feeling. "Sometimes I think she does two things real good—make a mess of her diapers and scream. Sure did me a world of good to sleep in."

"You do look better." Again Morgan cleared his throat. Then he suddenly blurted, "Luke, I'm gay."

Luke stared, not sure what to say. "Are you?" he finally replied.

Color stung Morgan's cheeks as he swallowed. Obviously this was hard for Luke.

"I just thought you should know," Morgan said. "I don't keep it a secret, so folks in town do."

"Okay then," Luke said, still feeling blank. He guessed Morgan wanted him to know since they'd be living together. Uh, under the same roof, that was. "I'm sorry I slept so long. I wanted to get an early start… take a look at your roof."

Morgan breathed out a sigh. "No… worry over that later. When Jessie's ready to eat, bring her to the kitchen since Gena should be by soon. I know you'll want to meet her. Oh, and the bathroom's through the kitchen. There is a pack of fresh razors under the sink and lots of other stuff on hand if you need anything."

Morgan was still avoiding his eyes, but he had relaxed his shoulders. He hesitated and then made to head back down the stairs.

Luke called, "I don't care."

"Excuse me?" Morgan's blue eyes shot to Luke's face.

Luke swallowed. "I don't care if you're gay." He ran his hands over his jeans in a nervous gesture. "Jessie slept through the night. Thank you."

Morgan's face thawed. "I'm making scrambled eggs."

Chapter Three

MORGAN'S HOUSEKEEPER, Gena, had a curvaceous figure and bright red hair and green eyes, reminding Luke vaguely of a pretty Christmas ornament. In her thirties, she was normally Luke's type for a one-nighter, though he felt nothing this morning other than relief Jessie had experienced her first good night since he became her full-time father.

Or maybe it wasn't merely parenthood that had crushed his libido into the dust. Before he knew Jessie existed, he was dissatisfied, restlessly searching for... something. He had spent most of his life wandering since he moved out from his former rodeo-star father's apartment. The funny thing was Luke always wanted a home, a family, roots... but somehow no woman he met seemed like the person he'd been searching for.

Now with Jessie on his hands, maybe it was better he'd given up. He didn't have the time or freedom to meet someone special. And who would want a cowboy who had no money and a kid? At this point he could barely afford to rent a DVD to watch with someone.

So he ignored Gena's speculative glances when Morgan first introduced her before the doc headed into his clinic to see his morning patients.

"You know Morgan's gay, right?" she asked once they were alone in the kitchen. Jessie was in Luke's arms, sleepy again from her breakfast. She was very relaxed under Morgan's roof; in the past when Luke would be pulling out of the parking lot of a motel at this time of the morning, she got fretful, as if she needed to stay somewhere. Feel safe.

Luke hadn't been able to give her that, and it killed him.

"He told me." Luke's voice was a little chilly, like the autumn morning shining golden through the kitchen windows.

"You disapprove?" Gena took a sip of her coffee, watching Luke.

"No.... Not of him. I mean." Luke sighed, wishing he was better with words, but he'd barely finished high school. "I just don't feel comfortable with talking about him."

Gena's face softened. "You've really taken to him." She cleared her throat. "I mean as a friend and employee, of course."

"Of course," Luke echoed.

"I'm glad. Morgan's a really good man. I think he works too much because he's lonely. Having a friend would be a good thing for him."

"It might be a good thing for me too," Luke said with some feeling.

"So Jessie's mom just… dumped Jessie and ran?"

"Pretty much. I woke up with a hangover and a baby on the bed next to me," Luke remembered ruefully. "She did write me a note on how to take care of Jessie."

"That's some morning after!" Morgan put in, coming into the kitchen to refill his coffee mug.

He was wearing a medical coat, his brown hair still damp around his ears, Luke noticed. Well, they'd had to share the bathroom to shave since Luke was out of shaving cream. It was a bit strange to be in the same steamy space, both of them wearing towels around their waists, Jessie propped up with pillows at the bathroom door so Luke could keep an eye on her. Strange because he was wildly conscious of Morgan's confession he was gay. He'd scolded himself it was no different from sharing space with a guy in the gym, but Luke found himself wondering if Morgan might find him attractive.

"It was definitely a morning after for the record books," Luke agreed now, glad to push aside the unsettling thoughts of sharing a bathroom with Morgan. "But if I can just find regular work, I won't complain."

"You know I'll need a lot done around here, and I still want to talk about maybe fixing up the barn so I can keep a couple of riding horses," Morgan said seriously. "But I know that Leif Gunnar is always looking for workers for his construction company, and Charlie LaFountaine runs a big spread not far from here. He also always needs good men."

Luke scratched his chin, considering. Suddenly it seemed like he had options. Too weird considering how black his prospects seemed for the past weeks. Probably getting a decent night's sleep helped. And Morgan.

"I'll be happy to get started looking at your roof now. When do you want the barn rebuilt?"

"Rebuilt? It's that bad, huh?"

"More than half of it is in fall-down shape," Luke said. He looked down at his daughter and then over at Gena, who was sipping her coffee and listening silently to the conversation with interest. He bit his lip. "But I can repair the corral with fresh wood this week after a trip to the lumberyard."

"Look, why don't you just keep coming in here to check on Jessie?" Morgan suggested, as if easily reading the unease in Luke's gut. "Gena will watch her while she cleans the house and does some cooking, and I'll be in and out. If you get a little worried, just leave what you're doing and look in on her, and if she needs you, stay with her."

Luke's throat tightened. He cleared it. "Thank you," he said, liking Morgan more and more. The guy had to be crazy if he thought the fact he was gay was enough to drive Luke from staying here! Jessie liked this place. She was calmer. Had she been picking up on Luke's growing depression and worry?

"Do you mind if I keep her in my office for a little while?" Morgan asked, face softening as he reached out and gently brushed a finger against Jessie's cheek. "I have some paperwork to do."

Luke lifted Jessie up, and Morgan took her. "She really likes you," Luke noted. It was stupid. Just yesterday he was thinking he'd have to give Jessie up, and now he felt a little anxious that someone else had her. He took a deep breath, reminding himself he wasn't going far. He was going to work around the cabin today and check out the barn. If he could rig up something temporary for the corral, he'd shoo Sable out so the horse could get a little exercise.

"You're lucky to have her," Morgan said.

Lucky. Luke hadn't felt that way since Jessie came into his life. But maybe… yeah.

When Morgan left, Luke finished his coffee, feeling oddly self-conscious with Gena watching him. She did so with a slight smile, not even looking away.

"You got something to say?" he finally demanded.

"Just thinking about the law of attraction."

"Whoa—"

"Dummy, not you and me!" she laughed. "Haven't you heard of the law of attraction?"

"I got a baby; what do you think?"

That made Gena laugh even harder. Luke flushed, feeling dumb as a stump. Like when older kids had asked him if he was a virgin when he was six and he said yes and they laughed, so he changed his answer and they thought that was even funnier. He hated being so ignorant. Morgan had floor-to-ceiling bookcases in his great room. Luke had never been a great reader, but he'd like to try, maybe pick up some things.

Gena's gaze softened. "It's a movie called *The Secret*. It's basically about the premise that like draws like. I was just thinking that here you are, lonely and not knowing how to be a family with Jessie, and there is Morgan, also lonely and wishing more than anything he could have one, only he's convinced himself it'll never happen, so he spends too much time fussing over his patients." She shrugged. "So you encounter each other 'coincidentally.'"

"Sounds like a chick flick."

She laughed again. "I like you, Luke."

"Okay." He was blushing. He hated when he did that. But he liked Gena too. Morgan seemed to attract good people, if that's what Gena meant by her law of attraction stuff.

And he was kind of sorry for Morgan, seeing him through fresh eyes. He guessed he *was* lucky, having that baby.

MORGAN SAT back in his office chair, the rattle of a ladder just outside his window as Luke moved it into place to check the roof. He'd been at it for a while with only two visits so far to check on Jessie, who was currently sleeping in the leather chair opposite Morgan.

Luke appeared in the window just then, and his hazel eyes went to his daughter, so he missed the way Morgan clenched his hands on his pen and had to take a deep breath… because Luke had removed his shirt and was wearing just worn blue jeans, cowboy boots, and healthy sweat.

Morgan forced himself to look away. *Get a grip, Gallagher!* He had shared a bathroom with Luke just that morning. It had to be his kink for cowboys firing his response, and yet why was it the more he saw him, the more attractive he seemed?

Nope, it was becoming a kink for Luke Walker.

"FINISHED YOUR paperwork?" Luke climbed down the ladder to greet Morgan, who had Jessie on his lap as he sat on a log bench in the sunshine.

"No, I just wanted to get out for a little while. Not too many nice days like this one before winter comes," Morgan said. "And I think Jessie appreciates it too."

Luke lifted his white T-shirt and put it back on, feeling weirdly self-conscious with Morgan there. Why? But it felt like something was humming in the air. He used a corner of his shirt to wipe the sweat from his face and caught Morgan looking at his stomach. He almost looked down at it himself to see what Morgan was looking at.

"Did you finish looking over the roof?" Morgan asked after he cleared his throat.

"Yes, sir. I think the bats are getting in through a hole near the fireplace. I can probably patch it, but you'll need to replace the roof in a few years."

"But it's all right for now?" Morgan looked relieved, which made sense, with the work he wanted done on the outbuildings.

"I think so. The woman who built this place knew what she was doing."

Morgan grimaced. "Better than me. I was hoping I'd get to see your horse."

Luke nodded. "I'm off to the barn now. I checked on Sable earlier, but if I can rig something up, I'd love to let him loose in the corral."

"I'll help you," Morgan offered. "I've had enough of sitting around for one morning; I like to keep in shape."

"You're not bad for a doctor," Luke said, taking his daughter.

NOT BAD? Did that mean Luke thought Morgan was attractive? *You really are a pathetic bastard,* Morgan scolded himself.

But it was Luke who brought it up. "Do you, uh, think I'm hot or something?"

Morgan took a deep breath and then forced himself to meet Luke's eyes, to be honest. God, he hoped he wouldn't get punched. Anything was possible when a man like him took a risk like this.

"Yes," he said flatly.

Luke considered him with his hazel gaze. "But that's not why you offered me the job here."

"No," Morgan said, disgust heavy in his tone. "I'd never…. Jesus."

Luke was nodding. "Didn't think so."

BUT LUKE found himself curious about Morgan as they put Jessie down nearby and worked to lift some fallen logs to close off the corral temporarily. "What is it like, being gay?"

"Challenging sometimes. My mom paid for medical school since my father just about disowned me. I was lucky to have her. She worked two jobs to support me and my sister, managing to put us both through school."

"Do you see her and your sister often?"

Morgan smiled. "Mom's coming out for Christmas, I think. She worries I work too hard. My sister Heather is a pediatrician, married about ten years now, so I don't get to see her unless I visit Boston, usually."

"Your mom sounds like a neat lady." Luke used a wooden mallet to hammer in a post, gathering his thoughts. "This is a nice spread you have here. A place with roots," Luke praised.

"That's what I thought when I bought it. I always wanted a home and, uh, you know, someone to share it with," Morgan finished awkwardly.

"Are you dating someone?" Luke blushed when the question just blurted out. What the hell…? But he'd always been impulsive.

"I do visit someone," Morgan said. "He lives in a smaller town not too far from here, and we've been good friends for a while."

"Oh." Luke closed his mouth, forcing himself not to ask any more questions. Geez! Morgan hadn't been so probing about his love life, not that he had one anymore.

"I go there for sex," Morgan confessed baldly. He was flushing, but again he held Luke's eyes, as if wanting him to get the message Morgan wouldn't be chasing after him.

"Uh-huh," Luke said. He took a deep breath, and then suddenly, he had to go into the barn because this conversation…. "Watch Jessie for a sec?" he rasped.

He strode into the concealing shadows, seeing Sable raise his head. Soothed, he went to his horse, reaching out to stroke his dark head. He took a couple of deep breaths, his heart pounding.

"Shit," he muttered, wondering what had come over him.

Chapter Four

LUKE AND Jessie had been living under Morgan's roof a week when the subject of Morgan's boyfriend came up again. During that time Luke had shoved his unsettling thoughts pretty much from his head, successful because of Jessie, who mostly slept through the nights now—but not always—and the hard work of rebuilding Morgan's barn.

Morgan had hired Leif Gunnar's local construction company, so his guys worked with Luke during the days, as the autumn sun still had the power to make it pretty warm.

During this time Luke also tried to make a little room for exercising Sable, though he still wasn't comfortable riding too far from Morgan's house and away from Jessie. Most days he settled for riding back and forth over the unpaved road that led from the log cabin to the turnoff onto the local road. It was also a good way to take a closer look at the outbuildings Morgan wanted restored.

One night Jessie wouldn't settle, and Luke was pacing the loft with her, the lamp by the bed providing dim light. He was hoping she wouldn't wake up Morgan, who had had a long day treating some patients with early flu bugs, and a cowboy from a nearby ranch who had fallen off his horse and broken his leg. But when he heard the creak of the step just out of eyesight, he knew he'd failed.

"Sorry we woke you," he called, letting Morgan know it was okay to come up. Morgan was respectful of Luke and Jessie's space and never came all the way up the stairs without an invitation.

Morgan appeared, brown hair mussed around his face from sleep, eyes heavy. Luke figured he probably looked the same way. Only Jessie wanted to be up at this hour!

"I could make some hot cocoa for us," Morgan offered. "Why don't you come into the kitchen with her and we'll have some."

Luke nodded. Sometimes when he gave up trying to get Jess back to sleep and resigned himself to being awake, she'd fall asleep. Babies were very contrary, he'd discovered.

He followed Morgan down the stairs, the little mobile tinkling softly from the air disturbed by their passage. Since Luke had repaired the gap in the roof, they no longer had bats winging just below the peaked ceiling anymore. The cabin was a little shabby, but sound and comfortable. What Luke liked best about it was listening to the wind moving through the trees beyond his window in the loft; that and the soft starlight that lit his room.

In the kitchen Morgan poured milk into a saucepan, yawning. He was wearing a blue T-shirt that fit tightly around his chest, and some gray boxers. Luke noticed, not for the first time, his new boss was lean and muscular for a doctor. Morgan ran. Sometimes he'd get up even earlier than Luke and take off running in the woods. Luke sometimes would watch him when he came back, sweaty and heaving for breath.

He looked away from Morgan to his daughter and settled in one of the wooden chairs with her. "Are you sure you aren't sick of us?" he asked Morgan for the tenth time. He couldn't imagine why anyone in their right mind would want to be in the same house with a newborn night after night.

"I told you I'm used to snatching sleep when I can," Morgan said, looking peaceful. "And sometimes medicine… it's damned depressing. Telling someone they have cancer, or stitching them up and knowing they are in pain. It's nice to be around a healthy baby."

"Did you ever want kids?" Luke dared to ask, remembering Gena's hints. It had to be the late night inviting confidences since he'd carefully avoided asking Morgan any more personal questions since that first time. He felt out of sorts for days afterward, sometimes unable to sleep even when Jessie didn't wake him up.

"Yeah, but it's unlikely," Morgan said, pulling out some mugs. "I don't have a partner, and I'd want to be able to offer a two-parent home with my crazy hours. I'll have to settle for vicariously enjoying your Jessica."

"You're certainly getting to enjoy her tonight," Luke said dryly. But Morgan really didn't seem to mind. The truth was he was as easy to live with as his house. He spent a lot of his time wearing glasses—doing paperwork or reading in the evenings—so Luke was left on his own. Sometimes Luke brought Jessie down to the great room and sat with Morgan, or walked through the woods near the cabin while Morgan watched her, which offered Luke time on his own.

Morgan never pressed his company on Luke.

"What a way to spend Friday night," Luke continued. "In a million years, I never saw myself doing this."

"But you don't regret it now," Morgan said. He was mixing the cocoa powder into the milk now and adding a little sugar and nutmeg, which was his own twist on it. Jessie had settled in Luke's arms, blinking up at him, calmer now, as if she liked listening to the voices of Luke and Morgan talking.

"No, just... sometimes. I guess it's like if you suddenly buy a dog, and then you have to go out and walk him in a snowstorm. Times one thousand."

Morgan handed Luke his drink, settling in the chair opposite him. "Um," he agreed.

"So... why aren't you with your boyfriend?" Luke kept his eyes focused on the steam rising from his mug. "It being Friday night."

"He's not—" Morgan cut himself off and bit his lip. "It's casual with us."

"Oh." Luke felt out of his depth. He could feel his cheeks heating. "Right."

"He's a professor at the local university," Morgan went on to explain. "So usually we'll do something cultural, like see foreign films."

"I'm more into action movies than, well…. Guess I'm a cliché, huh?" He had so little in common with Morgan. He worked with his back and his hands, not his mind, and he was used to roughing it. He was used to one-nighters. Even if this thing Morgan had going was casual, it was sure as hell more settled than anything Luke had ever experienced.

"I always had a thing for cowboys," Morgan confessed, his gaze on Luke's tanned hands where he held Jesse. "Laconic, capable, muscled, hard men in cowboy boots and jeans. There was this one gay stripper I used to…." Then he put his cup down abruptly. "Excuse me; I hope I didn't make you feel uncomfortable. I think I'm a little punchy."

"You didn't," Luke said. Wow. Did Morgan ever imagine Luke stripping out of his jeans? He swallowed hard. "So will you see your... friend on Saturday night?"

"Actually I will," Morgan said. "I invited him here for dinner."

That freaked Luke out more than the cowboy stripper thing. What would he have to say to a professor, someone into foreign films? Or would Morgan expect the hired help and his daughter to make themselves scarce so he could be alone with the guy?

Morgan gave a rusty laugh. "I invited him here since I thought it might make you more comfortable with me." He shook his head. "From the look on your face, I missed something. But last week when you asked me those questions, I could see you were a little... confused."

"I wasn't sure what I was feeling," Luke confessed, trying to match Morgan's honesty. "You didn't have to do that, invite him here for me. It's your house."

"But I share it with you and Jessie now," Morgan said. Then he flushed. "I think I overcompensated."

"What will I say to him?" Luke asked. "I mean, I have never seen a film where they don't speak English."

"You don't have to impress him," Morgan said gently. "Any more than I guess I needed to reassure you. Now I wish I hadn't invited Steven…."

Luke wished he hadn't either, but it was Morgan's house and his friend. But just how close were they, and would this Steven kiss and touch Morgan?

Shit, what a crazy thing to think about.

But Luke couldn't stop himself. He asked himself honestly if the idea bothered him because it was, well, two guys.

And yeah, it did. If he was honest, it did. Not that he was a hater. He once saw two male deer hang out together during mating season. Even in animals some things were just natural. Not that he'd share that with Morgan since he'd probably think Luke's thinking was what you'd expect of a hick.

But Morgan *ached* for a family.

Luke wasn't blind. He could see it. Gena could see it. And Morgan did overcompensate by working himself too much. Sometimes he'd come back so late and bushed that Luke had to suppress the urge to give him what for. Yeah, like what? A nagging wife? Je-sus.

But he cared about Morgan, damn it. And Morgan wasn't a player. He acted like he was, like he was experienced and worldly, like he was okay seeing movies with someone once in a while, but Morgan ached to be a family.

Probably this Steven guy was just playing Morgan. If he cared about him, truly cared, then he'd man up and…offer a ring? In the cities he knew some gay men and women married now.

Steven should offer Morgan a real commitment. Seeing movies together was bullshit.

SPLITTING LOGS by the barn the next morning, his shirt off, his body getting into the groove, Luke asked himself again why he'd had such a dumb thought about Morgan and Steven kissing in front of him. Why did it bother him so much? He honestly didn't care when Morgan told him he was gay, other than hoping he wouldn't somehow say the wrong thing to him. His father was a very tolerant man, maybe because he had been a working man all his life, and he'd tried to teach Luke to respect people based on their actions, not their differences.

Whump!

Splinters shot out and sections of log fell like slices from an orange. Would Morgan and Steven go into Morgan's room when Steven visited?

Whump!

The axe got caught in the spine of wood and Luke left it, walking away with his hands on his hips. A person had to be careful handling an axe when they were…confused. No, he answered his own question. Morgan was really focused on making Luke feel comfortable. He'd never do that, have sex with Steven in the same house. But would that mean Morgan would follow his friend home after their dinner?

Luke shoved his hair off his forehead, annoyed with himself. What the hell was he thinking about this shit for all the time? It was none of his business.

"You look like a man with a lot on his mind," Leif Gunnar noted. The tall, Nordic-looking guy was the owner of the construction company restoring the barn. He came by once or twice a day to make sure work was going smoothly.

Luke gave Leif a rueful look as he rubbed the back of his neck. "Yeah, I guess."

Leif moved his gray gaze over Luke's face. "It must be rough, being a new father," he said.

That wasn't what was eating at Luke, but of course, he couldn't bring up the burr under his saddle over Morgan. It was too strange. "Can be," he agreed.

"I have the opposite problem," Leif said. "My father can be a handful."

Luke nodded since he'd heard that from Leif's men. Leif's father had dementia, making it hard for Leif to structure his life. Still, Leif wanted to keep him home as long as he could, and Luke respected him for that. It couldn't be easy being a caregiver in such a situation.

"Are you finding it… easy living here with Morgan?" Leif asked, his gaze on his work gloves as he tugged them on.

Luke instantly knew it was the gay thing, like when Gena asked him. But as with Gena, he sensed this wasn't idle gossip. "It's different from what I'm used to," he confessed.

"My partner Mal just moved in for the season," Leif said, a quiet glow lighting up his face. And oh boy, that was why he brought up the topic with Luke…. "His cottage needs more work before it's ready for a long winter."

Luke understood Leif was letting him know he was someone Luke could talk to, if he needed. Someone not Morgan. "I find myself thinking about him a lot," he said. "Uh, that sounded odd. What I mean is… he has a boyfriend."

"And that makes you uncomfortable?" Leif asked mildly.

"*Yes!*"

Leif's eyes widened.

Luke nudged a log so it rolled toward the woodpile he was building for winter. He was so finished with this topic.

"The corral you built is good work," Leif finally said. "If you ever want a job, look me up."

"Thanks," Luke called, watching Leif walk away. He went back to the axe resting in the log, tugging it free and swinging again.

"STEAKS, SALAD… french bread." Morgan was itemizing with Gena when Luke walked in. His hair was cold around his neck since he'd used the hose outside to wash off his head and chest. Now his blue work shirt stuck in damp patches to his skin.

Morgan moved his gaze over him before looking quickly away. "You like steak, don't you?" he asked Luke.

"Sure," Luke said. At least it sounded like the menu was normal. He was worried this guy Steven would expect something fancy Luke would have to choke down, with a name he couldn't possibly pronounce.

"Jessie's sleeping here with us," Gena put in, seeing Luke looking for his daughter. "She's been an angel all morning."

"We can't decide what to have for dessert," Morgan went on absently.

"How about sawdust," Luke growled under his breath as he headed for the bathroom. But he heard Gena suggest apple pie.

Chapter Five

"LUKE, CAN you bring out the steaks?" Morgan called from the wooden patio off the great room. As Luke grudgingly did as asked, he passed the long dining table, made up for company for the first time since he'd come to live with Morgan. Gena even put reddened wild rose hips, late strawberries, and bright fall leaves in a vase in the center of the table. It did look nice, which didn't seem to lighten Luke's mood.

"Here," he said, handing a big plate to Morgan, who was looking pleased as he fired up what looked like a space-age grill.

"This is the first time I'm cooking like a real country man," Morgan said.

"Just be sure you don't put a foot through the decking out here," Luke said dourly. "I need to get around to replacing it; it's falling apart."

Morgan frowned. "Is something wrong?"

"Why would there be?" Luke raised his brows.

"Nothing… you just seem in a bad mood."

"I'm not in a bad mood!"

"If you say so."

"I just did."

Morgan sighed. "Add stubborn to the cowboy thing."

That made Luke smile a bit. Morgan had said he liked cowboys. "You have to be stubborn considering all the times you rough it outdoors, get your foot stepped on by a cow or your horse, or wind up on your ass in the dirt."

"You're sure you're not apprehensive about meeting Steven?" Morgan probed, sloshing whiskey onto the steaks to marinate them. Despite his grumpiness, Luke was looking forward to dinner. He was damn hungry after cutting firewood and working on the barn.

"Why would I be?"

Morgan shrugged. "I don't know. I'm trying to understand you. It's strange the way we met in the mission and I just… knew I needed to help you. And it turned out we could help each other." He looked at Luke, his blue eyes grave. "In just a short time, you've made my home much more comfortable. I like having Jessie here, and I like looking out the window and seeing you riding Sable."

Luke relaxed his stiff shoulders a little. "I like it too."

"Do the guys you work with tease you about working for a gay man?"

Luke shook his head. "No, probably because Leif is…."

"Yes." Morgan nodded. "I had kind of a crush on him before he met his lover Mal."

Luke ground his teeth. "Huh."

There was a knock on the door, so Luke gave Morgan a tight smile. "I'll get it. By the way, what is Steven's last name? You didn't mention it."

Now it was Morgan who looked a little apprehensive. "Chalmers."

"Right. Don't let the steaks burn."

LUKE LIKED being the one to open Morgan's front door, as if this were really his home. He smiled at the black-haired man waiting, who had a bottle of something under his arm. He was wearing glasses over serious gray eyes. His hair was pretty long, almost ponytail length, and he was slender, kind of nerdy looking. Like one of those freaking elves in *Lord of the Rings*.

And Luke realized he was looking at the other man in a new light, trying to see what made him attractive. Weird. He held the screen door open. "I'm Luke Walker," he said.

Chalmers adjusted his glasses. "Yes, Morgan told me he'd hired someone to help around the homestead."

"Uh-huh," Luke said. "Morgan's just getting the steaks started."

Inside the kitchen Steven handed Luke the bottle. It was white wine. Geez, who'd want to drink that? Luke always thought the stuff tasted like day-old piss. He didn't mind red so much, but he was definitely a beer man.

"I hope you like white wine," Steven said.

"I don't," Luke answered.

THE LONG handmade wooden table had an island of salad mixed by Gena, fresh-baked french bread, and a platter of steaks Morgan proudly laid down. Jessie was sitting on the chair next to Luke, and that left Steven sitting next to Morgan.

Morgan looked at Luke and Steven and wanted to sigh. Were he and Jessie the only ones having a good time?

Morgan also noticed Luke was drinking fruit juice while he and Steven had white wine. Probably because he didn't want to drink anything alcoholic when his daughter might need him, since Morgan did keep some beer in the fridge. For someone who only recently became a father, he was a conscientious one.

God, Morgan loved that about Luke.

And Christ, he was not going to go there anymore.

"There's a scene in *A Room with a View* that I really enjoyed," Steven was saying to Luke, obviously working to be friendly. Morgan couldn't figure out what Luke's problem was. He was speaking in monosyllables like a surly brat. So much for this evening making him more comfortable living here with Morgan.

"Is that in English?" Luke asked, taking a bite out of some of his french bread.

"Yes," Steven said, laughing. "It literally is English."

"Oh," Luke said.

Morgan took a sip of his white wine when Steven raised his brows at him. Yep, his first Western dinner party was turning out really great.

IN THE kitchen Morgan cornered him when Luke came in to warm some formula for Jessie. His head was thumping, and he just wanted to go up to the loft. Morgan and Steven had started talking about cities they'd visited in Europe. Like Luke knew anything about Frankfurt or Paris.

"Why are you being such a jerk to Steven?" Morgan demanded, closing the door softly between the kitchen and dining room so they wouldn't be overheard.

"I'm...." But Luke couldn't deny it. He'd barely said two words. No wonder the other two men started ignoring him. "I don't know, all right?"

"Something's wrong. Tell me what it is," Morgan pressed.

Shit, he looked worried, which raised Luke's frustration a notch. "Nothing is wrong. I just have a headache, and I'm hoping Jessie will let me sleep it off." And that sounded pissy, even to his own ears. Crap.

"I thought this evening would make you more comfortable."

"I'm *not*," Luke said. "Are you going home with him?" He put his palm flat against the log wall next to Morgan's head. Morgan's blue eyes widened.

"Excuse me?" Morgan glared at Luke.

"Just answer the question," Luke said. This was closer than he'd ever stood to Morgan. He had freckles the same color as his silky brown hair, which was usually in his blue eyes. And there were flecks of gray and green in with the blue of those eyes. Luke had never noticed that before.

"I wouldn't stay here and…."

"I know that." Luke's irritation softened. "I know you wouldn't play around with him while me and Jess are here in the house with you."

"Luke…?" Morgan obviously still wanted to know what was wrong.

Luke swallowed thickly. His heart was pounding. "You don't need to bring him here to make me feel more comfortable living with you just because you're gay. I like to go riding on my own in the meadows here. I like to walk your land and fix up your house. And I like you, Morgan. You saved my life."

MORGAN FELT something simmering between him and Luke as he did that first time their eyes connected in the mission. "You were going to give her up, weren't you?" he rasped.

Luke gave a slow nod. "I thought it was best for her."

"What's best for her is *you*, Luke."

Luke dropped his gaze, and Morgan reached out. He almost brought his hand up to Luke's cheek, but he let it fall at the last moment to his shoulder. He squeezed it gently.

"I'm beginning to see that now because of you," Luke admitted, his beautiful hazel eyes lifting again to hold Morgan's. The moment stretched….

"Hey, can I help with dessert, Morgan?" Steven called from behind the closed door.

Morgan let out a breath as Luke pulled away, turning his back. He cleared his throat. "No, I'm just getting some ice cream to go with the pie. Be right out," he called.

AFTER DESSERT Morgan took Steven for a tour of the half-finished barn, insisting Luke go with them so he could point out what they were doing. Morgan thought it would be a good opportunity to show off Luke's skills.

"The rear of the barn was in okay shape, so after we got the corral fixed up, I put Sable out there during the day while we reinforced it and replaced some of the boards," Luke said, switching on the lights, which were newly wired inside the barn. From the back Sable's eyes shone as he looked up from his stall.

"The silver wood is beautiful," Steven noted, looking around. "Like driftwood."

"Yeah," Luke said, seeming to soften a little at the honest admiration. "That's what I love about older structures. They really are worth preserving."

"Leif Gunnar has his men helping Luke out," Morgan said. "In another week the work should be done, and I'll be able to get a couple of riding horses. Maybe… you and I could go riding?" He looked hopefully to Steven.

Steven shrugged. "I'm not a really good rider. Never had the time to learn, I'm afraid."

"I'm sure Luke could teach you. He is an excellent rider."

Luke's jaw ticked. "Excuse me," he said. "I should get back to my daughter."

"Gena's watching her," Morgan said since Gena had returned from seeing a movie with friends specifically to make sure Jessie had someone to watch her while Morgan and Luke entertained.

Luke ignored his mild comment, nodding to Steven. "It was nice, uh…."

"Likewise. I'm glad that Morgan found such a capable handyman."

"I'm not a handyman," Luke corrected. Then his eyes took on a gleam. "That would be Leif Gunnar. Did you know Morgan has a thing for carpenters as well as cowboys? Good night."

Steven gave Morgan an inquiring look, and Morgan let out a deep sigh, his head falling back. Well, hadn't that been fun.

MORGAN FLIPPED on a single light in the great room, not wanting to wake Luke and Jessie, but he saw after a moment Luke was still up, kneeling by the stone fireplace, where a fire was going. Jessie was lying on the couch nearby, sleeping.

Luke looked up, hazel eyes tracking Morgan as he hesitantly approached, his boots thudding dully over the bound rugs.

"So you went back to his place," Luke said.

Morgan flushed at the censure in Luke's tone. "I'm an adult and I have needs."

"Boy, do you. Apparently you have a thing for a lot of guys," Luke said, turning his back to look at the flames.

"I do not!" Morgan hissed. He'd had it with Luke being so surly. "You knocked up some girl who worked in a bar, so I hardly think—"

"I know," Luke said. He looked up at Morgan again. "Maybe that's why I don't approve of casual… stuff anymore."

"I don't need your approval, Luke," Morgan said coldly, pulling off his silk-and-cotton turtleneck sweater so he was just in his T-shirt and jeans. It felt more comfortable with Luke and Jessie, whom he didn't have to dress up for.

But after a moment, Morgan settled down beside Luke on the braided rug in front of the fire. "I don't like being at odds with you. Since you've come here, we've gotten along so well."

Luke nodded, but his face was still stiff, his jaw a hard line as he stared at the fire.

"Do you want to toast some marshmallows?" Morgan coaxed. "We could have them and some hot cocoa. I noticed you didn't touch your pie."

"It's late, and you must be tired after…."

"I didn't stay long," Morgan said. And then when Luke looked at him, he admitted, "I didn't sleep with Steven. He, uh, had an early day tomorrow, some tutoring he's doing with some of his graduate students."

"Right," Luke said, his voice hushed.

Morgan was conscious that they were sitting close together, close like they were in the kitchen earlier. He'd tried to push that moment aside, thinking he was imagining—

"I just want to try one thing…," Luke whispered. He studied Morgan's face carefully, as if Morgan were a grizzly bear he was wary of approaching. "So don't move."

"What?" Morgan asked.

Luke leaned close, his fawn hair falling into his eyes, and then softly brushed his lips against Morgan's.

Chapter Six

LUKE WAS conscious of the fire warming one side of his body, of his torso twisted so he could kiss Morgan properly. Of the smooth texture of Morgan's closed lips and then the rasp of his heavier night beard against Luke's. *Weird,* Luke thought, but then Morgan opened his mouth and his tongue caressed Luke's, and Luke—

Panting, flushed, he broke away.

Morgan frowned, looking cranky. "What was that?"

Luke blinked. "From where I'm sitting, it was a kiss."

"I mean why did you kiss *me*?" Morgan demanded. He shoved his brown hair out of his eyes, and Luke noticed his hand was shaking. He could affect the cool, collected doc that much?

"I just wanted to know what it would be like, Doc," Luke admitted. He had a feeling he was saying the wrong thing.

"I am not a straight guy. When someone kisses me like that—"

"You liked it?"

"I expect... I want—!" Morgan got up and paced.

Luke pulled his knees closer to his body. His heart was still pounding from the gentle brush of lips. He put his head on his knees, squeezing his eyes shut. "I can be impulsive," he admitted. "I was pissed off, and I kept thinking about you with him, and he's not treating you right and you goddamned deserve it, and..."

After a moment he heard the rustle of clothing as Morgan knelt next to him again. "Oh, Luke. You don't know what you're doing," Morgan said. He touched Luke's shoulder and then slipped his hand into Luke's hair, stroking. The kiss... everything changed by the kiss.

Now tension was there, sparkling like static in the air.

I kissed him, I kissed him.

"Luke, how do you expect me to sleep?" Morgan's eyes were heavy with a kind of sorrow. "You don't see yourself. You don't. You hate yourself for wanting to give up Jessie when most men would have dumped her somewhere. You build things, you hold your child, and I—" Morgan's voice cracked.

"I'm sorry," Luke whispered. "I'm sorry, it was a mistake."

"Was it?" Morgan asked. Then he sighed. "Shit, of *course* it was. You work for me, you're a new father, which has to be scary as hell, and I… helped you out."

"I didn't kiss you because I feel grateful," Luke grumped, raising his head. "I did it because I couldn't *not* do it."

"You don't make it sound like something you wanted to do," Morgan said.

"Because it's not." Luke got up, feeling even pissier than he had earlier in the evening. His father would say his blood was up, but it wasn't just his blood, it turned out. "It's a mistake, so we'll forget it." He went to Jessie and gently picked her up.

Morgan's blue eyes were shadowed as he watched Luke head up the log stairs on bare feet. "Can we forget?" he asked.

Luke had no idea.

LUKE STRETCHED out on his double bed, the light on, Jessie sleeping beside him. If he ever felt sleepy again, he'd shift her back to her cradle since he was afraid of rolling over and crushing her if he fell asleep.

But now… she was a comfort to him. Reaching out and gently stroking her open hand, he studied her chubby baby face. Did she really have his chin, like Morgan suggested?

"Can't sleep?" Morgan's deep voice called from the foot of the stairs.

Luke sighed. "No."

"May I come up?"

"Yeah." He guessed he couldn't put off seeing Morgan again because they were sharing the same cabin.

Morgan's eyes were even more tired than previously, and his brown hair was wild around his unshaven face, but then, it was much later. He looked like he hadn't had any more luck sleeping than Luke.

"I used to think she was my biggest mistake," Luke admitted softly, his gaze on his daughter. "But now I think she might be the only good thing I've done as a man."

"Don't count yourself too short." Morgan had a trace of amusement in his eyes. "Speaking as a man who enjoyed your kiss…."

Luke shifted. "I don't know what I'm doing."

Morgan sighed. "It has to be a mistake, Luke. You said it yourself; you're impulsive. So you were just… experimenting with the dark side."

"You're probably right." Luke sounded depressed to his own ears.

Morgan looked around the loft and seemed to remember there wasn't a single chair up there. Luke gestured to the other side of the bed, and after a pause, Morgan sat down on the edge, joining Luke in studying his sleeping daughter. "You're lucky you have her. I feel instantly Zen sitting here looking at her."

Luke nodded. "My worst nights, just listening to her breathe made me feel better, like somehow despite being so fucking scared, things would work out."

"I hope those nights are over now you're here under my roof," Morgan said. "Sylvan's a good place; it gives a man time to think, time to find himself. I know it helped me."

Luke sagged back against the headboard, and somehow Morgan's bare feet were propped up on his side of the bed as he settled next to Luke. "I don't worry so much. I sleep more, and sleeping is something I will never goddamned take for granted again. Sometimes I get a hit of anxiety, but I'm not alone on the road anymore. There are people I can talk to, just in passing."

Morgan's face smoothed into something peaceful, and Luke looked over at him. Morgan looked so sleepy it seemed okay to just stare at him.

Their hands collided as they stroked Jessie's wispy hair, and there was another electric pause, just like that bit of lightning that manifested the first time their eyes met in the mission church. Luke meshed the bottom of his fingers through Morgan's in a tentative net.

Morgan parted his lips as if he were about to speak, but Luke said, "You look tired. Why don't we just rest now, Doc? I know I'm more impulsive than you are, but shit, aren't you sick of thinking?"

"Just for a moment," Morgan mumbled. "And yeah, I'm so exhausted my head hurts."

"I wonder if Steven's favorite moment in *A Room with a View* was when all the men go skinny dipping," Luke mused softly as he went over the evening again.

Morgan's eyes widened. "You had too seen that movie!"

Luke smiled. "Yeah."

"Playing the hick cowboy. What am I going to do with you?" Morgan growled.

"I have no idea." Luke looked pensive. "I don't know any women here in Sylvan yet, and I think it's a bad idea to ask Gena out… but maybe I should visit a roadhouse. Maybe that's what's wrong with me, why I… did what I did tonight."

Morgan swallowed, nodding in understanding. "I was going to go stay with Steven tonight."

"I figured, Doc," Luke said. He turned his head and stared openly at Morgan, studying him. Then he leaned close again, inevitably, like one of the leaves outdoors falling from a tree. His lips met Morgan's, warmly.

This time Morgan wasn't hesitant. He reached out and dug his hands into Luke's bare shoulders. "Oh," he whispered as he ran his palms over Luke's skin, his fingers seeming to appreciate the hard slopes of muscle.

Luke licked into Morgan's mouth, Morgan shuddering at the first caress of tongue on tongue. Rasping for breath, Morgan pulled away. "We'll crush Jessie!"

Holding Morgan's gaze, Luke sat up and gently lifted his sleeping daughter. He turned away to carefully settle her in the crib by the bed. His hand was trembling as he smoothed her hair before he got up and walked to the opposite side of the bed, where Morgan was lying.

As he sat on the edge of the mattress, he heard the bed creak, and then Morgan's body was behind his, pressed against him as Morgan wound his arms around him, kissing his neck. "Luke, God…! You can't want this."

Luke's head fell back against Morgan's solid body when Morgan ran his hands over his smooth chest. When he tweaked a nipple, Luke gasped. "Shit!"

Morgan gave a rough laugh, running one hand back and forth over Luke's flat lower belly and the line of his worn blue jeans. "Jessie's beautiful, sleeping like that. Almost as beautiful as you are," Morgan said.

Luke turned his head and made a face. "Beautiful?"

"You are." Morgan studied him with hot blue eyes, the eyes of a lover, and Luke could feel himself blush to be seen in that light. "Your hair reminds me of the color of a fawn's coat, and your eyes…. Expressive. They were what caught me that first time I saw you."

"Ordinary hazel," Luke dismissed with a self-conscious shrug.

"Extraordinary hazel, like a hunk of labradorite gemstone I have on the mantel. And your body…." Morgan clenched his fingers over the pad of muscle on Luke's chest. "I kept having to look away from you when you took your shirt off. Tall, blond, cowboy boots, muscle and sweat. I was afraid you'd see how sexy I find you!"

"Is *that* why you invited Steven here? So I wouldn't be threatened?"

"I was so attracted to you I was afraid somehow it was leaking out of my eyeballs," Morgan admitted ruefully. He flushed and dropped his gaze. "You shouldn't let me touch you, Luke."

"Why not?" Luke pushed himself shamelessly into Morgan's touch. "It feels good," he added in a whisper.

"I'LL WANT more." Morgan ran his index finger over the rim of the top of Luke's jeans. When Luke didn't do anything, he held his gaze and undid the first button. Luke again didn't react except to lick his lips. Morgan couldn't resist homing in on those lips, covering them with his own. Oh God, it was heaven, kissing that mouth. He'd struggled with the visceral need for this man right from the beginning.

But Luke was forbidden. Until now.

He reached his hand in the gap of Luke's open, wash-softened jeans, and his eyes widened at what he found.

Luke laughed at his expression. "Usually women want to back off about now." Then he sobered. "I have to go real slow."

"I'm not a woman," Morgan said, stroking the hardness he'd uncovered. He wanted to see Luke. He wanted to drop to his knees by the bed and suck and worship him, but he was afraid of breaking this spell.

"Yeah." Luke's voice was rusty. "I sure noticed."

Luke was open to him, his body braced against Morgan's, his sex under his touch and control. It had to be enough. Morgan couldn't ask for more. In the morning wouldn't Luke be wondering what the hell he was doing to let another man touch him?

But Morgan couldn't stop himself from gripping Luke gently through his boxers, running his fingers up and down. "I want to see you come," he said.

Luke wasn't as coherent. "Uh, Doc!" His eyelids were tightly shut, and he was panting, thrusting into Morgan's touch. It could be just he was deprived and shut down and anyone's touch would feel good, but—

Morgan gloried at his control over his cowboy. *His* cowboy.

Luke was shivering finely in his arms as if living for every brush of fingers against the erection prodding through his boxers. Impatient, Morgan pushed them down and Luke sprang free, curving toward his stomach, his cock smooth and warm and velvet over iron so that Morgan's mouth watered with the need to taste. Oh God, if only he could…. But could Luke accept a gay man going down on him? A hand job was nothing. They could forget it, put it down to the darkness, to being tired, lonely….

"Touch me!" Luke's hand gripped Morgan's. "Oh fuck…!"

"You like that?" Morgan's mouth was open against the side of Luke's face, tasting his skin the way he longed to taste his cock. "You're hot for it, aren't you?"

Luke thrust into his hand, impatient for his relief, and Morgan laughed. All Luke's muscle and tanned skin, spread out and open for him, begging for his touch. Luke needed him, needed his hand on him. He couldn't come, couldn't have his moment, without Morgan giving it to him.

Morgan used the tricks he'd learned from his encounters with other men to make the moment last. This was the only time he'd touch Luke, and he wanted him to always remember another man had given him the most pleasure, knew exactly how to hold and pet him. He reached down and squeezed Luke's sac gently, Luke just about shouting at the touch. Oh, he was sensitive there! Morgan again wished he could put his mouth to Luke, suck his balls.

"Beautiful," Morgan whispered. Luke had broken out in a fine sweat, his eyelids quivering, his body strung tight.

"Morgan…." Luke hissed out his name, and Morgan loved the sound of it on his lips. He sounded so needy.

"Come for me," Morgan urged, pumping Luke. "Come for me; I want to see it."

Luke's bare feet thudded against the hardwood as his neck arched and he hissed, "*Fuck, Morgan!*" His relief spilled hot on Morgan's hand as Morgan held Luke, made him come.

Chapter Seven

"UH, GUYS?"

Luke blinked his eyes, not wanting to wake up since he was snuggled against a warm, firm body that had an arm around him. He couldn't remember feeling this good in forever. His body was heavy and relaxed and sexually satisfied. He liked the possessive fist curled in his hair. His head resting against a… flat chest?

He opened his eyes and met a flash of worried blue. Morgan. Morgan with his brown hair in his eyes and his lean body in his bed. He'd slept in Morgan's arms.

Luke's heartbeat kicked up.

He yanked free of Morgan's gentle hold, turning his back to look at his daughter. Still asleep? The sun was shining in through the window, warming the bed like a spotlight, unlike the kinder starlight from the night before.

In that light Luke was able to do what he wanted. To do the forbidden. Now in daylight?

Gena had her arms crossed as she stood just below floor level on the loft stairs. "Morgan, you have patients waiting," she prompted. "And Leif Gunnar wants to talk to Luke about restoring one of the outbuildings."

"Shit!" Jessie woke up and, predictably, let Luke know she wasn't happy, but hungry. Struggling to also wake up, to assimilate the night before, Luke felt a wash of familiar helplessness, looking at her. He needed to reboot, but he also needed to take care of her.

"I'll take her," Gena offered. "Since you look seriously hungover."

Without a look in Luke's direction, Morgan barreled past her.

Luke swallowed.

Gena raised one eyebrow.

"I'm not hungover except from not getting enough sleep," he said. "I don't know exactly what happened last night."

"Yeah, that seems to happen to you a lot," Gena noted, taking Jessie. "You might want to cover yourself with, uh, a towel."

Luke's face flamed as he realized his morning erection, which had grown tall innocently against Morgan's solid warmth, was prodding his boxers. The same ones that last night Morgan had—

Embarrassed, he snatched one of the generous beach towels that were folded neatly on the end of the bed and covered himself.

"You know, Morgan's a really good guy," Gena said in a severe tone. "And he's really lonely. Remember how I told you he works too much?"

"Don't you think I know that?" Luke asked. "He's…." He remembered how he'd pulled away from Morgan just a few moments ago. How would Morgan see that?

Shit.

But did it matter? Maybe… maybe they could let it go. Maybe it was better if it never happened again. Kisses in the darkness… they could stay there, stay safely there.

Christ knew Morgan would never push it, especially when Luke obviously freaked out to wake up with him.

"Something's brewing between you two," Gena said. "I felt it right from the start even though I told myself…. Well, you have a kid, so…. But I'm saying he's more vulnerable than he seems."

Luke's shoulders sagged as Gena rocked Jessie. "I guess I behaved like a total cliché this morning."

"You've got some time to think on it." Gena and headed down the stairs with Jessie to give the baby her feeding, leaving Luke with tousled hair, a morning beard, and his guts in his cowboy boots.

LUKE HAD no time to talk to Morgan alone that morning, not that he knew what he'd fucking say. He still felt as if he'd just woken up from a strange, erotic dream, as if at night Morgan was his perfect lover, handling him confidently, stroking his chest, making him come, but now…. He managed to shower, shave, and grab one of Gena's fresh-baked bran muffins before striding out to find Leif Gunnar.

Because it was still chilly that morning, he was wearing a blue work shirt over his white T-shirt, faded jeans, boots, and his hat. He paused when hot eyes raked him and then looked away.

Morgan.

Beautiful. Luke, you are beautiful.

Luke flushed. Did Morgan really whisper those words in his ear when Luke was wrapped in Morgan's possessive arms, coming on command last night?

And... like... was he? It was weird thinking of himself like that. He peered into the new windows of the barn but just saw plain old Luke. He hadn't had time to shave and his hair was doing a rooster impression.

Beautiful Luke.

Right.

Then he flushed when the other two men continued to regard him, obviously waiting for him to get with the program.

"Morgan is out here on a break between patients," Leif explained as he snapped his work gloves against his thigh. When Luke caught up with the others, he avoided looking at Morgan, trying to force his mind to business. They headed toward the first of the outbuildings, which had once been a bunkhouse. "He wants this place fixed up pronto for you and your daughter."

Luke stared at the long roof, covered with moss, a sapling shooting out near the crooked lightning rod. The windows in the long row were dusty, some broken. It had no heating, no electricity, and no running water. Then what Leif said impacted. *Morgan wants me to move into my own place. He doesn't want me living under the same roof anymore after last night?*

Beautiful. You're so fucking beautiful, Luke, it hurts me.

Disorientated with Morgan's behavior, Luke rubbed his forehead.

"He's the boss," Luke rasped, still avoiding Morgan's gaze though he felt it on him. He struggled to shove down emotion and concentrate on the task at hand. "Leif, this is going to be a major project before winter sets in."

Leif nodded. "Last I knew Morgan here was content to wait till spring. It was going to be a guest house for when his mother or sister visit."

"Guess things have changed." Luke was pale, sweating, like when he had a hangover—no wonder Gena figured he'd done the crime and was doin' the time.

And wasn't that exactly how he always played it? Went to a roadhouse or a bar and got piss drunk and went home—or sometimes only to the bathroom and got it on. His love life was a car accident, flashes of limbs and weary smiles and creeping out the next morning, his head thumping like a bitch.

Somehow, deep inside, he always knew there was no chance of anything more for him. And why was that?

Luke wasn't sure he was ready for the truth.

The last time he felt this confused was when he woke up with Jessie and found out he'd be a full-time daddy, ready or not.

"Luke, are you all right?" Leif suddenly asked him gently.

Feeling Morgan's gaze still lasering in on him, Luke merely shook his head. He didn't know. Christ, he really didn't know.

"Funny how you and Morgan both look like you got hit by the same truck," Leif observed dryly.

AT NOON Luke was resolved to talk to Morgan. His head was splitting and he was tired, but they should talk, shouldn't they? Or was Morgan going to pretend it never happened?

Shit, did that mean he was supposed to pretend as well? Morgan had touched his cock, pleasured him. How the fuck was he supposed to forget it ever happened?

So he was just going to move into the newly renovated building with his daughter, and what? Morgan could freely entertain Steven? Snuggle with him and watch foreign fucking movies?

He fisted his hands. So fine, fuck around with good old dumb Luke, touch him, tell him he was *beautiful,* and then get back with Steven.

Was that all in a gay man's life?

But then Luke flushed, recognizing he was stereotyping because that was *his* MO, wham-bam-slam, and he had no reason to think Morgan played that way.

Or was he even playing? Was he just lonely and Luke... Well, Luke kissed him first.

Why the hell had he done that? Burning lips against his. Urgency, fire, oh God, he couldn't get that kiss out of his head.

He rubbed his palms over his jeans nervously as he entered the kitchen, spotting Gena spooning out some soup, Morgan sitting at the table, blue eyes even more shadowed than they were this morning, and—

Luke's stomach twisted, sick.

No, oh no.

A voluptuous woman with brown hair and green eyes was leaning against the counter by the window, nursing Jessie with a bottle.

"Your fiancée is here to see you, Luke," Gena said, raising her eyebrows coolly in Luke's direction. Morgan looked away. "She said she got your text."

"Zelda?" Zelda Mancuso, who dumped Jessie with him weeks ago in a shitty little motel room. Who up until now had ignored all the texts Luke had sent her.

Luke wanted to snatch Jessie from her, but he couldn't help but notice she was holding their baby much more adeptly than Luke ever managed. Shit, a week ago he would have been thrilled to see her. He might even have given in to her demands to marry her. Anything for Jessie.

Morgan lifted his gaze and caught Luke's, and Luke knew all his pain and uncertainty must be written on his face.

What now? Oh Christ.

Gena's words from that morning repeated themselves in his mind. *You've got some time to think on it.* Luke took a deep breath, and then he moved forward and held his arms out to take Jessie back.

ZELDA SPENT the night.

Luke slept in the great room on one of the long couches. No way he was sleeping next to Zelda. Shit, they had a lot to figure out. Now, living here with Morgan, he felt like he had a fingerhold at handling being a father. Would handing Jessie off to her mother really be the best thing in light of the way she'd left her with Luke?

But she was so eager to be around Jessie, and so good with her, putting Luke to shame, that he didn't put up any fight when she kept the baby up in the loft with her.

Now Luke lay staring at the dying fire. When Jessie fussed, he threw the blanket aside, ready to climb upstairs... and heard Zelda's soft voice as she crooned to their baby.

Morgan's door opened, and he stood in his room, looking at Luke. He was wearing pajama bottoms and not a shirt.

When Luke didn't look away, he crept quietly to the chair opposite Luke.

Both of them listened to the soft sounds coming from above, watching the fire, saying nothing.

The silence pulsed with feeling, but damn if Luke had anything in him left to say.

"You promised to marry her?" Morgan finally asked.

Luke burned to deny it, but he couldn't do that, not yet. Not without clearing the air with Zelda. He had a past, and he had to face it. "We've got stuff."

Something about his tone must have spoken to Morgan. He didn't look as frozen.

"Luke, she's a part of your life. You share a child."

"I know." He rubbed his jaw. No wonder Jessie hadn't missed him today. He looked bad. He hadn't even showered. "She's real good with Jess."

Morgan narrowed one eye. "Oh no, you don't."

"What?"

"You think because she's a woman it comes naturally to her, taking care of the baby?" Morgan laughed without humor. "Gender has nothing to do with being a parent. She had two months plus, taking care of Jessica. It's sink or swim when you're a new parent."

"Don't I know it," Luke said ruefully. "Mostly sinking."

"You were holding your own."

"I had my head eye level with the water most days. And that's only because of you." Luke sucked in a breath. Morgan was... he was still his friend. Thank God, because Luke needed one right now. "Zelda comes from money. She fought with her parents, but if she went back home... they'd want that baby. Probably hire a nurse and everything."

"And that would trump her real daddy?"

Luke swallowed. "Maybe."

"You can't think that!" Morgan fumed. "It's trite, but money is not love. It's not *you*."

"And I'm so damn special I've fucked over my life. I was going to give her up, Morgan. You know it. I know it. I thought about....." Luke squeezed his eyes shut. He had to say it. He had to man up and get it out. "You think I was in that church by accident? I was casing the place out. I thought of just leaving her there."

"Oh, Luke." Morgan's eyes expressed how much he bled for him. "I think maybe more was at work that day we met in the church."

Luke's gaze snapped to Morgan's. "You believe that?"

"Luke, I work with life and death all the time. If I didn't believe in more than what makes up this"—he held up his hand—"I couldn't do it. It would *break* me."

"When I looked in your eyes." Luke sucked in a breath. "I wanted to be the man who didn't leave his daughter alone in a church. I wanted to be better than that."

"You got your wish. Instant dharma."

Luke rubbed his eyes. They both pretended he wasn't crying. "Thanks," he muttered.

"No problem. You, um... you try to get some sleep. For Jessie."

"Sure." But Luke wasn't sure it mattered.

He was a better man than the one who walked into a small-town church bent on abandoning his daughter, but could he be strong enough to make the right choice for her?

Even if it killed him?

"LEAVING JESSICA with you was the worst thing I've ever done; I know that," Zelda said as she and Luke sat together the next morning over coffee.

Gena and Morgan had discreetly left them alone with their baby.

Morgan had looked back over his shoulder at Luke, and Luke was warmed, seeing Morgan nod at him, as if he trusted Luke to do right.

Luke only hoped he could figure out what that was.

He felt like his old life had broken like a beer glass, and now he was trying not to cut himself on the shards.

"I don't judge you." How could he after nearly doing the same thing himself? He reached out, hesitant, and squeezed her hand. He didn't even remember the night they made Jessie. It made him ashamed.

"I judge me."

"Yeah, you gotta stop doing that. It doesn't help, believe me." Luke smiled at her, and she smiled back, faintly. Now that he was more relaxed, Luke saw her freckles stood out. She was pale and much thinner even than before she carried Jessie.

It shot him out of his selfish place. He thought having a baby was the end of his world. How was it for Zelda, who was only nineteen? At least Luke was older, more beat up by life. She was just a kid.

"Is there someone?"

She started. "Why do you ask?"

"Simple. Girls sleep with me for two reasons: horniness or heartbreak."

"Flattering."

"I'm not. I'm being honest. What's worse is with girls like you, the ones who are hurting? I knew and didn't care. It helped, of course, that I was usually drunk." He cleared his throat. This raw honesty burned. "I hope it was good for you, at least."

The faint smile was back. "Sorry. I, uh—"

"You don't remember?" He shook his head. "We got to make a pact, girl, to never tell our daughter that. She deserves better."

Zelda nodded. "You're right."

"Zelda, I can't marry you. I don't even know if I can be a father right now. Being a husband.... I wouldn't make you happy."

"I know." Tears welled in her eyes, spilled over. Luke felt like shit. "I just wanted so bad to have someone. Like when I met you that night, you seemed so happy—"

"It was a lie. I was a lie. I see that now, Zelda. The only good thing that came from that night is Jessie." He swallowed. "Two lonely people made something beautiful."

Her shoulders relaxed. "I'm glad you're being so understanding, Luke. And you know, you haven't had Jessie that long, so it's probably going to be such a relief when I take her."

"Relief?" Luke's voice cracked. "Sure, of course it will be."

MORGAN FOUND traces that Luke had mucked out Sable's stall when he entered the barn later that afternoon. He noticed the tack room had been organized, some of the old gear repaired, hanging up neatly, the leftover debris from the new flooring cleaned up.

His barn was ready to house the riding horses he wanted. Rubbing the back of his neck, Morgan wondered when he'd get around to that. He'd imagined bringing Luke with him, getting his opinion of some of Charlie LaFountaine's horses before buying one or two. But now….

Morgan had had a very bad feeling all morning long. He was restless in his office, snappish with Gena.

Where was Luke?

Morgan paused to rub Sable's head, liking the calm, dark eyes of Luke's horse before he wandered deeper under the loft…. And then he caught it—the sound of water falling. Luke must be using the old sun shower on the outside of the barn to get cleaned up. Morgan had been a bit dubious about it, but Luke convinced him to let him restore it. During the day the sun warmed collected rainwater in a tank on the side of the barn roof. It was only practical when the weather was warm, of course. Today had been that. One of the last really fine fall days.

Morgan hesitated, heart thudding. He should go back to the house. What happened between them was an impulsive mistake. Luke pushed him away. Luke had a fiancée.

LUKE'S ASS gleamed white against the brown of his back and thighs, highlighting his butt and making Morgan want to dig his fingers into it in appreciation, kiss Luke's neck as he touched him, made love to him—

As if feeling Morgan's gaze from the shadows, Luke spun around, daylight hiding nothing, not the muscles, slick with water, the rounded arms above his head, his hair back from his high forehead, his lips wet and soft… his heavy hanging cock and luxuriant pubic hair.

His gaze collided with Morgan's, and he parted his lips.

Caught.

Caught looking. Caught wanting.

Morgan knew he should look away, give Luke some privacy.

Luke swallowed as the moment stretched between them. There was something in his eyes….

Morgan tried to read it. Couldn't make it out. Desolation? He needed to walk it off, this desire for Luke. Walk it off so he could be his friend again.

Unbelievably Luke held out a hand. "Coming in?" he croaked.

"Luke, what's wrong?"

Luke turned his back and leaned an arm against the building. Morgan couldn't see his face, and he wanted to, more than anything. "Luke?"

"Come and try the shower. The water's about gone." Luke stepped out of the spill, reaching for his jeans. His face was still carefully averted.

What to do? Morgan had a feeling he had to walk on eggshells here. He didn't want to push Luke to talk, but Luke sure as hell needed to.

Patience.

Morgan yanked off one boot, hopping, stumbled over Luke's discarded boots, and laughed breathlessly. "Shit!"

But his clown act served its purpose: Luke smiled back, white teeth against tanned skin, breathtaking. "Whoa."

"That's my line," Morgan growled.

He didn't give a fuck about why he should stay away, how crazy this was. Luke's wet skin beckoned. He needed to taste Luke's stiffening sex, needed to be on his knees to take it into his mouth….

He yanked off his T-shirt and walked into the sun-warmed water, his boxers saturating and hiding nothing of his own aching erection, staring into beautiful eyes, capturing him. "Jesus, Luke," he whispered. "I just can't stay away from you."

Luke yanked him close, desperate, and their lips crashed in a kiss. Morgan moaned, running his hands down Luke's back to his bare ass, cupping, loving the hard, round shape filling his palms. God, he wanted to fuck that ass. He wanted Luke bent over, hands clawing the wall as Morgan took him.

He squeezed his eyes shut, feeling the hurt from earlier making his throat ache, but not caring now. Luke. Luke against his body, naked, wild, briefly his.

He fell to his knees in the sand, glimpsing startled hazel eyes as he clenched his hands over Luke's hips, and then he opened his mouth and took the hardened tip of Luke's penis in his mouth.

He moaned again, and Luke cried out, "*Morgan, fuck!*"

Morgan broke away, water hitting his face as he looked up, licking his lips and the taste of Luke. "I wanted to do this last night. I want to suck your cock. I want to do it all the time, get on my knees, pull your jeans down, and let you fuck my mouth…."

Luke's eyes were huge. "God almighty…!" Then he raked his hands in Morgan's wet hair. "Take it. I want to see you take it all—" he ordered.

Morgan opened his mouth obediently and let Luke thrust into it. Luke stiffened and arched his body, his prick growing huge in Morgan's mouth, hungry, needing sensation.

Morgan licked at it, taking Luke deep, sucking strong. To fuck with technique! Fast, hard, Luke slammed into him again, all of him, long, thick, and then he spilled hot with a choked cry….

Morgan tasted and then pulled away a little, and Luke shot against his skin. As Luke's come slid down his lips and chin in the water, he saw Luke staring at him under heavy lids, his eyelashes clumped together from the shower, digging his fingers into Morgan's skull, huffing. "God, that's hot," he rasped.

Chapter Eight

MORGAN RESTED his forehead against Luke's thigh, breath huffing himself. He struggled with his own arousal. He couldn't.... Luke was innocent to men being with men. Morgan didn't want to turn him off. Surely he couldn't want—

"Water's running down," Luke said calmly, and Morgan blinked, seeing that only the occasional drop was spattering from above them.

"We...." He looked up at Luke, and his breath caught. Luke's eyes again reminded him of labradorite gemstones, lit by the autumn sunshine. "We need to talk."

"Talk later, Doc," Luke rasped. "Action first." And with that, he lifted Morgan up and over his shoulder.

"*Luke!*" Morgan gasped. No one had ever treated Morgan this way! There was always witty conversation and light anticipation and fine food before bed. In contrast Luke just kissed him, invited him into the sun shower, threw him over his muscular shoulder, and carried him up to the loft in the barn....

"Cowboy," Morgan murmured. Luke put him down in a fresh bed of straw. It prickled a little against Morgan's back, and Morgan almost sneezed, so he turned over onto his hands and knees, looking over his shoulder at Luke.

"Yes, sir, I am," Luke murmured. He ran his gaze over Morgan's raised ass with his wrinkled boxers; Luke knelt behind Morgan and carefully removed them, catching Morgan's gasp with his lips when the saturated cloth caught on his erection. "Better?" he whispered.

"Yes," Morgan whispered back. "But Luke... wait. I should have resisted you earlier...."

Luke cut him off with a kiss. "Why?"

"Because something's wrong, damn it!"

But Luke wasn't talking.

"And you were experimenting. You're conflicted."

Luke sighed. "I'm going to get no peace until I talk. You're such a woman."

Perversely that made Morgan grin. "Sexist."

"Yeah, yeah. I haven't been honest with you, with myself. You aren't the first guy I...." Luke shrugged. "Liked."

"You've been with someone?" Dark jealousy swamped Morgan. He wanted to punch the guy's lights out, whoever it was. And wasn't that a kicker coming from a sophisticated, urbane doctor?

"Technically no."

"Why not?"

"It would be too real."

"Okay." There was so much more he wanted to know, so much more they had to talk about, but God, he could feel the imprint of Luke's cock against his rear end, stiffening with renewed interest, brushing Morgan's cooler skin and making him shiver. He could still taste Luke coating his lips. Morgan was no saint.

Luke brushing his lips against his back made Morgan arch, his penis hanging heavy between his legs, aching for relief. Morgan swallowed, able to count his heartbeats in the throbbing of his sex. He looked over his shoulder again as Luke mounted him from behind, rubbing his cock against Morgan's ass.

"I need to do this," Luke's voice was stilted. "Morgan…?"

In answer Morgan pushed his rear higher, and Luke wrapped his arms tightly around him, panting hot against the chilled skin of Morgan's neck as he thrust, needing to hump Morgan.

Luke hesitantly wrapped his hand around him, caressing the rim of Morgan's penis with his thumb. Morgan groaned, unable to keep from thrusting into that callused grip. "Luke, God, touch it!"

"You like it, huh, Doc?" Luke's blank, unfocused hazel eyes were hazy with passion as he rubbed himself against Morgan. He reached down and touched Morgan's balls, rolling them in the way he probably did his own when he masturbated, weighing him. "I've never held one of these 'cept my own."

Morgan thrust against Luke's touch, and Luke made a channel for him with his moist fingers. Then Luke tightened his hands, choking Morgan's cock as hot come splashed his ass.

"You needed… to fuck me," Morgan huffed as lightning shot through his nipples, his tight balls, his strangled penis, and he creamed Luke's hand full, dripping.

"Yeah, but don't know how." Luke wobbled, thighs trembling.

LUKE HEFTED Morgan onto his back, his hand leaving a slippery imprint of Morgan's spill on his chest as he collapsed on top of him. Sticky, straw prickling, they crushed close together. Morgan rubbed Luke's heaving back, feeling the rapid thump of his heart as their bodies lay skin to skin. He knew next time he'd let Luke fuck him.

Luke whispered, "Do you think I'm going to lose my little girl?"

Morgan pulled him closer, knowing this, at last, was Luke's pain. Here in the semidarkness he could confide in Morgan. "I don't know, Luke. All I know is you aren't alone."

LUKE PUT *Die Hard* in the DVD player and then came back to the couch in the great room where Morgan waited with Jessie. Morgan handed his daughter to him and then hesitantly cuddled up behind him, putting one hand on Luke's hip. When Luke didn't stiffen, he relaxed slightly.

"I think Jess likes action movies," Luke reflected. "She especially likes Bruce."

"How did Zelda get pregnant?" Morgan asked, obviously refusing to leave the touchy shit alone. But he ruffled Luke's hair, stroking it.

"We used protection," Luke answered. "I guess it didn't work. At first… when she met me at a roadhouse with Jessie, I was…." Luke swallowed.

"It's all right," Morgan encouraged.

"I didn't *want* her, Morgan. I didn't want my own daughter. Christ, I didn't even want to see Zelda again," Luke admitted. "Stuff never seemed to work out with girls, and I was okay with that. Looking back, it's kind of obvious why."

Luke saw the curious light in Morgan's eyes and wasn't surprised when Morgan asked, "Ever think of men?"

"Yeah," Luke said. "But I never let myself go there. Not until you, Morgan. You don't judge me. You just…."

"Care?" Morgan said, smiling a little. "I do, Luke."

"I know," Luke said. "My old man was tolerant, and he raised me to have an open mind." He looked at Jess. "I want that for her. I guess I'll have to find out how Zelda feels about shit like that."

Morgan rubbed Luke's shoulder, curving his fingers over muscle as if he appreciated it. Jess was a little puddle in Luke's arms, avidly slurping her formula as Bruce arrived in L.A. for his first adventure. "You don't even know that much about her, her attitudes?"

"We just…." Luke's jaw ticked. "We got drunk and fucked. Now I guess she's in my life forever."

Morgan nodded. "Yes, Luke."

"I guess I also got impulsive with you," Luke said. "I get real physical when I like someone. I need to fuck."

"I noticed," Morgan said, his voice a little droll.

Luke flushed, remembering how he'd positioned Morgan so he could rut against his ass.

Morgan cupped his cheek. "I didn't mind."

Luke searched his eyes. "Can we do it again, Doc?"

"I thought you only did one-nighters?"

"I used to, but Jess changed me like the side of a mountain after a wildfire, you know? I feel stripped down."

"I think you should see a lawyer and protect your rights," Morgan suggested. "Even though you are going to have to talk to Zelda, negotiate with her over Jessica."

Luke sighed. "She wanted me to go dancing with her when she first showed up."

"Sounds like she hasn't given up the party lifestyle." Morgan's voice was carefully neutral.

"Like me, you mean? I was usually too tired except for Saturday nights," Luke said. "And she's *not* my fiancée. I never asked her."

Morgan swallowed. "Oh?"

"I didn't love her," Luke admitted. He studied Morgan. "I guess men don't love other men in your world."

"Leif and Mal seem to love each other," Morgan countered. "But I've never…."

"But you have that casual thing with Steven."

"It's good for both of us. I have needs, Luke."

"I don't like him," Luke said.

Morgan's eyes widened. "No, really?"

"Guess it was obvious."

"It was neon." Morgan shook his head. "Luke, you have so much going on in your life right now. I'm not sure it's a good time for you to think about… a relationship."

Luke felt like a boulder rolled onto his back at the R-word. Whenever a girl had brought it up, he'd moved on to another town. "Is that what I have to have with you?"

Morgan sighed. "No, that's what you might *want* with me. I don't want you to have to do anything."

"Will you sleep in my bed tonight?" Luke wanted those arms around him again. It was stupid, but he felt grounded with Morgan there. He liked his smell and the rasp of his night beard against his hair.

"I think we should take some time," Morgan said.

"That means 'no,' right?" No Morgan in his bed. Not that Luke could blame him. He'd made a mess of his life. The only good thing in it was Jess. Luke would have to prove himself if he wanted Morgan.

"That means 'not just yet,'" Morgan said gently, holding Luke's gaze. "We have time. Time to sort things out."

"It's funny, but ever since I came to this town, people have said that," Luke noted. "And Jess is sleeping through the night now, mostly."

Morgan pulled Luke closer, and Luke soaked up the feeling.

"Are there things you want to do with your life?" Morgan asked after a moment. They were both ignoring the movie now, but Jessie seemed to like the flashes of explosions coming from the screen.

"I was a foreman in an outfit that took tenderfoot tourists into the foothills for trail riding when I met Zelda," Luke mused. "I loved that, giving people a real taste of the West."

"The foothills aren't so far from here," Morgan noted. "And the barn is large enough to house quite a few riding horses. Once the outbuildings are restored, this could be a good place to run something like that."

Luke chewed his lip, thoughtful.

Morgan cleared his throat. "That is… if you decide to stay here." What he didn't say, but what Luke heard, was *with me*.

AT CHARLIE LaFountaine's ranch, Morgan watched as Luke shook hands with Charlie, a tall man with a single black braid down his back, wearing the typical dusty boots, jean jacket, and jeans. Charlie was a fixture in Sylvan, running both cattle into the foothills of his spread and some of the best riding horses in the area. Today Morgan and Luke had come there to purchase a couple for Morgan's use.

Charlie had them wait outside the ring by the barn and brought out the first of the horses, a Tennessee Walker named Meg. After watching her move around the ring, Luke climbed over and joined Charlie, and Morgan was immediately taken by how affectionately Meg responded to Luke.

"Come and try her out," Luke called.

"I haven't ridden in…." Morgan shrugged. He barely had time, but sometimes made it over to Charlie's for an afternoon.

"She's smooth as silk," Luke reassured him.

With Luke's recommendation Morgan climbed into the saddle, settling for a moment as Luke handed him the reins and stepped back to join Charlie, sitting on the corral. The two men watched as Morgan tentatively did some circuits. By the second one, Morgan smiled, feeling more at ease. He would not be saddle sore from riding Meg, who didn't seem to care he was still a beginner.

The sun was hot and warm against the skin when Luke joined him on Ed, a small Blazer with a calm disposition. They set out on a trail that ran behind Charlie's ranch house, the horses' hooves crunching on fall leaves from arching birch trees.

They dismounted by a stream, and Morgan watched as Luke hunted for late wild strawberries, gathering them in the palm of his hand before bringing them back to share.

When he ate the first one, sweet from the combination of frost and sunshine, Luke watched him, eyes on his lips, before brushing his mouth against Morgan's. Morgan stiffened a little, aching to surrender.

"What?" Luke asked, licking the last of the strawberry from his pink-stained palm.

"Someone might see us. I'm not sure…." Morgan shrugged.

"I just wanted to kiss you."

"I couldn't sleep last night," Morgan found himself admitting. He'd lain in his bed, staring at the log door, imagining opening it and going upstairs to Luke. Jessie would be sleeping in her cradle, and he could be in Luke's arms, though he knew Luke's hot temperament enough to know that they wouldn't sleep, not right away.

Luke would want him, would press him into the mattress….

"Me neither," Luke said, grimacing. "Sleeping alone sucks, Doc."

"But just the fact you haven't thought of what it would be like to be out with me says you need some time," Morgan cautioned. "You're so impulsive. Besides, Zelda might come back any day now from visiting her folks. And that might prove… awkward. You need to be sure of who you are."

Luke put his palms flat above the willow tree Morgan was leaning against. He glanced his lips against Morgan's, the caress singing through Morgan's skin, through his beading nipples and hardening cock.

"And I'm so easy," Luke whispered. "I'll wait for you, Doc."

Chapter Nine

A FEW weeks later, Morgan jolted from sleep at the sound of a fist hammering on his bedroom door. He shoved his hair back, sitting up and grimacing at his erection. He'd had another hot dream about Luke.

It wasn't easy, living alone with Luke and resisting him. Zelda had disappeared again after telling them she'd be back. They both figured she'd gone back to the party life.

It gave Luke a breather and time for them to be together, though Luke made it clear he didn't want Morgan seeing Steven. Morgan had acquiesced. He didn't want anyone but Luke anyway, and it was stupid to pretend differently.

And so far Luke hadn't shown any desire to return to his old ways. He worked with the horses, repaired the old buildings, and spent all of his free time with Morgan and Jess.

And in the end, Luke had racked up lots more time as a father. Morgan had taught him how to take care of Jessica. He reached for her instinctively now, knew without looking if her diaper was too tight, if she was hungry, if she just wanted to walk around the room in his arms.

They were beginning to feel like a family, and that made Morgan happier than he'd ever been in his life.

As well as more scared.

"Doc?"

Luke's voice, muffled by the wood. "You gotta wake up!"

Morgan opened his door, then gripped Luke's bare shoulder. "What's wrong?" he immediately demanded.

"Jess—I think she has another fever—for real this time! She was fucking choking and her legs were all rigid...!"

"I'm right behind you," Morgan reassured him, snatching for his robe as Luke's bare feet pounded up the stairs to the loft ahead of him.

Jessie. Shit. He took a deep breath, but he couldn't be detached. This was Luke's baby, and somehow Luke had become his... as well as Jessica.

"WHAT HAPPENED?" Jessie was half-undressed, as if Luke had tried peeling free the layers in an attempt to help her. She was lying in her crib with her eyes open, drooling, looking innocent-baby blank.

"She made some soft sounds, and I woke up," Luke fired out rapidly, shoving his bed hair out of his eyes. He was wearing jeans and nothing else, and his pants weren't zipped, so they were about ready to fall off his butt. "Scared the fuck out of me! When I looked at her, her legs and arms were jerking like a zombie's...."

Morgan touched the baby's forehead carefully with the back of his hand. "She's damp and warm. How long did she behave like that?"

"Not long," Luke rasped, wide-eyed as Morgan gently removed Jessie from her crib, heading down the stairs at a rapid pace for his clinic. "It looked like some kind of... seizure. I was about to shout for you, Christ...! But then she just stopped, as if everything was back to fucking normal!" Luke laughed, but Morgan heard the panicked tears he was suppressing.

"It may have been a febrile seizure," Morgan agreed absently. Seeing the panic in Luke's face, he reassured, "That's the first sign of a fever sometimes, and it's good it didn't last long. I'm going to check her over now for the cause. Can you switch on all the lights, please?"

Swallowing thickly, Luke nodded. He rubbed his eyes. "Is she going to be okay, Doc?"

Compassion lodged in Morgan's throat after one quick glance at Luke. His face was so pale that his freckles stood out from his tan. Morgan wanted to take more time to reassure him, even pull him into his arms, but there was no time for that now. He had to take care of Jessie for Luke.

LUKE WAS slumped against the wall of Morgan's examination room.

Water tinkled. Morgan was using a facecloth and lukewarm water to rub Jessie down, carefully avoiding her ears and eyes. The baby waved her arms weakly, giving an irritated cry, as if she really wanted to howl but felt too shitty.

Luke took a deep breath as his eyes stung. Shit. *Shit.* Kids got sick all the time, right? And he was so fucking lucky, living with a doctor.

Did I do something? Was Jess sick because I—

Luke swallowed around the dry boulder lodged in his throat. His phone vibrated, so he checked it.

Hey, I got your message! Let me know how Jessica is doing. I'm sure she'll be okay. I met someone!!! Talk later, Zelda.

"Fuck," Luke muttered, scrubbing his unshaven jaw. Looked like he was all Jessie had, and he was no prize. He didn't even want her for the first… maybe twenty-seven hours of sheer black panic. Then she fell asleep in his arms, and he held her and ached, worrying about what kind of formula to buy, and whether she should sleep on a bed or if a drawer was better since he didn't have any baby shit….

His phone vibrated again. Zelda again, responding to his first text message.

Okay, I'm coming over. I've had a little bit to drink so the bartender is giving me a ride to your place. Be there soon, okay?

"Luke," Morgan called softly.

"Yes, sir? God!" Luke nearly dropped his phone, heart thudding. The sounds from the examination table weren't ominous, and neither was Morgan's expression, but shit, who knew…?

Morgan looked tired, with wrinkles creased into the dark rings around his eyes and his face unshaven, but he didn't look alarmed.

He reached out and squeezed Luke's shoulder gently. "Jess has an ear infection. It spiked a fever, which I'm treating along with her ear."

"So…." Luke swallowed, his saliva sparking off a feeling of nausea. He felt kind of spacey. "She's going to be okay?"

"Yes," Morgan said, looking both calm and tired.

And Luke whispered, "It wasn't anything I did?"

Morgan took a deep breath. "Oh shit. *No.* Come here, Daddy."

Luke went into Morgan's arms. He was trembling. Tomorrow he'd be embarrassed, he knew. Morgan felt so good, so comforting. He didn't let himself close to Luke very often since neither of them could trust Luke's hot blood.

"She's really… small, you know?"

"She is," Morgan agreed.

"You're a doctor." Luke pulled back to look into Morgan's eyes. "This shit happens all the time, right?"

"She's… yours," Morgan said. "And she lives under my roof. This was scary for me too." He huffed out a sigh. "We're both car wrecks now, but she'll probably sleep this off."

"I don't think I can sleep. Zelda's coming over."

Morgan nodded. "Good. She should be here."

"Can I take her into the great room?" There was a rocking chair there. Jess normally loved lying in Luke's arms, sleeping while he slowly swayed back and forth.

"I'll light a fire," Morgan offered.

"We'd like that, Jess and me," Luke said.

MORGAN LEANED against the base of the rocking chair, his hand on the armrest, occasionally rocking it as he and Luke held their vigil.

Luke cleared his throat. "You haven't had Steven over for dinner since that good-bye deal," he noted. Morgan had invited the other man once because he refused to stop taking his calls the way Luke wanted—but Luke could admit to himself he liked that about Morgan, how he was kind. Luke didn't handle the dinner with any maturity, preferring to go riding when Steven was here.

"Luke, I told you that other than a single polite kiss, we didn't…."

Luke's head fell back. "That single kiss makes me a little crazy. I've never been jealous before. It sucks."

Morgan's gaze touched on the sleeping baby before he knelt higher, his face upturned. Holding his gaze, Luke bent down and their lips connected. "Oh man…," Luke whispered.

Morgan swallowed. "Yeah." He scratched his stubble, rueful. A hard-on wouldn't kill him. "Want some granola and yogurt? It's just about breakfast time. In Tibet."

Luke cracked up a little. "Granola? Doc, what am I going to do with you?"

Lights arched through the great room from a vehicle, and both men heard a car door slam.

Luke said, "Zelda."

Morgan nodded. "I'll put on some coffee."

ZELDA SLEPT on the couch by the far window. Jessie was still lodged in his arms since Luke couldn't bring himself to let her go, as if there were a web of skin stretching from him to his kid. Instead he paced the great room.

Morgan was right. Jess had scared the shit out of them both and then slept it off like someone recovering from a bender.

"I always knew you'd do this, Jess. Put me through it," Luke told her. "But that's okay."

Morgan came in from seeing a patient, looking pale and wasted, and went to Luke, putting his arms around him from behind. It felt good just to breathe then, not saying anything for a moment. Almost as good as it was to wake up next to Morgan. Luke was sick of sleeping alone.

"Jessie's lucky to have you," Morgan said. It was his campaign to make Luke feel better as a dad, Luke knew. Sometimes his words penetrated like rain hitting the forest floor through thick trees.

Zelda's eyes opened. "Oh wow," she said, staring at them together.

Morgan stiffened, but Luke only said, "Yeah."

"Kind of makes me feel better," she rasped.

"Do you want some more coffee?" Morgan asked politely. He was always nice to Zelda, though Luke felt a kind of buried lightning in him when she was around. On a gut level, he got that; it was what he experienced with Steven.

"No, thanks. Matt, the bartender from last night, wanted to have brunch with me at the diner," Zelda said, looking pleased. "He was impressed I cut loose a good-looking cowboy to come see if my kid was okay. He was raised by a single mom."

"Thanks for coming," Luke said.

"You know, if you weren't the way you are, I'd have to take care of her all the time." Zelda chewed her lip. "And I love her, but I don't want that. And even though I know my parents would take her…."

Luke stiffened.

"She's not their responsibility. I know that. I just wish I was as ready to be a mama as you are a daddy, Luke."

"It's okay." Luke looked away, flushing. "I, uh, didn't want it at first either."

"But now you're a family," Zelda said, looking at Luke and Jess… and Morgan.

Chapter Ten

ZELDA PASSED Luke another gourd along with some wired pinecones and acorns. He attached it to the swag over the doorway.

"So are you planning on dancing naked tonight?"

"I can't dance, as you might remember," Luke said absently, taking a frost-ripe apple from Gena, who was decorating the outside of the single window of the little cottage Leif and his team just finished restoring in time for winter. "And I'm a bisexual cowboy, not a pagan. This whole festival idea… it was Gena's."

"Hey, I'm not named Gena Gardenia for nothing. Now I need more ivy," Gena said. "And hand me some of the corn." She took a handful from Zelda.

"Morgan's going to flip," Zelda said, looking inside where a fire was already lit as the sun glimmered golden through the trees, lighting tufts of yellowed grass and damp leaves.

Luke climbed down the ladder and then carried it down the stairs, replacing it by the cabin wall. "I hope he'll like it," he said. "I'm about ready to go insane if he doesn't." He looked at his two friends, thinking it weird Zelda had become just that in the months since Luke lived here with Morgan. She came and went and was a good babysitter when Morgan simply had to see one of those foreign films. Even hating them, Luke went with him. "Okay, I think we got everything ready."

"Let's hope Morgan's ready," Gena said.

"God, I hope so." Luke had tried to show Morgan that he considered them a family, but Morgan held back.

Luke knew he was afraid.

Thing was, so was Luke.

"LUKE, I don't know…."

The first thing to go wrong was Morgan got a call just before their scheduled horseback ride. He'd been gone for hours, and now it was dark and cold, not the scenic sunset ride Luke had pictured.

The second thing was Luke twisted his ankle over a slippery pothole walking back to the house. It was throbbing now, telling him to give it up tonight and send up a white flag.

"Gena and Zelda are having a manicure party while they watch Jess. If we stay there's a chance we'll wind up with a pedicure," Luke warned. Shit, maybe he should call this off. If it wasn't Jess with an ear infection or one of the horses with a strained leg, it was Morgan out late. It seemed like they'd never get things straightened out between them.

Luke tightened his jaw. No, fuck that. He was sick of their current arrangement. What if Morgan called Steven again and they exchanged another "friendly" kiss? He'd go out of his mind. And damn it, he'd come out, at least to his ex-one-night-stand mother of his child and two gay men who worked with him. That was a start, right?

"But…." Morgan looked like he'd argue some more despite Luke luring him into the stable. Okay, the carrot had worked. Now it was time for the stick….

"That's *it*, Doc." From his seat in Sable's saddle, Luke leaned down and fucking hefted Morgan up. Sable snorted, and for a moment, it seemed as if they'd both take a tumble, but then Morgan settled behind him, hands clenched around Luke's waist.

He gaped at Luke.

"You said you liked cowboys," Luke muttered, face burning. "And you just got yourself taken by one."

THE CLEAR string of bulbs from the cabin glittered like fairy lights through the brush as Sable walked them to their destination. Leaves rotated slowly from the trees, and Sable huffed out a breath, white dragon's mist in the autumn night. Morgan relaxed his hands around Luke's hips, and Luke began to hope again.

When they arrived, Luke dismounted first and then held a hand out for Morgan, who was staring at the cottage.

Luke rubbed his palms against his jeans. "It's, uh, Mabon, or autumn equinox," he said, watching as Morgan walked up the three steps to where the door waited, open. "I couldn't think of any special occasions this time of year. Gena suggested it."

Morgan flashed him a look of surprise.

"I wanted something…." He couldn't say "romantic." He could not say that. But would Morgan get it? "Gena said it was like a theme."

"A theme?" Morgan looked into the little cabin, where a table waited, festooned with pomegranates, dried milkweed, thistles, and reeds from Sylvan Lake, exploding with white tufts. And wine, both red and white since Luke hadn't known what Morgan might prefer. He was willing to drink the white if that impressed Morgan. "Luke, it's late, and this seems so impulsive—"

"No, Doc, it's *not,*" Luke growled, on surer ground now, even if it felt like a skim of ice over too-deep water. He swallowed and reached his fingers toward Morgan's as they stood on opposite sides of the open doorway; at the last moment he let his own fall. But then he moved closer so his breath brushed Morgan's lips. "Don't keep closing your door and leaving me on the outside. I know our schedules are fucked. I know I fucked up a lot in the past with my one-nighters, but don't lock me out anymore, Doc."

Morgan studied him, blue eyes calm and mysterious as the starlight over the lakeside. What was he thinking?

Luke swallowed again since his throat was already dry. "I want you for a lover." He flushed but held Morgan's gaze. "Doc, show me…."

This time when he put his hand out, Morgan took it, and Luke knew it would be okay.

"IT'S BEEF stew," Luke said, shrugging as if the meal he'd procured was no big deal, but he was watching Morgan closely for signs he liked it. "I didn't make it, and I'm sorry I couldn't get you something fancier." What would be fancier, Luke didn't know exactly. "It was on special in the diner, and Gina said it had the right vegetables for her theme."

Morgan twitched his lips, and Luke colored when Morgan took a sip of his wine—red, thank fuck—and looked over his shoulder at the waiting bed, made up with pressed white sheets and also decorated with ivy and pinecones. The women had gone a little overboard, so it resembled a wedding bed, but everything felt significant somehow, like a sign left on a trail. Luke just didn't know where it led.

But he wanted to.

"Luke, when Jess got sick, I found myself worrying it was meningitis," Morgan admitted. "And I never do that before diagnosing a patient."

"You were scared too?" Somehow that seemed important.

"Yeah." Morgan put his fork down, having apparently enjoyed his stew. Luke was too nerved up to eat much himself, like a groom at his own wedding. "I think this is the first time we've ever been alone together. Without Jess, I mean."

Luke got up from the table and walked to the window, looking outside at the forlorn trees holding rags of leaves. What seemed almost magical earlier had evaporated like a soap bubble. What was he doing? Maybe Morgan was right... impulsive. He'd never been with another man. Could he please him?

He started when Morgan wrapped his arms around him from behind, but then the steady heartbeat and lean body and rasp of Morgan's beard against the skin of his neck settled him. Weird. He never thought he could feel—

"I'm a little nervous," Morgan confessed.

"Yeah!" Luke breathed out a laugh. Morgan felt that way too? "At least you've been here before."

Morgan's gaze was solemn. "No, I really think I haven't."

Luke's throat tightened. "I want it nice. I want to make it nice for you...."

"Just kiss me the way you did that first time," Morgan said, his eyes on Luke's lips, and then Luke cupped his face, bent down, and met Morgan warmly, caressing him with his tongue. He moaned at tasting him, pulling him closer.

His erection ground against Morgan's, nudging, and there was no guessing now. He knew he was wanted. He cupped Morgan's ass in his hands, squeezing, and then Morgan gave a little leap, almost like he was mounting Luke's horse again....

Luke crashed against the side of the wall, and some of the decorations clattered to the floor. He gasped out a laugh, Morgan's legs hooked around his hips. "What are you doing?"

"I'm a bottom, well, mostly," Morgan whispered, gaze roaming Luke's face until they ground together again, perfect, and Morgan's head fell back. "So I'm doing what comes naturally."

Luke felt another moment of uncertainty prickle his spine and mix with the cocktail of wanting to just rut himself against Morgan again. Oh yeah, spill his come on his legs, his penis, and look into his eyes and know that he belonged to Luke alone. But he was supposed to be the one to...?

Morgan hooked a leg higher, and Luke spun around so Morgan was lodged half on the wall, half on a side table under the window. A lamp fell, rolled, and the cabin was abruptly a little darker.

Morgan cupped Luke's neck, his eyes promising—

Luke's breath panted a rapid tattoo against Morgan's skin as he reached down and freed himself while Morgan pushed down his own jeans so they sagged.

"Condom?" Morgan prompted.

"In my pocket, Doc," Luke said, but he needed to press himself against Morgan's groin again. He wanted to rub his cock there, dominate Morgan....

Morgan fumbled, touching more than Luke's pocket so Luke thought he'd shoot in the other man's hand. Oh God. He wanted Morgan all the time now. He'd wanted him the first time in the mission when it had felt like lightning hit him, meeting his eyes, though he wasn't ready to process it then, and now he wanted him when he was rocking Jess in his arms, listening to Morgan talk about his day, and he wanted him when they went riding and got soaked in the rain, so he imagined pulling him down to the mud and climbing him—

"Here," Morgan offered, but Luke dropped it.

"Shit!"

"It's all right." Morgan's eyes were dilated so that the black iris only left a thin rim of blue, seeming to swallow Luke's reflection.

"Doc...." Luke found the goddamned thing, but he couldn't get it on himself. Fuck! He'd been putting them on for years, but he was shaking so hard—

Morgan rolled it on, hands competent, smooth, though he was also panting. "It's lubed," he said.

Lubed. That meant.... One of Morgan's legs was up on Luke's shoulder, and the table was trembling like it would fall like the lamp, but he needed to fuck, needed to fuck Morgan, and he positioned himself and pushed, sweat running down his back. Slow? He had to... he couldn't just use the other man like a stallion.

Morgan hissed and clenched his hands on Luke's arms, locking him in place, and Luke didn't know if he was doing this right, but Morgan's hot tight body was fitting him snug, milking his cock. The table wobbled as they slid to the floor, and Luke pressed Morgan so his back was against the wall, but he couldn't.... Gravity made it awkward, Morgan still sliding.... Luke lifted him with desperate hands, digging into his ass, hammering into him at a shallow angle because it was the only goddamned angle he had, and Morgan growled out a curse as if Luke had touched on something that really made him live. Morgan's arms were around him, and Luke had meant to make love to him, but this was fucking.

"Morgan, take it!"

"Luke!" Morgan's body tightened and jerked, and then Luke felt hot jizz splash his skin where his T-shirt was shoved aside, and he pressed his lips against Morgan's as he spent inside him, nailing him against the wall….

LUKE'S ANKLE throbbed, swollen in his boot, and he stared at his hand, which was fisted possessively in Morgan's twisted T-shirt. He blinked, damp in places, chilling, hard floor, sore knees, and his face stung since he'd kissed someone who had a beard shadow.

He jolted away, but Morgan was there with him, completely there, as if he'd been waiting, and his eyes were serene as he smoothed a hand down Luke's cheek.

"So much for ambiance, cowboy," Morgan drawled. "I think you broke me for the saddle."

"What? Really?" Luke stiffened, trying to untangle his sticky body from Morgan's while Morgan's legs were practically around his neck in some kind of fucking yoga position, and all Luke wanted to do was melt his body into Morgan's.

"Oh yeah," Morgan whispered, and Luke blushed, self-conscious now he'd finished ramming into Morgan like a spring bull.

"I guess it's nothing like what you'd…. No culture or foreign films."

"Just someone who wanted me the way I've never been wanted before," Morgan agreed, smiling faintly, eyes heavy and satisfied. "Are you all right?" His brow wrinkled in concern.

"I want to stay here with you and Jess until spring," Luke blurted. "Can we, Doc?" He wanted to ask if they could stay the next year… or more, but spring seemed less intimidating, a smaller jump to take.

Morgan was up now, wobbly, reaching for one of the linen napkins to rub off his spunk from his body… and Luke's. "Oops, dropped it," he said, kneeling, but his face was between Luke's spread legs, and he pressed it against Luke's thigh, nuzzling him with open lips. "I love you," he whispered.

"You'll get fucked again, doing that," Luke warned. He swallowed. Morgan's words…. He guessed that meant he could stay.

Morgan's eyes glinted.

But Luke's smartphone buzzed from their dining table, and Luke reached for it, sighing but not surprised. "Jess won't settle."

"No, she's used to us both putting her to bed," Morgan agreed, also not surprised. He kissed Luke's leg, then climbed to his feet and finished wiping away their spill more briskly. They both pulled up their jeans, Luke raking a still-trembling hand through his hair.

"I heard what you said, Doc," Luke said. He cleared his throat. "I guess two men can… love each other." *Say it. Tell him. You're afraid, but just tell him.*

But Morgan's eyes said he knew already. And then the smartphone buzzed again, and the message read, *For God's sake, get back here! It's too early for Jess to be teething, right???*

"We didn't get to use the fancy bed," Luke lamented as they both left the cabin, closing the door behind them.

"It'll keep, cowboy," Morgan said, putting a hand in Luke's back pocket and squeezing his ass.

Luke smiled, feeling that. "Let's put our girl to bed," he said.

Epilogue

"SHHHHH, JESSIE girl," Morgan whispered. Although he was focused on settling the baby in his arms, he was aware of the whispers behind him in Sylvan's mission church. Morgan was there, Jessica's biological mother and sometimes babysitter, Zelda, was there…. The church was in fact packed with neighbors and friends and patients, all there at sundown to attend little Jessica's christening with the two men who were raising her.

The only one conspicuously absent was Luke.

"I'm sure it's the usual stuff. One of the new foals needs the vet, or…." Gena shrugged, standing near Reverend Doyle as they waited on Luke. "If it's not you I have to hold dinner for some nights, it's Luke."

Morgan sighed. "I know." Ever since Luke took Morgan at his word and started up his trail-riding business, he'd been working like a man possessed. He called in favors from the other operations he'd worked for, getting advice, renting horses, and hiring two experienced hands. And Luke also had to go out with the tenderfoot tourists and guide them through the foothills, giving them a taste of real Western life.

"He'll be here. He's very responsible!" Zelda added. "Just like you, Morgan."

Morgan hid a grin. Yes, he and Luke took their responsibilities very seriously: Morgan to his patients and to Jess and Luke, and Luke to his new business as well as Morgan and their child. But even when they were stiff with exhaustion, once they were under Morgan's handmade quilt, Luke was definitely hot to explore lovemaking with Morgan. And he especially enjoyed making love to him on the trail rides they went on when they could cobble together the time.

The mission door banged open, and a perspiring Luke ran into the church. There was a cough from the pews that sounded like a stifled laugh. Luke flushed, yanking off his cowboy hat and hitting his chaps to knock off some of the dust, which were also crusted with mud. His fawn-colored hair was sticking to his neck in sweaty ringlets, but his labradorite gaze ensnared Morgan like the first time they'd met there in the mission.

Their gazes held, and feeling built like wood stacked for a bonfire.

Then Luke took a deep breath and gave a rueful half smile before walking more sedately to where Morgan and Jess waited.

"Hey, Doc," he drawled. "Sorry I'm late." He reached out and touched Jessica's yellow christening gown in awe. "Whew! She looks like a porcelain flower. I'm almost afraid to touch her."

"She was waiting for her daddy," Morgan said softly.

"Look, before we do this…." Luke huffed out a breath, color touching his tanned cheeks. "I was never one to ask for help." He faltered, and Morgan knew Luke was remembering the first night they met, when a desperate cowboy had come to the mission.

"I know, Luke," Morgan said, wanting his lover to know he understood. "But it was more than you who found what you needed that night. I'd been asking too."

Luke swallowed thickly, staring into Morgan's eyes, and Morgan could read the love there. Sometimes deep in the night, Luke whispered the words against Morgan's skin.

Luke put his arm around Morgan and Jessie. "Well, all right, then, Doc."

Afterword

I WROTE this story when I was in a dark place in my life and it was pure comfort. It seemed to give joy to the people I shared it with and to the readers who later found it. I'm so pleased to have the opportunity to go back to Sylvan and live again with Luke and Morgan, adding a little more to their story.

Sylvan is based on a real place where I used to spend summers growing up. Morgan's log cabin is like the one my grandfather built on land he homesteaded long ago.

Even the mobile and the bats were real.

Nathaniel

There are no unimportant acts of kindness.
—Anonymous

Chapter One

"FREAK!"

Jeremy shoved Samuel into the gully between the unpaved country road and a stand of birch trees.

Samuel didn't know what else to do, so he got back on his feet, feeling raw skin on one knee. He blinked at the other eight-year-old boys from Sylvan's country school who had followed him.

"Nothing to say, freak?" Jeremy asked him, raising his dark brows. He had asked the same thing when Samuel brought Mrs. Henderson the basket of eggs to school that morning.

Samuel's gaze went from one hostile gaze to another. He swallowed and then shook his head.

"Can't talk, can't talk," Andy, Jeremy's friend, chanted. "Freak can't talk!"

Jeremy pushed him again, but this time Samuel didn't fall. He stood his ground.

"Fucktard!" Jeremy and Andy and the rest pushed him into the trench, pounding and kicking him until he was on his knees, covering his head. "Eat this!" He smelled it before they smeared it on him, rotted droppings from the side of the road.

"Hey, what the fuck!" The voice of a warrior. Samuel blinked up through the crud attached to his face to see the tall cowboy called Happy get down from his saddle. Samuel's belly clenched, and his face heated. He pulled into himself like a small sparrow.

The other boys scattered. They ran down the road, looking back over their shoulders and shouting in high, excited voices as they left Samuel alone with Happy, who took off his cowboy hat and swiped a hand over his sweat-damp brow. Above, the sky was a blue bowl over tall, bleached grass, making Samuel feel even smaller.

"Aw, they picked on you, huh?" Happy said. His eyes, reminding Samuel of gray smoke, were fixed on his face. Samuel dropped his head, not wanting to meet those eyes.

Happy frightened him.

He was loud. He laughed and smiled. He liked music. He danced sometimes, all on his own.

Despite the stink of the stuff clinging to him, Happy didn't hesitate in offering his hand to Samuel. Samuel stared at it, the stiff work glove loose along his rangy bones, the dark hairs on the back of Happy's forearms.

When he didn't take it, it didn't fall aside—Happy's hand still outstretched, waiting—

Samuel let Happy help him from the ground, avoiding his eyes as the big man knelt beside him, cocking his head. "Sam," he murmured, and his voice wasn't too loud this time, but sad and soft, like a quilt he wanted to wrap around Samuel. Hearing it, Samuel's throat tightened. "Poor little soldier."

Samuel could smell himself. Smell the horseshit on his face, his clothes.

"Let's get you back to the ranch," Happy said. "Your papa will worry if you're late getting home."

Samuel shook his head, not wanting….

Happy raised his dark brows. "You don't want him to see you like this?" Happy chewed his bottom lip. "Okay, kid. There's a sun shower we can use on the way home at the doc's place to get you cleaned up. Have you met Morgan Gallagher yet? He has a girl just a little younger than you are, called Jessica."

Happy took off his glove and gripped Samuel's dirty hand. He didn't seem to care about the stink. "Sam," he whispered. "Sam, kid, it'll get better, you'll see."

SAMUEL ALMOST forgot about the shit stuck to his skin as he sat at the front of Happy's saddle. Happy let the big Appaloosa walk, clip-clopping down a winding pebbled road to the homestead Samuel could make out ahead. There were patches of snow on the ground, and the puddles were iced over, cracked where traffic had impacted them. Despite that, the day felt warm and dusty, the Indian summer hanging on into early December.

Samuel curved his lips, and he let himself lean back against Happy. He liked being up on the horse. He liked the sun on his face and the way Happy wasn't hurrying to get him home.

When they reached a brand-new-looking barn, a blond man came out. He was as tall as Happy, with slender hips and changeable hazel eyes. He smiled, looking at Samuel, who hunched down, making himself small again.

"Luke," Happy said, swinging down easily from the saddle. He reached out for Samuel, lifting him free and back to the hard-packed dirt. "This is Sam."

Luke tipped his cowboy hat back on his head, his straw-colored hair matted by sweat to his face. "Sam." He offered his hand. Didn't he smell Samuel?

Samuel rubbed his hand over his dark trousers and then took Luke's big, callused palm, shaking it. Luke looked straight into his eyes, not smiling. "Nice to meet a friend of Happy's," Luke said. When Samuel didn't say anything, he lifted his gaze to Happy's.

"Kid doesn't talk, Luke," Happy said. "Not since he and his papa showed up on the ranch, leastways."

"Okay," Luke said as if it didn't matter. "Let me guess. You're here to hog my sun shower? I swear, Happy, you never leave any water for me and Morgan." Happy coughed, and Luke colored. "Uh. Well, it's around back. Help yourself. If Sam needs anything like bandaging or some clothes, bring him to the kitchen. Hell, do it anyway. Jessica made cupcakes." Now Luke smiled.

"Cupcakes!" Happy tied his horse to the side of the corral and then put a hand on Samuel's shoulder, guiding him toward the back of the barn. "We'll be there, though I gotta get the boy home soon. Don't want his papa to worry."

"See you then." Luke strode away with a wave, smacking his work gloves against his thigh.

HAPPY HANDED him soap that smelled strong, like the herbs his papa tended, and then stood back, pulling on a leather cord. Water fell, warm water, and Samuel lifted his head.

He was smiling when Happy handed him a towel.

"CUPCAKES," HAPPY said as he lifted Samuel into the saddle again. "You sure you never had them before?"

Samuel shook his head. He had one gripped in his hand, a perfect one with sprinkles. The little girl with blond hair and blue eyes had given it to him before she hid behind one of her tall fathers.

"You're going to love them," Happy said. He spoke to the horse, and they set off at a trot. After a moment Happy asked, "Want to go faster?"

Samuel nodded vehemently, and Happy gave a little laugh, kicking the horse to greater speed. Somehow Samuel held carefully to his treat as they thundered down the road toward the Rocking M Ranch where Happy and his papa worked. The wind feathered through his hair.

It was funny how life was.

He'd been so ashamed, not wanting to go home. And now it turned out to be the best day of his life.

Happy had lived up to his name.

"SAMUEL!"

His papa was standing outside the kitchen where he cooked for the hands. He walked over to Happy, still on horseback, and took Samuel from him, lifting him from the saddle.

"Aaron, Sam had a little trouble. I hope you don't mind, but there were cupcakes after I got him cleaned up."

"Trouble, Nathaniel?" Papa asked. He was the only one to call Happy by that name. He told the cowboy once it was a good name, with a good meaning. Samuel looked it up at school with his teacher's help, and it meant "gift of God." It was one of the names of the twelve apostles.

Happy climbed down from the horse, standing with the reins in his hands, shifting his feet as he held Papa's eyes. "Yessir, some kids from the school were kinda… unfriendly with your boy."

Papa lifted Samuel's face gently. "You're going to be colorful," he said.

Samuel nodded.

"The kid is real brave," Happy said. "I guess your people…. I guess you grew up with the whole pacifism thing."

Papa stared at him a moment like he did some mornings when Happy came by to eat. Happy was too restless to do it inside, so Papa filled a plate for him and the cowboy stood under a tree, eating quietly. Sometimes when he brought Happy his food, Happy would tease him until even Papa had to smile.

"Thank you for bringing him back to me, Nathaniel."

Happy pulled a face. "Nate. If you don't want to call me the other name, that's fine, hell, I don't care, but I'm Nate, Aaron." He held Papa's dark eyes before taking a step back, bumping into his horse. His face was flushed. He put his hands in his pockets. "Ah, I better go."

Papa nodded, and Samuel noticed Papa's face was also warm, probably from all the cooking. He pulled Samuel to him, and just from that touch, Samuel felt himself calming, like a leaf settling into place when he felt his father's broad, strong hands on his shoulders.

AARON KING pulled the quilt higher around his son as Samuel settled into the single bunk that had come with the cabin. He stroked a hand down Samuel's swelling cheek before getting to his feet and stepping from the room. He turned out the light and left only the Mickey Mouse night-light to beam from near the floor. It was fancy, something the community they'd lived in would never have approved of, but then, they hadn't had electricity for such things.

It was the first thing he had bought Samuel when they came here. A new life.

"Good night, Samuel," he whispered. He knew his son wouldn't answer. He bowed his head, feeling something seethe like dragon's breath under his breastbone. He was supposed to have faith Samuel would recover. Faith!

Alone in the great room, Aaron felt familiar restlessness rise. He was used to evenings spent with the company of his father, his brothers. Now there was only this empty cabin where many people had lived. A yellowed plastic clock ticked from the stone mantel, counting the hours until Aaron would serve food to the cowboys again, until he'd see Nathaniel and maybe exchange a handful of words. So far Happy was the only one to truly talk to Aaron.

He made jokes, but sometimes he said profound things, things Aaron had to think about all day until he could comment back to Nathaniel. And sometimes his observations about the land, about people in town, were poetic. He knew Nathaniel would wince at being described as a poet, but he was. He'd have said he spent so much time alone in the saddle that he had plenty of "thinking" time.

Needing to breathe fresh air and stand under the stars, Aaron left the cottage, leaving the door open behind him. It was crisp outside, the water that melted during the heat of the day freezing into icicles that clung to the edge of the roof like silvered teeth. Aaron reached up and broke one off, holding it in his palm.

"When I was a kid, I used to like to break those off and chew on them," said a familiar voice.

Nathaniel. He stood in the dark of the bending trees, holding a tin cup in one hand.

Aaron's heart picked up. "Me too," he admitted.

Nathaniel stepped into the light from the porch, slim hips swaying, boots clomping. He took his hat off and placed it on the bench, his dark hair mussed around his face, stubble on his jaw. His smoky-quartz eyes latched on to Aaron's.

"Some nights seem longer than others."

Aaron grunted an agreement. He nodded to Nathaniel's cup. "Coffee so late will make it hard for you to sleep."

Nathaniel shrugged. "I had a date. I'm just winding down." He sat on the bench and let the air out of his lungs in a long sigh, as if it were the first time he'd sat down all day. Aaron could believe that since Nathaniel Jefferson seemed always to be in motion, smiling, joking, even dancing, swinging those hips from side to side. He was like an unbroken colt, free-spirited. He attracted the eye so that sometimes Aaron would catch himself watching him, fascinated.

"Is she someone who lives nearby?" Aaron asked. This was something he could navigate in the strange outside world he'd been forced to embrace, talk of courting. He would never marry again, *never,* but Nathaniel was so remarkable it made Aaron wonder what kind of woman would appeal to him. Would she be quiet and content to let him sparkle the way he did, or was she like him?

"He's a guy named Sean I met at a rodeo a while back. He's a really good rider," Nathaniel said.

Aaron's breath caught in his chest. He didn't look at Nathaniel, heat rising in his face. Oh. Nathaniel was one of those kinds of people. Lost.

Nathaniel finally made a soft sound, as if disgusted with himself. "Night, Aaron," he said, retrieving his hat and getting up to leave.

Heart thudding, Aaron listened to Nathaniel's boots crunch on the gravel. He parted his lips, trying to think of something to say.

Nate. He ached to call him that. The name sounded simple, clean, like the man. *Are you lost? Because it seems to me it is I who is lost. You seem so free, so happy. And my heart is ashes. Who am I... to judge you?*

But it was too late to call Nate back. Instead Aaron walked out from the cabin onto the middle of the darkened path as Nate returned to the bunkhouse, never once looking back to where Aaron watched him.

Chapter Two

ON MONDAY Nathaniel danced in the dust outside Aaron's cabin, his boots kicking up little tufts of dirty air that hung suspended, as if lazy in the morning heat.

It all began as Aaron dished out pancakes, something he'd learned to make from a mix to which he added only water. He still wasn't sure what was in this mix. Everything seemed like a chemical, making him uncomfortable with the result. He couldn't help but think what his wife, Anna, would have thought of it, but then if she were still alive, he wouldn't be there.

The hands he fed thanked him, their gazes touching on his face, his shaggy beard, suspenders, and homespun clothing, and then darting away. Aaron didn't know what to say to them; they were like Happy Nathaniel, speedy hand gestures, laughter. He knew they thought he was strange, quaint. He should not feel pride, but pride locked up his words.

Only Nathaniel ever treated him as if he were just like anyone else on the Rocking M Ranch, his eyes alight like the water in nearby Sylvan Lake, sparkling under sunlight. But now he barely looked at Aaron, and Aaron felt like a closed-up house, truly stuck inside now, his fault.

"How was your date, playboy?" Albert asked Nathaniel when they stood next in line. Aaron's hand jerked as he handed a plate of bacon and pancakes to Nathaniel's friend. Albert and Nathaniel's eyes flashed to him, and Aaron reddened, dropping his gaze.

Lost. He knows I thought him lost.

"Fine," Nathaniel snapped off, but his tone said more. It said, *Not here, not in front of him; he doesn't get it.*

Nathaniel had never sounded like that before. Always before he included Aaron, even taking the time to explain things like movies Aaron had never seen. Aaron's throat tightened, but he silently poured out coffee, remembering who liked it with sugar, who with cream, who plain.

The work was a comfort at least. He had the work still, the rhythm of being useful. He thought of that when he handed out Albert's cup and his hand somehow collided with Nathaniel's.

Coffee spilled all over Nathaniel, and he gave a soft cry of pain.

"No!" Aaron said, grabbing a cloth, standing there with it in his hand. He stood frozen. Should he hand it to Nathaniel rather than touch him? What was proper? "No, I didn't mean to—"

"Save it," Nathaniel said, eyes heavy with some kind of cynicism Aaron could not begin to understand or relate to.

"Ouch, you okay?" Albert asked, ignoring Aaron, who stood there like a stupid big mountain, watching, wanting to say... wanting to—

I do not mean to judge you.

Nathaniel took the cloth, giving a wry twist of his lips. "Fine. Good thing I'm wearing blue today; stains won't show up as much, huh?"

Albert rolled his eyes. "You are hardly going to meet any hot men mending fences."

"Au contraire, my friend, there are hot men all over this ranch," Nathaniel teased. Just then his gaze caught on Aaron's before he dropped it just as quickly.

Albert shrugged. "Sheila and I went to the diner for meatloaf. She wanted me to talk about my feelings and shit again. I think you're lucky, sticking with guys."

Albert and Nathaniel were almost at the door of Aaron's kitchen now. Aaron watched Nathaniel reach out and rub some of the basil between his fingers Aaron had planted for a window garden. Aaron noticed he did it every morning, as if he liked the pungent scent.

"I am sorry," Aaron boomed.

All the hands froze at the sound of his loudness, and Aaron swallowed, feeling eyes on him. This was a serious matter. Huge. He was... had been one of the plain people. You did not attract attention to yourself.

Nathaniel had been saying something to Albert, his lips still stretched in a smile. He'd smiled like that at Aaron just two days before. He turned his head, and his gaze again collided with Aaron's.

"I am sorry," Aaron repeated in a softer voice.

Nathaniel frowned as if he were trying to make something out. He gave a stiff little nod, and then he stepped outside, leaving Aaron and his empty kitchen.

HE WAS wiping up the kitchen table, long maple planks scored like a picnic table with dents and carved initials, when a shadow fell at the door. He looked up, and there stood Nathaniel, his hands full of dishes. He used to return them, but lately, no, he hadn't done that.

Aaron had felt that aching loss. He'd tried, days ago, to say he was sorry, but he had done something wrong. He had embarrassed himself and driven Nathaniel further away.

His only friend.

Now Nathaniel hesitated, and Aaron went to him, taking the dirty plates. He wished he could take more than them, could take his hesitation and his shyness and his judgment away.

"I can scrape out the stuff for your, uh, recycling."

Aaron blinked. "Recycling?"

"The stuff you put on that heap of earth in the vegetable garden," Nathaniel said.

"Oh, that is a compost heap. Next year I will scatter it on the garden," Aaron said. "Better-tasting vegetables."

"That's hard to believe. Your tomatoes are really great."

Aaron dropped his gaze, basking a little now. He knew he shouldn't, but he liked that Nathaniel noticed the superior quality of the stock he grew. He hadn't even been there a full year yet since he was hired on at the ranch in February.

"The pail is under the counter," he said, even though it was unnecessary since they'd done this before. He stacked the plates by the sink, but then paused to watch Nathaniel as he began the chore. He was so easy to watch, the easy swing of his hips as he dipped to drop leavings in the pail and the way his chaps seemed to emphasize where he was a man.

Nathaniel looked over his shoulder at Aaron and then huffed out a breath. "Okay, are you homophobic?"

Aaron blinked. It sounded like one of the ingredients in the mix he disapproved of. "I don't like chemicals," he said.

Nathaniel's too-serious face cracked into a smile. "Oh, Aaron. Do I even ask?"

Aaron guessed this was one of the things he didn't understand. He had picked up as much as he could, but it was a like a quilt with gaps in the sewing. "I don't like that you stay away now," he said. He cleared his throat. "Samuel misses you."

Nathaniel held Aaron's gaze, for once not dancing or talking and smiling. He contemplated.

Familiar with thinking time, Aaron felt his muscles relax.

"You may not know much about the outside world, but you're a confident man; it's sexy."

Aaron blinked. "I am… sexy?"

Now Nathaniel smiled again. "Yep." He winked, as if encouraging Aaron not to take him too seriously.

"Why did your friend call you a playboy?"

"Do you know what it means?"

"Yes." Aaron was short. He wasn't stupid. They had all rented a movie with James Bond and watched it in the bunkhouse. From this Aaron understood what a playboy was.

"I, uh, date a lot of guys," Nathaniel said.

"Taste a lot of flowers," Aaron said.

Nathaniel blinked, and then he grinned. "Yeah."

Nathaniel returned to his scraping. Silence hung between them, but now Aaron didn't feel like he was inside the locked-up house. He felt content to listen or to let it be.

"Can I ask you something?" Nathaniel's eyes were a thundercloud gray now, and somehow Aaron knew what he would ask.

"Samuel," he said.

"Yeah. He…. Can he talk?"

"When I left my community, I took him to a specialist," Aaron said. "He can speak."

Nathaniel finished up and rinsed out the plates before turning to face Aaron, crossing his arms. "Why doesn't he?"

"It is not something I like to think of," Aaron admitted.

"You're sad," Nathaniel said softly. "You and your son have the saddest eyes."

This was something he could not speak about. It was too much, the past…. It built up in his chest and lodged in his throat. But Nathaniel was speaking to him again. He had to find something to say. Something not stupid and ignorant.

"Samuel liked his horseback ride."

Now Nathaniel's eyes lightened, as Aaron hoped they would. He liked the Nathaniel who danced and laughed.

"Yeah, your boy is really horse-crazy. I'll be sure to take him for another ride, if you don't mind. I know you're protective of him."

Aaron didn't know what to say to that. He was Samuel's father.

"And yet you let him go back to that school." Nathaniel chewed his lip. "Did you speak to the teacher about those bullies?"

Aaron shook his head.

"Why not?" Now Nathaniel sounded annoyed again.

"Samuel…. He must live in the world. We are alone now." He knew Nathaniel had no idea of the enormity of what he was speaking about. They were alone. There were no grandparents, uncles, and aunts for Samuel. There were no boys his age who dressed as he did, were raised as he was. And at night there was only this empty place where Aaron wished he belonged, with the clock ticking until the next day.

No one to pass the time with, to steal a joke.

No one but Nathaniel, and Aaron's stupid ignorance about this world had nearly driven him away.

Nathaniel gusted out a disgusted sigh, and he shifted his hands from his belt to his thighs, restless. If he touched him, Aaron almost thought he'd catch a spark of electrical current. "You can talk to someone at the school administration. He doesn't have to go through shit like this."

Aaron returned to cleaning up after the meal.

"Aaron, listen, I know your people… whatever, I figure they are pacifists, right?"

"Yes, they are." Aaron wasn't sure anymore who he was. Nathaniel called him protective of Samuel. He knew he wanted to yell at the children who gave Samuel shame and bruises.

He wanted to make it right, but he did not know how.

"But that kid is hurting so bad…." Nathaniel walked to him, snagging the hand Aaron was using to wipe the sideboard. "He's hurting, Aaron."

Heart thudding, Aaron felt that electricity now like a wire shorting out. He couldn't make sense of the impulses in his head, his body. Did he pull away from Nathaniel? Would that offend him somehow? Nathaniel's hand over his was warm, callused the way Aaron's was, the hand of a working man.

Touching like this reminded him of Peter. They had been very young, and when Peter had touched him, he didn't know it was bad. They had been discovered, and it could never happen again. Aaron's own papa made it clear. He didn't punish Aaron; he simply told him he must never be alone with Peter again, or he'd be lost.

And Aaron never was. He was a good son, a good husband, tried now to be a good father.

But he was lost anyway.

"I know he is hurting. I do not know what it is I can do it about it," Aaron rasped.

Nathaniel paused and then stepped back a little, and Aaron could think again. He felt a bit like he and Nathaniel were two planets, and when they got close, there was the heat of friction. It was better they stayed separate.

"You don't know what to do, how to handle it, right?"

Aaron didn't look up. There was a coffee stain. He had to scrub—

"Aaron, I can come to the school and talk to the teacher with you."

Aaron looked up into Nathaniel's serious eyes. "You would do that?"

"Sure." Now Nathaniel smiled again slightly, his expression easing. "I had a tough time in school, but Sam doesn't have to be miserable. You can step in and make things better for him. There's a new awareness now of the problems with bullying, even in small towns like Sylvan."

"Nathaniel, I would be so grateful if you would help us," Aaron said simply.

Nathaniel's eyes softened. "Some of the guys think the beard is a little… archaic. But I like it."

Aaron wasn't sure what to make of this. "Oh."

Nathaniel laughed. "I'm making you bashful."

"Yes, you are." Aaron nodded in agreement.

"Can I ask you something else?"

"You can ask…." Aaron let his reply trail off and saw the appreciation of his subtle poke come through in Nathaniel's eyes. The young cowboy understood he was being gently teased.

"I figure you're from some Amish community. Why did you leave?"

"Not Amish," Aaron said. "A little different." To him there were big differences between the families who followed his grandfather's strict example and the Amish, but he sensed Nathaniel would not quite see that.

"Uh-huh."

"I left for Samuel," Aaron said simply, his chest aching as he thought of his son. "Because he wouldn't talk. I needed to go out into the world to find a way… and there was no doing that. If I left it meant I did not have faith, but he was my son, my child…." His voice cracked and he flushed. "So I left."

"Of course you did," Nathaniel said. After a moment he took a step back.

"Well, I hope you repair all your fences," Aaron said.

"I think I just repaired one big one." Nathaniel's lips tipped up the way they did when he made a joke. "But yeah, some of the horses got out through a downed fence in the upper meadow. I found the bones of a foal in the foothills—cougar."

"The cougar must eat."

"The boss would rather he didn't eat our herd, and so would I," Nathaniel said. "So should we go over to the school this afternoon?"

Aaron nodded.

"I can take Samuel for another ride."

"He would like that."

Aaron followed Nathaniel to the kitchen door, watching him. He thought of all he had to do. He had to look through the eggs, take some to the little roadside stand he'd lately set up to sell his overstock. He had to cut late dahlias from the cutting garden before they dried completely from the freezing nights, and he had to shear the grass that was a foot high around the cabin.

Instead he watched as Nathaniel danced. The cowboy faced his way, smiling, dust rising, singing something under his breath. "There's a time to grieve, Aaron," Nathaniel called softly. "And a time to dance. One day maybe you'll come out here and try it."

Aaron felt he never would. But when he held Nathaniel's smiling gray eyes, he found he wasn't absolutely sure anymore.

Chapter Three

AARON WAS waiting outside the country school when Nate drove up in one of the ranch vehicles. He could see Aaron had dressed up for their appointment, his clothes freshly pressed, his beard combed, the color white-blond like prairie wood, the same shade as his hair. It was a startling contrast to his serious brown eyes.

Hell, Nate had it bad for that beard. He kept wondering what it would feel like rubbed against his nipples, between his legs. It looked so soft.... He could imagine himself in bed with Aaron, lying on some of those sheets Aaron hung out to dry in the wind, his body spread and open as Aaron came over him, touched him, kissed him.

Disgusted with himself for dwelling on something that sure as fuck would never happen and only served to make him as hard as a plank, he climbed out of the truck and slammed the door behind him, nodding to Aaron. He could see Samuel on the small swing set painted the same white as the old wooden schoolhouse. Sylvan didn't need a larger school since it was still sparsely populated.

"I'm sorry I'm late," Nate huffed, aware he looked like crap, still dusty and sweaty from working hard. He'd taken a closer look at the remains of the foal after he repaired the fence in that stretch of the property, and it left him with a few questions he planned to bring up with their boss, Tom Jackson.

"No need to apologize," Aaron said. "We are glad you are here."

"I hope Sam's teacher is still around."

"She is." Aaron walked beside him, and Nate appreciated how comfortable the other man seemed. He still wasn't sure what Aaron had meant about chemicals, but he seemed to have adjusted to the bombshell Nate dropped on him when he talked about his date. As they entered the one-room building, Nate wondered why he'd been so blunt. It was almost as if part of him wanted Aaron to know about him.

"Mrs. Henderson," Nate greeted, relaxing into a smile at the familiar gray-haired woman. He looked at Aaron. "She taught me a long ways back."

"Not so long," she said, getting up to shake Nate's hand. She nodded to Aaron, her eyes curious and yet kind as she took in his quaint style of dress. Aaron nodded shyly in return. "It's good to see you. You have to watch this one," she told Aaron. "He's a scamp."

"I know this," Aaron agreed.

"Hey, can we get down to business here?" Nate interrupted their teasing. Secretly he liked that Aaron teased him. He was so stiff and silent when he first came to work as a cook on the ranch. It took all of Nate's charm to coax him to smile sometimes.

"I gather this has something to do with Samuel?" Mrs. Henderson asked.

"Yeah," Nate said, and then filled his former teacher in on discovering the kid getting bullied.

She sighed. "It's tough. Children don't always embrace differences. And Samuel...." She looked at Aaron. "Quite frankly I've wondered if he should have some special schooling."

"Special schooling?" Aaron asked.

"In sign language," she said, folding her hands on her desk.

"*No*," Aaron said.

"Mr. King...."

Aaron's mouth became a straight line. He didn't say anything more, but Nate could almost feel the knot of feeling he wanted to express. "I think Aaron's concern is that Sam might not resume speaking normally if he has a crutch."

"He can't go on the way he is forever," Mrs. Henderson pointed out. "Right now he and I have worked out a system so we can communicate, but it does take a lot of extra time."

"I appreciate you taking that time," Nate said, knowing the woman probably went to a lot of extra work for Sam. "Uh, I mean, Aaron does."

"The point is, if this drags on much longer, you may not be doing Samuel a service by delaying exploring other options," she said.

"But if he learns this sign language, he might not...." With worried hands, Aaron worked the hat he'd taken off when he entered the school house. "He might not speak again, yes?"

"From what you told me, it was your wife's death that triggered his inability."

Aaron nodded.

She raised her brows. "How long...?"

"Eight months now," Aaron said. "The house was so quiet after she died. I waited and waited for Samuel to speak, but he never did."

Unable to help himself, Nate reached out and gripped Aaron's broad shoulder. Aaron dropped his head as he took in a deep breath. "Please, Mrs. Henderson…."

"You might also think about therapy, Mr. King. If your son is still grieving…." Mrs. Henderson leaned back, and Nate guessed she probably recognized Aaron had very little money. "I will speak to the boys who bullied Samuel. They will *not* do it again. And… I think we can wait until after the holidays to resolve the issue of sign language. But no longer than that," she warned.

"THANK YOU," Aaron said when he and Nate exited the school. Nate couldn't help but see he looked tired… but also relieved.

"I'm happy to help," Nate said sincerely. He cleared his throat. "I'm sorry for your loss."

Aaron looked away. "Yes… Samuel was very close to his mother."

Nate wanted to ask if Aaron had also been close to her, but quashed the question. It wasn't right to ask him that. He knew he had self-serving reasons behind it.

"So I had to bring the truck out here to make it on time. Can I offer you and Samuel a lift back to the ranch?"

Aaron nodded. "That would be good." He called to Sam, but the boy didn't respond. The chain of the swing clanged softly as he twisted and twisted, his posture slumped. Aaron sighed.

"Go talk to him," Nate encouraged. "No rush." He leaned against the truck, content to enjoy the break.

He watched Aaron go to his son, saw him kneel beside him, say something. After a moment Aaron climbed awkwardly into the swing next to Sam, which was far too small for his giant's body.

And right then, watching Aaron patiently swing back and forth, his gaze fixed on his son, Nate felt them tugging at his heart.

"MILKSHAKES BEFORE horseback riding," Nate offered, stopping in at a pastel-colored drive-in shack that stood sentinel over dust, cracked asphalt, and the endless waving yellow grass. It was still hot from the sun, but at night, it would go below freezing again. "This place has been here since I was a kid."

Aaron sat at the passenger side with Sam between both of them. Nate caught his eye when Sam didn't look enthused. Aaron shook his head.

Okay, so it wasn't going to be as easy as ice cream, but Nate still wanted to spoil Sam. After they ordered and picked up their shakes, they sipped them on the way back to the ranch. Nate honked and waved to people he passed on the trip.

"You fit in here," Aaron noted, and Nate caught the envy in his voice. "You have many friends."

"Yeah. It's a nice town. Not perfect, but what is? I grew up swimming in the lake, horseback riding, and camping in the foothills."

"Does your family still live here?"

"There was just my mom. Never knew who my dad was," Nate said. "Mom's a retired nurse. She married a doctor from the local hospital where she worked, and they're in Florida now."

"You must miss her," Aaron said.

Nate gave him an appreciative look. He might be too serious, but he was also sensitive. Damn, Nate liked that quality. Liked a man who watched his face to touch him, take in his every reaction, and he could just picture Aaron in that role.

He rubbed one eyebrow as he turned into the drive to the ranch. He had to stop thinking about Aaron. He needed a friend, not…. He had better hook up with Sean again, try to forget about Aaron for a while.

"I must get out here and cut that tall grass," Aaron said, looking at the weeds in disapproval.

"Better hurry; we could get the big dump any day."

Aaron widened his eyes. "Oh, you mean the snows."

Nate nodded. "They're overdue this year, which is kind of worrisome." The countryside had been very dry, with wildfires in the foothills, deer, bear, and other animals coming down in search of berries that weren't shriveled, and streams still flowing. "It'll be a relief when the cold comes."

He pulled up outside Aaron's cabin. Aaron climbed out first, and Sam rushed by him, running into the cottage. The screen door slapped hard.

Aaron expelled a breath. "I think he is upset that we intervened with the boys. He is… ashamed."

"He'll get over it," Nate said. "I hate to think of him walking home with those kids dogging him. They could really hurt him, him being smaller."

Aaron nodded. He looked at Nate, and Nate suddenly felt self-conscious without Sam there between them. "Well, I guess I better get back to the bunkhouse." The hands usually fed themselves dinner from the refrigerator Aaron kept stocked. Lunch was bagged sandwiches, and only breakfast was served en masse unless the boss put on a barbecue.

"Nate."

Nate's eyes widened. Aaron usually called him by the longer version of his name. "Nate" sounded intimate. "Yeah?"

"I am not used to spending so much time alone," Aaron said, his shoulders stiff. "I would like to invite you to eat supper with Samuel and me."

"Wow."

"If that is all right with you. If… you don't have another date."

"No." He didn't blurt out that lately all he'd been able to think about was Aaron. He meant to go out this Saturday night, maybe hit one of the larger towns and hook up with someone. He was not going to dwell on a guy who was never going to be in his bed, but he still couldn't resist tonight's invitation. "I'd like that. I'll just go back to my room and clean up first."

Aaron nodded, his face softening. "We will see you."

"Yep." Nate opened the truck door. His hands were shaking. He had to get a grip. This wasn't a real date or anything. He was just going to eat with Aaron and Sam.

AARON WASN'T sure if he should serve the eggplant.

He wasn't really fond of eggplant, but there had been a sale on the seeds and he decided to try it, try something new. And he liked the color of it, sleek purple and plump in his vegetable patch. He just wasn't sure he liked the taste.

When he had his casserole in the oven, he cut up fresh greens from the garden, noting a bitter quality now. The season had stretched on longer than it normally did, so he was lucky to have fresh vegetables at all. Perhaps he should take heed of Nate's warning and harvest them all now while he could.

After setting the table, he stared around his kitchen, trying to see if he had forgotten anything. He wanted to show his appreciation to Nate for helping with Samuel. Everything sparkled, worn but clean. He'd scrubbed the table so hard the ink staining it had bleached out.

Flowers! Sometimes he had Samuel go out and pick some for the table. His wife had done it, and it made the table seem friendly. Was there time to pick any? He checked the ticking yellow clock and saw he might have just enough time. He grabbed a coat because it was chilly now, and rushed outside, stumbling a little over one of the porch steps.

Flushed and triumphant, Aaron arrived back at his front door just when Nate did. He stared at him, taking in his combed hair, his freshly shaved chin. He was wearing jeans, a T-shirt, and a jean jacket.... He looked nice.

"For me?" Nate teased as he looked at the bouquet Aaron gripped tightly.

"Yes," Aaron said.

Nate's eyes softened as if Aaron had said something quaint. Aaron growled under his breath, and Nate grinned.

He opened the door, and they hesitated on the threshold before they entered the warm, fragrant kitchen.

Chapter Four

"WHAT'S THAT scent?" Nate immediately asked Aaron.

Aaron smiled, thinking he'd finally shown something new to the worldly cowboy.

"It is cardamom. I put it in the spice cake. I noticed… you like basil, you like herbs and spices." Aaron nodded to the clump of light-green leaves in his windowsill Nate liked to finger every morning.

"Well." Nate rubbed his hands on his jeans and then took off his jacket, standing there.

After a moment Aaron took it from him and hung it on a peg by the door. He pointed to the table. "Sit."

"Right." Nate sat down, reaching out to run a hand over his utensils. Aaron stared at him. "What?"

"It is strange, having a man friend over for supper," Aaron said as he sat down.

"Man friend." Nate grinned.

Aaron remembered the flowers, picking them up from the table where he left them and taking them to the sink. He filled an empty jam jar with water and plunked them in before setting them on the table.

"Dinner smells amazing."

"I used eggplant in the casserole. I am still…. I did not cook before coming here, but it was the only job available."

"What did you do?" Nate settled back to listen, and Aaron found himself relaxing. It felt good to talk to someone again.

"I grew crops, vegetables, repaired equipment, and kept some chickens for eggs. The month before I left, I whitewashed the inside of my barn."

"That's kind of like white paint, right?"

"Not a paint; it is an old recipe. In our barn I would apply it once a year. It was a good antibacterial."

Aaron thought of that house. How he'd closed the shutters, swept the porch, and then taken Samuel's hand, leading him away from it.

How big a step it was to walk out from the only life he had ever known, into the void. No one spoke to him after he made his decision. He was dead to his family and friends.

"I can't imagine what it would be like, leaving everything I was used to behind," Nate said. He reached out, as if to touch Aaron's hand. Aaron felt a strange ache under his breastbone at the aborted gesture.

He stood up from his chair. "I will check on the casserole," he said, opening the oven so a waft of dry, scented air washed over him. He pulled out the bubbling creation. It looked good, the eggplant overlaid with fresh potatoes and other vegetables from his garden.

"Oh boy," Nate muttered. He leaned over to sniff the food when Aaron placed it on the center of the table, pleasing Aaron so he flushed from more than the heat of the stove.

Samuel came in then, saving Aaron from having to call him. Aaron nodded to him, and he brought milk in a jug from the fridge, pouring it fresh for Nate and then Aaron, and last of all himself. He was dressed neatly for company, Aaron noted with approval.

When the food was all on the table, Aaron bowed his head and Samuel did the same. He glanced under his eyelashes at Nate and saw him lower his head after a hesitation. Aaron gave thanks for the meal and then thanks for the company. He saw Nate color as he said the last.

They passed the food, and at first, Aaron didn't say much, used to eating in silence with Samuel after all these months.

Nate told a story of how he had one of the horses step on his foot the other day, so that after a while, Aaron noticed they'd all finished, and he and his son were watching Nate, who was living up to his other name, Happy, with his hand gestures and his teasing.

Samuel had a faint smile on his face.

"So how's school going, buddy?" Nate asked him.

Samuel dropped his head.

Aaron cut into the cake and served portions before pouring out hot coffee for the adults. He knew Nate took it "black as sin," as he always said. Aaron always chided his choice of words, but that only made the cowboy grin. It had become a joke between them.

"When I was your age, I got beat up a lot. It was scary and humiliating," Nate told Samuel. "Back then, you know, we just thought it was something all kids had to go through sometime, like a rite of passage, and if you complained about it, you were a whiner. But it's really about standing up and saying 'I deserve better.'"

Samuel collected the plates. Nate looked over at Aaron, giving him a rueful little shrug. Aaron sipped from his coffee. The cardamom tasted strange to his plain tastes. He wasn't sure he'd gotten it right, but Nate seemed to like the cake. Samuel only ate half of his, dumping the rest into the compost bin.

"Do you have homework?" Aaron asked his son.

Samuel shook his head but then gestured to the door.

"Yes," Aaron said, watching as his son put on his coat before leaving the cabin quietly.

Nate raised his brows.

"He is going to check on our goat, Martha, and our hens," Aaron said. "He likes spending time with the animals we keep in the shed."

"Then this is a good place you brought him to."

Aaron nodded, sitting back in satisfaction. Perhaps the meal wasn't perfect, but he felt full and grateful not to be alone right now. So often he cleaned up and then, after putting Samuel to bed, wandered outside, heart heavy.

He ached for someone to talk to, to share his worries about Samuel.

"I couldn't take Samuel to the city." Then Aaron shrugged. "No, that is not true. I knew if I went there, I would die."

Nate didn't seem to think that was overdramatic. He merely nodded. "You're old Mennonite, aren't you?"

Aaron raised his brows before nodding.

"I, uh, did some research on the computer in the bunkhouse," Nate admitted. "When you said you weren't Amish, I wanted to know more about you."

"My grandfather broke away from a larger community and brought my family and some other families with him. He wanted to live a stricter life. He was very…." Aaron spread his hands. "People liked to follow him."

"Charismatic."

"We would not say that."

"Probably not, but it sounds like it."

"Yes," Aaron admitted. "I thought I'd live all my days in my community. But Samuel… I felt him moving further and further away. I looked for answers, talked to the fellowship, prayed." He expelled a deep breath. "But as the days stretched on, I became afraid, Nate. More and more afraid. In my heart… I knew we had to leave."

"You're as brave as your son."

Aaron shook his head. "No. I left for him. I did not leave for myself. I was always too afraid to leave for myself."

Nate frowned, but before he could ask the question Aaron saw in his eyes, the door creaked open, and Samuel appeared. His eyes were wide, and his face was flushed from the cold.

"Time for bed," Aaron said, relieved the conversation should break now like the icicle he'd snapped in his hand the other night.

Samuel shook his head frantically, pointing toward the open door.

Aaron and Nate stood up and walked out onto the porch with Samuel, who gestured toward the trees across from the cabin, which was set in a high crease of the foothills. They stretched for miles, slowly climbing up into the mountains that blocked some of the stars on the far horizon. Outside it was very dark, dark the way it was in the country, so at first Aaron couldn't make out what his son wanted to show him and Nate.

Samuel took his hand and led him down to the path, and in the cracked earth, with ice forming hard peaks, he made out fresh horse tracks.

"Oh...." Instinctively he placed his hands on Samuel's shoulders. "You saw some horses?"

"Not one of ours," Nate said, kneeling to take a closer look. "That's what I wanted to tell the boss. That dead foal I found wasn't one of ours; it was a mustang."

Samuel was a warm and relaxed, sturdy shape under his hands. Aaron could feel his happiness, and it made his spirits pick up. Perhaps things would work out here. Seeing the horses had clearly moved Samuel from his isolation.

When they returned indoors, Nate was shaking his head. "The wild horses have been gone for a long time from this area. They were rounded up and hunted down about twenty years ago."

"It has been very dry," Aaron noted.

Nate nodded. "Yeah. They might have come down here because of all the irrigation."

Samuel left them then, heading toward his room. Aaron let out a deep sigh. "Seeing them made him happy."

"Maybe things are turning around for him," Nate said, echoing Aaron's earlier thought. They didn't return to the table but lingered by the front door. Aaron knew soon Nate would leave. They both had an early morning the next day.

"That is what I hope," Aaron said.

"I noticed you put your hands on his shoulders. Touch is a powerful way to communicate," Nate said. "My mother… she's not only a retired nurse, but she practices energy healing through touch."

Aaron blinked. "Oh yes?"

Nate smiled. "Probably sounds very strange."

"Yes and no. It seems to make sense to me."

"You know it as truth in your body," Nate said. "I can see you use it with your son sometimes, reaching him despite how he's tried to close everyone out."

"You think that is what he is doing?" But Aaron felt it too. He sighed, rubbing the tight muscles on the back of his neck. "He has locked me out."

"It has to be very lonely, but you aren't alone here, Aaron. There are good people on this ranch. You might also take him to see Doc Morgan sometime. He's an MD, but it might be he has some suggestions for helping Samuel."

"I have heard he is a good doctor," Aaron admitted. "I am not sure about the therapy that Mrs. Henderson described. I keep waiting for Samuel to share with me what has rolled a rock over his heart."

"I hope he does that sometime, Aaron," Nate said. "Maybe Morgan can suggest where there is some free counseling for kids. He's really good about helping people." He paused and added dryly, "You probably also heard the doc lives with another man."

Aaron's cheeks heated. "Yes."

"They have a little girl. I know this might be hard for you to accept, coming from such a strict place, but they have a good life."

"Is that what you want for yourself?" Aaron studied Nate, seeing his gray eyes were the color of heavy thunderclouds in the dim light.

Nate raised his chin. "Yes, I want someone to come home to. I want a family."

"And yet you date many men." Aaron had been glad Nate didn't have a date this night. He'd wanted him, his dancing spirit, for him and his son.

"I need touch," Nate said. "It can be lonely being single, and I like to be touched."

Aaron felt the return of the ache he'd experienced earlier when Nate almost touched him. "Yes," he rasped.

Nate studied him and then licked his lips. "I could touch you."

Aaron tensed.

"I mean, just touch to… to let you feel not so alone, Aaron. Like my mother taught me. Will you let me try?"

"Energy healing?" Aaron repeated what Nate outlined earlier. "I...."
He should say no. "What do I do?" Nate wasn't as tall as he was. He was
built on more slender lines, not like the awkward mountain of a man Aaron
often felt like. He had freckles on his nose, on his cheeks.

"If you could unbutton your shirt, just halfway down your chest,"
Nate said with his voice softer now, hushed as if he were trying to reassure
a small bird trapped inside a window.

Aaron hesitated, but as he stared into Nate's eyes, he felt trust. Nate
had helped him and Samuel. Still, his fingers trembled as he pulled aside
his suspenders and then went to the top button of his homespun shirt. He
unbuttoned it and saw Nate's gaze fall, watched him looking at Aaron's bare
skin as he revealed it.

He wasn't like Nate. He was pale as snow in contrast to the times he'd
seen Nate without a shirt, sun-browned like warm wood. He swallowed, his
heart thudding until at last his shirt was loosened.

"Now can you...." Nate cleared his throat. "Can you spread your shirt?"

The act of disrobing for someone was something he'd only done
for his wife, and then only in darkness. Breathing through his parted lips,
he opened the material and revealed his nipples and the little silky curl of
white-blond hair in the center of his chest. He saw Nate's eyes focus on that.

"You have the most incredible hair color, like something out of *Hansel
and Gretel*," Nate said.

Aaron could think of nothing to say to that. His hands fell to his sides.
As the plastic clock in the other room counted out the seconds, he balled
his fists.

Nate closed his eyes and took a deep breath, then another, his face
upturned as if in prayer.

Aaron watched him, holding his own breath. When Nate finally
reached out and laid both palms against Aaron's naked chest, Aaron gasped.

Nate's heavy eyelids flickered open to look at him, his eyes soft.
"Easy," he said in the same tone he used with his horses sometimes. "Easy,
Aaron, it's okay."

Aaron felt his blood rushing through his veins, fast, powerful, so he
felt like a conqueror, not a simple farmer. He looked down and saw Nate's
hands against his skin, the contrast of color, felt the texture of the calluses
on the pads of Nate's fingers. Nate's face looked serious, concentrating, but
all Aaron could feel was... hands on him....

"*Aaron!*"

Nate. Nate's voice. Aaron had lifted him, shoved him against the corner of the cabin between the door and the wall. Nate's smoky eyes were wide and shocked, his lips parted, his hands tangled in Aaron's shirt, which gaped open.

Aaron kissed him. He devoured him, eating Nate's mouth like a feast, and he was starving, starving to be a man again, blazing and standing between Nate's legs, which Nate curled around his hips. Nate locked his hands in Aaron's hair, stroking over his beard as he kissed back, letting Aaron have him.

Chapter Five

HEAT, FLESH, the sound of a whimper. *He* made that sound. *He* clawed Aaron's back. Nate broke away from the desperate kisses Aaron burned over his face, his neck.

"Shit!" Nate's legs slid, his groin brushing against Aaron so he felt him hard, swollen, and huge.

Nate sagged into the corner and held up a hand to ward Aaron away since Aaron looked like he was ready to toss Nate over his shoulder—*holy fuck!*

Puffing for breath, he put his hands on his hips. *A hard-on won't kill me. A hard-on won't kill me. Oh shit!*

When he glanced up, he saw Aaron looking just as shell-shocked as he felt, as if they'd set off a bomb when they touched. The big man leaned against the kitchen table where they'd eaten with Samuel just a short time ago. He trembled with his pupils blown.

"Aaron," Nate said softly, recognizing Aaron was in a state. Had he often experienced desire in his repressed life? He had a son, but… somehow Nate didn't think so.

Aaron rubbed a hand over his bare chest, as if retracing the experience, as if reliving Nate touching him there…. Nate watched that hand as Aaron moved it down and cupped his sizeable erection. Aaron stared at him, stroking himself. It was both the most dominant display Nate had ever seen, and the most innocent.

"Oh hell, will you stop doing that? You make me want to get on my knees for you."

Aaron's eyes flared.

Nate put up his hands. "What just happened? Did you just… oh my God, I just about came."

"Came?" Aaron was still out of it.

Nate laughed ruefully, running a hand over his jaw. "Came as in shot, climaxed, got off. Oh fuck…." Talking about it was *not* helping. "You're straight… aren't you?"

Aaron opened his mouth, closed it.

Nate felt rejected by Aaron's hesitance. This was just some kind of weird accident brought on by Aaron's isolation and loneliness. "You're straight unless you make it clear you're not," he said, folding his arms.

"You touched me, and I felt your electricity."

"And I felt yours!" Nate agreed with feeling. He turned to the door. "I'm leaving now."

Aaron moved to block his way. His hair was wild from Nate's hands. His lips were reddened from their wild kisses. "Nate…."

Nate let out a deep sigh and couldn't stop himself from connecting again with Aaron. He nuzzled him, their foreheads touching, Aaron threading his fingers through Nate's own. *Touch.* Holy crap, it gave all new meaning to the word, as if all this time Nate had only experienced it with half of his senses.

"In the morning you might hate me, yourself. I don't want that, Aaron," he whispered.

"No, never hate," Aaron said, his dark eyes as serious as a promise. "I am one of the lost ones, I think."

"Lost ones?" But Nate wasn't sure he was up to that conversation. He swallowed the big lump in his throat before he pulled himself away from Aaron, opening the door and letting the cool air in, and with it, hopefully, sanity.

Aaron followed him out onto the porch. When Nate's boots crunched on the gravel leading back toward the bunkhouse, Aaron called out, "You are my friend."

BEING NOBLE was a bitch and a half.

Nate couldn't sleep, throwing the covers off in disgust. His bare body was covered in perspiration, all worked up. He kept imagining what might have happened if he hadn't stopped Aaron. Aaron didn't seem to have a red light. He'd been all green for go.

He was so innocent he was primal. He reminded Nate a bit of Tarzan, a wild man.

Nate groaned at that thought. His cock flexed as if it felt the grip of Aaron's fingers wrapped around it. It was the second erection that night since Nate had taken care of the first one in the shower right after he returned to the bunkhouse.

He turned on his side, feeling a phantom large body behind him, spooning him. A callused hand running over his belly, stroking him until it found where he was needy.

Damn, he was never going to get any sleep at this rate, and he had a lot of work to do the next day. He stroked himself again, still wildly sensitive from coming so recently. He knew he had to back off, and he had to be cool about things. Aaron was clearly out of his mind, so he couldn't hold him to it. But he was so damn passionate. He didn't filter his responses. He was fearless, taking what he wanted.

"Shit!" Just the memory of those lips taking his, of Aaron lifting him, claiming him—

Nate came hard, his whole body shaking. Then he wrapped his arms around himself, listening to his pounding heart.

As much as he told himself not to hope, not to believe, Aaron's kiss— it changed everything.

THE NEXT morning Aaron found himself having difficulty showing patience with Samuel.

"You can do a better job of rinsing those dishes in the sink, Samuel! The wild horse tracks will still be there later if you want to look for them," Aaron chided. "And don't drop any eggs bringing them to the roadside stand this morning."

Samuel looked at him, and Aaron felt suddenly aware of how sharp he sounded. He hadn't spoken that way to his son since before his wife died. He had worked so hard to shove down how tired he felt, how he didn't know how to help Samuel, and how sometimes he even resented that Samuel made things so difficult for both of them....

It is Samuel's fault we had to leave our home.

No. He once thought that, was ashamed for thinking it, but lately since he'd lived here on this ranch, become friends with Nate, that dark snake of a thought hadn't whispered inside him.

He took a deep breath. "I am sorry," he said. "Samuel...."

The screen door slammed; he wasn't sure if Samuel heard him.

Miserable, Aaron focused on washing dishes. He was still washing the same plate when a knock on the door made him jump. He swung around to see Nate standing at the screen door, hands in his pockets, his smoky-quartz gaze fixed earnestly on Aaron, his hair mussed from the cowboy hat he'd left on the bench outside.

Aaron's heart gave a big *thump*. What would happen now? Would Nate tell him what happened between them was a mistake? Had he pushed Aaron away because... because he didn't like how Aaron kissed?

But why would he like how Aaron kissed? Aaron didn't know how, not really.

"I thought it would be easier if I came by before breakfast," Nate said. "Less weird than when there are other people around."

"Less weird, yes," Aaron agreed. He put the plate down and, after wiping his hands, went to the door, opening the screen in silent invitation. He couldn't hide from Nate. If he didn't want to be Aaron's friend anymore....

It would hurt.

"Hey, you look so sad!" Nate exclaimed. He hesitated, clenching and unclenching his hands at his sides before he took a half step toward Aaron. He reached up and touched his cheek. "Aaron, it's okay. We'll work it out."

Aaron dropped his head. "I have not had a friend since I left the community," he admitted. "People look at me and then away."

"You can't lose me," Nate whispered. Aaron wasn't sure how it happened. Whenever Nate came close to him now, there was the scent of his cologne, and the warmth of his body caused Aaron to crush him close.

"I was afraid...."

"Me too," Nate agreed. "I didn't sleep last night."

"I was cranky with Samuel this morning." Aaron's eyes were damp, so he squeezed them tight and took a deep breath. "I have been angry with him for a long time."

Nate rubbed his back. It felt good, like he found all the places that hurt inside Aaron. "He shut you out, and it hurts, Aaron." When Nate said it, it didn't seem so bad, so unforgivable Aaron would feel that way. "Hell, this morning before coming here, I yelled at my poor, dumb horse, but it was my fault I dropped a bucket. I—" He blew out a breath. "I'm totally fucking useless since you kissed me."

"I was good?"

Nate blinked as if he wasn't sure what Aaron meant, but then his expression relaxed into a smile. "So good I nearly... you know."

Aaron's cheeks turned pink. "Yes."

"I, uh, better step back. Folks will be by any minute," Nate said.

Aaron didn't want to let him go, but Nate said he had to, so he let his hands fall.

"You've had these feelings for other men before." Nate sounded so certain, and his certainty made it possible for Aaron to say it.

"I tried...." Aaron swallowed.

"You tried not to."

Aaron gave a tiny nod.

"It's what you meant when you said you left your community for Samuel, but not for you." Nate studied him. "Last night was…. But it was still just an accident. You didn't choose me, Aaron."

AARON BROUGHT his dark eyebrows down, and he seized hold of Nate's arms, shaking him. "My life, I don't know what it is. It is pebbles and rock sliding down a mountain, so I don't know where I am going. It is a barn that is on fire, and I can't put it out!" he rasped. "Most of all, I can't help my son."

"You try so hard." Nate sighed. "What about Christmas? Maybe we can think of something that might be special for Sam. Is it something you celebrate?"

"We do, but it is simple, not—"

"Not tons of toys under the tree," Nate said. He smoothed his hands over Aaron's arms. He couldn't help himself. He saw Aaron's eyes widen at his touch, his lips part. He wanted to kiss and suck on those lips. "That's not what he needs, anyway. I have an idea of something that might be special for Samuel."

"What?"

Nate shook his head. "Let me think about it, okay?"

A long moment passed. Nate could hear his heart thudding in his ears. His gaze touched Aaron's dark eyes, his flushed cheeks and lips.

"Nate…." Soft, pleading.

When Nate did not pull away, Aaron crushed his mouth over Nate's, bright, fiery, lighting him up where Nate had felt tired and depressed. "I can't think."

"You think too much," Aaron said.

Nate dug his fingers into Aaron's hard shoulders, feeling cloth under his hands when he wanted…. God, he wanted to see Aaron naked. He'd wondered about him for so long.

"Aaron… this is just going to make it worse," Nate groaned.

"Worse, better. It doesn't mean anything."

Aaron didn't seem to know what to do with him other than kiss him. When Nate put his tongue in Aaron's mouth, he stiffened. Nate paused, aware this must be the first time another man had caressed Aaron with his tongue.

"All right?"

Aaron poked his tongue out, a little timid, but then sliding it over Nate's so Nate gave a choked sound. So sensual, as if Aaron were licking his cock. Oh God, what would that be like? Would Aaron be disgusted by the idea?

Chapter Six

"MORE PIE, Mrs. Henderson?" Aaron asked Samuel's teacher.

She shook her gray head with a smile. Aaron was aware of her green eyes studying him as he poured more coffee into her cup. Samuel had gone off after dinner with a coloring book, this one a gift from Nate featuring horses and cowboys.

"It was nice of you to invite me for dinner, Aaron," she said. "I was a little surprised since word in Sylvan is you are a little aloof."

Aaron nodded. "It is my fault. Since Nate had to go out of town, I thought… it would be nice to have someone over."

"Well, I'm glad I'm the beneficiary of your wanting to reach out and get to know people. I've enjoyed the eggs you send me. Those hens are really beautiful."

Aaron had given the teacher a tour when she first arrived. She especially liked his bantams. "Not as many eggs, but they take care of themselves," he told Mrs. Henderson.

She leaned back in her chair, sipping from her coffee.

After a moment Aaron blurted, "I want to court someone!"

Her eyes widened, and she coughed. Aaron colored. There he went again, the big ox.

"I'm sure that if you want to do that, you'll find a way," she said. When Aaron didn't answer right away, she asked, extra gently, "Is it Nate?"

Throat tight, heart thudding, Aaron nodded.

"I felt something between you two when you came to visit me," she admitted. "He's a very good man."

"Yes," Aaron said. "But he is a man. I don't know how to…."

"You can always look up some things on the web if it makes you feel a little more confident, though be careful to take whatever you, ah, see with a grain of salt," Mrs. Henderson suggested. "But I think the best thing to do is spend time with Nate. I am sure he can guide the boat, so to speak." She smiled, and Aaron found himself relaxing for the first time that evening.

"I miss him," Aaron admitted.

"Here," Mrs. Henderson said, reaching into her bag and pulling out two paperback books. "These are rather entertaining."

Aaron took the books from the teacher. His eyes widened as he scanned the back blurbs. "A love story with men?"

"I have some favorite authors I can suggest if you like it. I wanted to give you something back for all the eggs you sent with Samuel." Her eyes twinkled. "And I had a feeling before I came here this evening that you might share my taste in reading."

Aaron put aside the titles by Mary Calmes and Kim Dare, although he was burning to open them. After a moment he reached out and shyly squeezed her weathered hand. "When I invited you here, I hoped most of all to make a friend."

"Then you have succeeded, Aaron," she said. "Now you asked about where Samuel was in his reading, so why don't we talk about that?"

"THIS IS what you wanted to show me?" Aaron asked two days later as he huffed up a steep path on the unused land beyond the ranch.

Nate nodded, putting his binoculars back into the knapsack slung over one shoulder as he waited on Aaron. "You told me how Sam has been looking for tracks from the wild horses. Well, turns out the boss was curious too after I told him that dead animal I found wasn't one of ours. He wants confirmation a herd has returned to this area."

Aaron joined him on the bluff, the rock spanned by roots and loose pebbles and scrub caught in pockets. The view was oddly intimate. Their perch jutted out over prairie, veiled by the huge bowl sky, the distant purple of mountains.

"This is a place to feel small, to feel a part of things," Aaron said. The air stung, chilly, but also exhilarating, nothing like the gentle land where he grew up. "I like it here."

Nate flashed a smile at him. "Me too."

"So why have you lured me from winter preparations for my vegetable garden today, Nathaniel?" Aaron asked.

"Partly because we haven't had time to talk since breakfast last week," Nate said. He'd left to deliver horses to a ranch out of state, leaving many things unsaid between them. "I, uh, thought it would be a good thing to spend some time alone. I also figured after a few days of thinking time, if you didn't want to go anywhere with me… you could let me know."

"But I *desire* you," Aaron said. "I am not going to hide in the cupboard."

"That's the closet." Nate laughed, but his face flushed at Aaron's bald declaration. "And I think you're pulling my leg. You know the expression."

"Yes," Aaron admitted. "I was kidding. But not about the desire."

Nate dropped his gaze, looking a little shy. Aaron decided he liked it. He could make the bold and experienced Nate feel bashful? "I'm glad you can joke about it," Nate continued. "I was worried, but I thought… it would be better, time apart."

"I spent a lot of time walking alone outside at night. I couldn't sleep."

"I couldn't sleep either. I had a lot of shower time, though," Nate said. "Thinking of you."

"Oh." Aaron now felt the shy one.

Nate's expression sobered. "Aaron, do you ever plan to go back to your community? I mean, what if Samuel…?"

Aaron shook his head. "I miss my family, but shortly after I met you, when we became friends, I knew I would be all right, that I could make a place for myself. And… Mrs. Henderson came by when you were gone. I made her dinner. I think she would like to be my friend also."

"I'm glad. It helps to have friends," Nate said. Then a frustrated look crossed his face, and he finished in a rush, "So do you, um, want to maybe try dating?"

Aaron's pulse picked up, racing like the wild horses they searched for traces of. "I don't know how to date you," he confessed. "I know nothing about how to keep a man like you."

"Keep?" Nate's eyes widened, and Aaron knew this was probably another thing he would consider quaint. "I think if you kiss me the way you did before, that would go a long way to—"

Aaron pulled Nate to him, at first hesitant. He was so awkward before, the way he first grabbed Nate. "I asked Mrs. Henderson about how to court you," he admitted. "I want you to like me, Nate."

"W-what?" There was surprise and laughter in Nate's voice.

"I did the wrong thing again?" With Nate's body so close to his now, Aaron felt a primitive satisfaction Nate wasn't as tall, wasn't quite as muscular, but instead had the slim hips and agile body of a natural rider.

"Wrong, I don't know…." Nate closed his eyes as Aaron kissed the side of his cheek, near his tempting lips. "I don't think you've ever done anything wrong."

"I want you to be mine," Aaron said. "Is that wrong?"

"Oh, hell no…." Nate's heavy eyes flared open when Aaron's palm covered him, touching him where he was hard and swollen. "Aaron, wait."

"She told me I could find information online. I used the computer in the bunkhouse, and I saw…. Nate…."

Nate gripped Aaron's wrist, licking his lips. He didn't exactly remove it, but Aaron knew he'd made some kind of blunder again. He'd seen pictures of men touching other men on their crotch. The thought had made him squirm, and he thought Nate might like it.

"I bet you saw some stuff that…," Nate said as a dimple appeared in the side of his cheek.

Aaron knew then it would be okay, whatever blunders he made. Nate laughing was always okay, and there was also something there in Nate's eyes Aaron was not sure he was ready to put a name to.

"Had to be a hell of an eye-opener. Just what did you see?"

"There were other people around, so I didn't look too long…." Aaron blushed, remembering how uncomfortable he felt in the common room, as if everyone could see his questions, his secret yearning.

"You didn't check out my porn stash?" Nate teased.

"No! Mrs. Henderson did give me some books to read. I have enjoyed them." Now Aaron was as red as the tomatoes he'd harvested before meeting Nate, piling their remains on his compost for the next year. "And I did see some pictures, very briefly…." There was one of a naked man kneeling at another's feet. He was sucking the other man, a cock buried deep in his mouth. Thinking of that, Aaron shifted, painfully excited. He'd been unable to get the image of Nate doing that to him, or him doing that to Nate, out of his mind for two days.

Nate leaned close. "What did you see, Aaron?" he whispered, his voice challenging, gently taunting. He treated Aaron like the man, like the equal he had always treated him. Hearing that, Aaron felt reassured. Here was his friend.

"I saw men, men together. Men… sucking." Aaron gently squeezed Nate. Nate gasped, and his head fell back.

"Okay, shit! Shit, we'll have to take care of that *right now*, or we'll be lusting all afternoon."

"Lusting…." *Oh yes.*

Aaron looked to Nate for direction. He was as much lost here as he would be up in these woods without Nate's guidance. "It's okay, baby," Nate said.

"Baby?" Aaron wasn't sure how he felt about being called such a name. "I am not."

Nate gently pushed Aaron's hand from where it was warming his crotch. There was high color in his cheeks, his eyes slightly wide, sparkling like a gray lake under sunlight. Aaron picked up on his mood, feeling buoyant, as if they were about to play some kind of game together.

"I want to see you. I know how shy you are, but... damn, I want to see you! Will you take off your clothes for me, Aaron?"

Aaron's eyes widened, and he looked around. "Here in the woods?"

"We might moon a couple of bunny rabbits up here," Nate said dryly.

"Very funny." *We*. "We" meant Nate would take off his clothes as well. Aaron wanted to see him, wanted to touch.

He pulled his suspenders from his shoulders.

"Hang on." Nate pulled his knapsack off and tugged out a small blanket, only a little larger than a towel. He flipped it out, spanning some rock shaded by an elderly pine tree. Aaron looked at that tree, thinking he'd like to come back here again, to this place, to where he first looked at Nate.

His attention snapped back to Nate when he tugged off his blue T-shirt, his muscles undulating under his browned skin. His nipples were smaller than Aaron's, tightly puckered from the chill.

Aaron couldn't resist reaching out and brushing the pad of his thumb over one.

"Oh fuck!" Nate cursed. He covered Aaron's hand, holding it to his chest. "Hang on... I need to know one thing, Aaron, and it's killing me."

"What?" Aaron grunted. He didn't want to talk. Why did Nate?

"You said stuff about the 'lost' people when we talked about your background...."

Aaron sighed. "Yes, I am lost. I accept this."

"It sounds kind of bad." Nate ran his hands through Aaron's hair. "As in wrong."

"I was taught to think so, but... living here, meeting people, making friends"—Aaron held Nate's gaze meaningfully—"I see it another way. I am lost... without you, yes?"

Nate chewed his lip. "If you mean strictly in a romantic sense."

"I am romantic."

Nate laughed. "Like a buccaneer is romantic, baby."

And that easily Aaron stopped worrying about what to do because Nate pulled him into a kiss. At the first brush of Nate's warm, wet mouth, he lost his head. He groaned as Nate parted his lips and brought his skillful tongue out to play, stroking Aaron's, making a kind of red, misty haze veil his thoughts. It was just like the other two times they'd kissed, when one moment he was Aaron and the next moment he became this beast, brought to life by Nate's touch.

"Easy," Nate whispered, putting a hand on Aaron's shoulder.

Could Nate feel him shaking?

"I want…," Aaron husked.

"Let's get this off you." Nate was unbuttoning his shirt. It reminded Aaron of that first time, when he'd been healing Aaron. Aaron's shirt fell open, and they both pulled it free. Nate parted his lips as he smoothed his hands over Aaron's big shoulders, and then he dipped closer to Aaron's chest with his tongue teasing a nipple.

"Ah!" Fire, Nate had *fire* inside him, and when he touched Aaron, he burned. And everything burned away. His past. His aching loneliness. His fear of not pleasing Nate.

"Oh yeah, you are so hot for it," Nate praised. He couldn't seem to stop touching or tasting Aaron's bare flesh. Nate reached one of his hands down to Aaron's belt and tugged it impatiently even as Nate sucked his nipple deep into his mouth, pulling hard.

Aaron's eyes rolled back. "Stop! Or I'll… I'll get off, shoot, come before we…."

Panting, Nate pulled away. "Race you," he said, his gaze deadly serious now. He dropped his hands to his own belt and tugged it free before Aaron caught on and did the same, falling out of his underwear and his pants with a groan, shoving away the constricting material, his socks, his boots….

He froze when he saw a nude Nate sitting on the blanket, studying him.

"Look at you!"

Aaron fought the need to cup a hand over himself. Anyway, it wouldn't be adequate because he was…. Nate stared at him with something like awe.

"You're definitely not a baby," he said. He lifted a hand, and Aaron took it, a little scared but burning now, burning so he couldn't do anything but let Nate burn him to ash.

Nate pulled him down, and they immediately crushed together. They wrapped their arms around each other, sliding them over one another's backs. Nate dared to reach down and touch one of Aaron's snowy buttocks and squeeze it. He gave a little snicker when Aaron jumped.

Aaron liked the sensation it caused him, making his cock flex. He definitely liked having his rear squeezed by Nate.

"Lie back on the blanket, Aaron," Nate encouraged. "It's a little cold, but we'll warm up when we…."

Panting, Aaron obeyed, staring up at Nate.

"Don't be afraid." Nate cupped his cheek. "I only want to make you feel good."

Aaron nodded so vehemently at that idea Nate laughed again.

"Spread your legs."

Feeling more vulnerable than he ever had in his life, conscious of the wind and sun on his bare body, exposed in so many new ways, Aaron obeyed Nate's gentle prompt, sitting up on his forearms to watch Nate crawl between his legs. The same wind that touched Aaron stirred Nate's brown hair.

Then Nate bent down and licked Aaron's cock.

"*Uh!*" Fire again.

"I keep wanting to channel kindness or intention or some goddamned thing into touching you, the way I tried at first, the way my mom taught me," Nate said, looking up to meet Aaron's eyes. "But I short out whenever we touch. It's like when I was in Hawaii once, and I would swim into the big waves and they'd catch me, and I'd roll over and over again until I struck beach. Touching you is like that."

"I have never been to Hawaii," Aaron said. *Please touch me again. Please put your lips…. Oh, there! Oh yes!*

"Mmmmm." Nate purred as he opened his mouth and took the tip of Aaron's cock in his mouth. "I love sucking you."

Aaron yelled, knotting his fists in the blanket, his body arching up so Nate was forced to take more of him, deeper, surrounding him in tormenting heat. "*Nate!*"

Nate pulled away as if to ask Aaron a question, but Aaron couldn't hear or understand him. There was only the roar of his blood, the need, and then he released, he released on a long groan and saw his spend hit Nate's lips, his chin, his neck, and chest.

Panting, sweaty, confused, feeling close to tears and close to shouting with the joy and sheer power of the act, Aaron stared, watching as Nate darted his tongue out and tasted Aaron's come on his lips. The sight incited him again, so he grabbed Nate's arms, tugging him up. He rolled on top of him, their bodies sliding, wet where Aaron had marked him, and then he crushed those wonderful, delicious lips under his.

Chapter Seven

"YOU LIKED that?" Nate asked, feeling a weird trace of anxiety. He had Aaron's come on his lips, but Aaron acted so untouched, so different from anyone Nate had ever been with. His heart thudded as he waited to hear from Aaron.

"I…. There are no words," Aaron said, sitting up. His pupils were blown, and he pushed his hips against Nate every now and then, as if still helplessly in the aftershock of climax.

"I love how you taste," Nate said. "I love sucking cock."

Now Aaron frowned. "Mine. *My* cock. No other, Nate."

Nate's eyes widened at this sign of possessiveness. "Okay." He guessed he could live with it. He'd dated because he thought there was no hope of ever being with Aaron, but all his fantasies had been focused on him. It was so hard sometimes, but Nate valued his time with Aaron and Sam and didn't want to fuck it up. He felt their isolation, wanted to help them both.

"But what about you, Nate?" Aaron shifted, exposing where Nathan remained hard and needy.

"Aaron, I don't want to scare you," Nate said, feeling that pinch of fear in his belly again when Aaron didn't immediately do or say anything. Shit, he was acting foolishly, but he couldn't help it.

"I am not scared of your cock, Nate," Aaron chided, looking up to give Nate a patient look. "I have one also."

Put that way, it did sound silly. Nate found himself grinning. "Prove it."

"Oh-ho, you challenge me?" Aaron lifted his dark brows.

"Aaron, just one thing. I—Touch your beard against it." Nate flushed at admitting something he'd wanted for months. "Against the tip, *oh God*…." The last he whispered as Aaron moved down his body and, after a brief hesitation, did as Nate asked. "Fuck, it's so soft! I've had so many fantasies about you between my legs, and that beard."

Aaron put his large, warm hands on either side of Nate's thighs, and Nate jumped a little by reflex, so wound up. He blew out a breath, recognizing he had to relax or he'd make Aaron afraid to explore.

"I want to look at you," Aaron said. "I like to take my time and look and think, Nate. You know this about me."

"I do know." Aaron also liked his thinking time. Nate just hoped he didn't die from the pleasure of it as he imagined Aaron seeing *all* of him, his distended cock, his balls, his opening. What was Aaron thinking?

Nate sat up on his forearms, his pulse crashing through his body as he watched Aaron studying him, occasionally grazing a curious finger over some part of Nate's sex. Nate couldn't stop from groaning when Aaron stroked over his butt with a finger. He wanted…. Oh shit, he couldn't say it. He didn't want to frighten Aaron, however bold he was acting.

"This is all mine now?" Aaron asked him in an absent voice.

Fuck, that was a sexy thought. "*Yes*," Nate agreed.

"You will let me do what I want?" Aaron's breath against his balls, and then, oh, and then he made contact, his lips brushing softly, his wonderful beard.

"As long as you promise not to shave that beard," Nate groaned, looking up at the lattice of pine branches and thinking he must look like some kind of male sacrifice, splayed out, Aaron playing with him how he wanted.

"You like it? I thought…." Aaron blinked up at him through heavy lids, as if what he did to Nate aroused him. "I thought to shave it off for you."

"No, oh no, please don't," Nate begged.

"But most of the other men don't have one. It is… old-fashioned." Aaron grimaced.

"So? I live on a ranch. I like old-fashioned," Nate said. "I like *you*. Your suspenders, the way you button your shirt all the way to the top, that floppy hat you wear in the garden. By the way, I could really get into gardening after watching you tend yours all summer. When you bend over, those trousers you wear really show off your, um…." Was Aaron ready to hear this?

"You were looking at my rear? I thought so." Aaron didn't look shocked, but smug. "Sometimes this summer I would catch your eyes on me, and you would blush."

"Yeah." Nate remembered. God, the thoughts he had about what he wanted to do to Aaron on his knees.

"I always thought you were a wonderful rider, and one day I saw it for myself." But now Aaron's expression darkened a little.

"What do you mean?" He heard something in Aaron's tone.

"I was stocking the fridge in the bunkhouse, and I heard you groaning. I thought you were in some kind of distress, so I went to your room, knocked on your door. It opened a little, so I saw you were sitting on someone. I couldn't see who it was. Back then I thought it was a woman."

"Oh no." Nate remembered a couple times getting it on with his rodeo friend Sean when the place was deserted. Ironically he'd been trying desperately to purge himself of his need for Aaron. "Aaron."

"I've tried not to think of it, what you looked like, your head thrown back, the way you were rocking as if you loved what you were doing."

Nate licked his lips. "I did like it. I like sex."

"Apparently you do." Aaron's voice sounded cool.

"Hey, it's not like I knew you'd ever want to be my boyfriend!" Nate retorted. He chewed his lip, feeling a little bit of uneasiness since he knew Sean, the guy Aaron saw him with, had been hired on full-time recently; he'd be living in the bunkhouse soon. How would Aaron deal with that?

"I do want to be your man friend." Aaron nuzzled between his thighs and then put his lips against Nate's opening. "I want you to be on top of me, Nate."

"Ah!" Nate couldn't hold back. He forked his hands through Aaron's hair as Nate twisted his head from side to side. If Aaron kept this up, he'd come all over him before he ever sucked Nate's cock.

"You make louder sounds when I touch you here," Aaron mused, touching Nate's opening with tentative fingers.

"That's because I need you there, Aaron. *God, I need you there so much!*" Was that his voice, confessing his most secret desire to his friend? "Please."

Aaron gently pushed a finger into Nate, and all Nate could do was tremble, loving the penetration, at last. He'd needed Aaron to fuck him for so long. "Put… put your mouth on me while you finger-fuck me," he directed. "I love that." He blinked. "If you, ah, want, that is…."

Aaron tentatively sucked on the tip of Nate's cock, spearing Nate with a second thick, callused finger, pushing now a little deeper so Nate felt the full feeling, the burn as Aaron played. Nate pictured himself riding Aaron as he had Sean, Aaron's thick cock deep inside him, his hands on his hips, urging Nate to take all of him.

"Aaron, pull back!" he gasped.

But Aaron only sucked him harder, and Nate cried out, arching up, giving Aaron his spend in long, luxurious contractions that wrung him out.

For a moment he could only lie there, Aaron's hair fisted in one hand, his body solid between his legs.

"Oh my God, are you okay?" He still huffed, but he sat up and cupped Aaron's cheek. He could see his come on the other man, so he used his T-shirt to wipe it off his lips, chin, and where it had dripped. Aaron obviously wasn't able to swallow it all.

Aaron cocked his head at him, as if still in his thinking mode, before pulling Nate into his arms. He was large, warm, and muscled, with that little bit of white-blond hair between his nipples Nate couldn't resist trailing a finger through. He smelled faintly of the herbs he was harvesting now in his garden. Nate laid his head against Aaron's shoulder, still shuddering from the intensity. Aaron patted him, a little awkward, as if he wasn't sure another man would want affection.

Nate's throat tightened. Truth was he needed that more than anything else. But only from Aaron.

Chapter Eight

AARON HAD saved the last biscuits from scratch for Nate. They had no chemicals in them. They were studded with late-fall strawberries he'd saved from the frost. He fussed by the stove, satisfied the other hands were enjoying breakfast but fretting over where Nate was. Why did he not come? Aaron wanted to see him, to watch him interact with the other people, to have him smile into Aaron's eyes. He was never late for breakfast. It had become their time together since they lived under two different roofs.

Aaron hated that, hated saying good night to Nate. Was it wrong he wanted him to climb the stairs up to the loft with him every night, to listen to the woodstove crackle below, and huddle under the wedding-ring quilt on Aaron's double bed?

Instead Aaron had to sneak kisses with Nate in the barn late at night before watching him go back to the bunkhouse. And with the last bit of harvest to attend to and the horses to move to other pastures, there wasn't time to be alone since that day on the bluff.

It was too cold to return there now.

Samuel brought some of the dirty plates to the sink, silently assisting him, and Aaron felt his throat tighten with guilt as he looked down at his son. Mrs. Henderson had come by recently and brought him more information on sign language, reminding him time was moving forward. After the coming holidays, Aaron would have to sit down with his son and let him know he wouldn't be allowed to close himself off any longer, but Aaron was afraid. What would Samuel do if Aaron pushed him? Would he pull further away from his father?

"Hey, I'm Sean, the new hand here, just off the rodeo circuit," a tall brunet said, interrupting Aaron's thoughts. He smiled as Aaron scooped out breakfast for him by reflex. "I'm a friend of Happy Nate's."

"Yes, hello." Aaron looked into Sean's hazel eyes, and suddenly he wondered if he was the man who had lain underneath Nate. It was a stupid thought, he knew. Nate had many friends. He didn't sleep with all the men on the ranch. Nevertheless, Aaron couldn't get the picture out of his head.

"Hey, watch out!" Nate finally appeared, flushing as Aaron stared from him to the new man, Sean. "You nearly dropped the eggs, Aaron."

Something in Nate's tone, the way he stood close to Sean.... Aaron swallowed thickly as he doled out more for Sean.

Nate's forehead crinkled. He opened his mouth as if he wanted to say something.

"How do you know Nathaniel?" Aaron asked Sean.

"Just friends, you know, though he is why I thought I'd winter on the ranch this year," Sean admitted.

Aaron looked at Nate again, who was shaking his head at him. What did that mean? Why was it Aaron was only just finding out this Sean had moved with Nate into the bunkhouse?

He reached up and wiped his forehead. What was wrong with him? He'd never felt so....

"Hey, any more pancakes?" Sean asked.

"No," Aaron said, even though there were more.

"Sean." Nate pulled the other man's head down so he could whisper something into his ear. Aaron could see only Nate's lips close to another man, lips he'd kissed the night before until he felt drugged on the sweetness of Nate.

He swung away, staring out the window.

"Aaron?" Nate asked. He touched Aaron's shoulder gently.

Aaron jerked away. "No more food today," he rasped.

AARON USED an old plow and Gitty, a placid Belgian draft horse, to dig up and turn over the remains of his vegetable garden. There were tractors and other equipment on the ranch, but this was familiar. Aaron needed his thinking time. When he'd come to fit Gitty out into harness, his hands were shaking. He'd had to calm himself because he didn't want to stir up the horse.

Even now, an hour later, as he looked in satisfaction at all the recycled bits of stalks mixed in with the soil, his eyes pricked. He could see only his Nathaniel with that man Sean, whispering to him.

They would be sleeping under the same roof this winter. Nate would see Aaron was boring, old-fashioned. He'd never been with another man, not in the same bed.

When a small hand banged his thigh, Aaron jumped, looking down to see Samuel wanted to show him another of his drawings of the wild horses. It was a familiar picture of a foal and mare, the mustang with her head bent close to her baby as they fed on grass near the road that led to Samuel's school. Aaron's forehead crinkled, and he was confronted with how frustrating it was to try to communicate with his son. He sensed the boy wanted to ask him something with all his pictures lately of the horses, but Aaron had no idea what it was.

"Very nice, Samuel," he said. "Did you finish your homework?"

Looking a little subdued at his father's answer, Samuel nodded.

Aaron cleared his throat. "Did you get the eggs safely to Mrs. Henderson?"

Again the boy nodded before turning away, as if to drift off, shutting Aaron out.

No. Aaron couldn't bear it. He tried to think what Nate would do, how the cowboy would laugh and tease and somehow bring Samuel out of his shell. "Would you like to ride Gitty?" Aaron asked, hitting on something Nate had used to reach Samuel before.

Samuel swung around and nodded enthusiastically.

"I have to take her harness off first, free her from the plow," Aaron said. "You could work on your drawing while I do that."

Samuel approached the fence that protected the blossoming vegetables and flowers from raiding deer. He leaned against it as he raised his pencil and continued sketching.

From time to time, Aaron watched him as he carefully detached Gitty. The horse dipped its head down to munch on weeds still green from the richness of Aaron's carefully tended soil, and at last, Aaron went to his son.

"I will lead you around on her," he said. "You will be all right without a saddle?"

Samuel nodded but then continued to stare up at his father, swallowing.

"Sam, what is it?" Aaron asked, very gently. The shortened name just slipped out, the one Nate always used. Nate had been changing him, changing even the way he saw his son.

Samuel handed him the drawing, and Aaron saw he'd written under it.

I see these horses sometime on the way to school, and
I've wanted to tell Nate 'cause I know he has been looking
for them. I want to tell him things all the time. Him and you.
Papa, I know we are poor. I know what that means
because we don't haf stuff. But if I do extra chores, if I work

hard, real hard for you this winter, do you think I could have a horse?

Please.

Your son, Sam.

Aaron blinked, automatically about to say no because he'd only had this job a short time and had not put enough money aside for something like a horse. They couldn't possibly....

He looked into his son's eyes, and he couldn't say it. Soon he would have to tell him about the sign language Mrs. Henderson was pushing. It might be Samuel would have to attend another school just when he was beginning to feel more at ease in the one he attended now.

"I will think on it," he found himself saying, and Samuel's eyes brightened.

As Aaron lifted him onto Gitty's broad back, he tried to think what odd jobs he might be able to take this winter that would bring in more cash.

NATE FOUND his two men in the ring, Aaron leading a patient Gitty around with Samuel riding the Belgian. He climbed onto the fence and watched them. Aaron looked up at him and then away. Samuel waved, flashing a brilliant smile. The kid came alive whenever he was around horses.

"I'll help you," he offered Aaron as he led Gitty back to the horse barn after giving Samuel a few more turns in the ring.

"If you want," Aaron grunted.

Nate huffed out an exasperated sigh. Jealous. Somehow his Aaron had figured out Sean was the guy Nate had seen off and on, and now he was jealous.

Sam shoved a wrinkled drawing into his hands, and Nate looked down to see another drawing of the mare and her foal. He nodded to the kid. "I think she might have gotten separated somehow from her herd. She's never with a stallion in your artwork."

He didn't add it wasn't a good thing for the wild mustang. Normally she was more than capable of protecting herself and her baby, but with the cougar prowling, she would do better to return to her herd.

"Show me the others, Sammy," Nate asked absently. If he could get a rough idea of where exactly the mustangs grazed.... He recognized part of the landscape as Samuel's path to school, an abandoned old farm that was just waste now. It ran along the country road. He'd heard from Luke that Morgan had thought of buying it and putting the land back into use.

As he skimmed through the collection, he found a sheet with a message written for Aaron. He read it and his jaw twitched.

"Here, kid," he said, handing the drawings back to Sam. "I need to go talk to your papa, okay?"

Samuel nodded, and Nate watched him head back to the cabin he shared with his father.

"WILL YOU just…!" Nate wanted to tear his hair out. Aaron had finished brushing the draft horse, all while coldly ignoring Nate. "I'm not going to sleep with Sean again."

Aaron gave him a look under his brows.

"I told him, okay?" Nate rubbed the tight cords in the back of his neck. "I told him that I… belong to someone now."

Aaron put down the brushes he was using.

"That is, if he still wants me." Nate hated that his voice came out sounding so uncertain, but he was scared. Aaron mattered to him.

"You should have told me about him," Aaron said.

"I know. I was working up to it." Aaron suddenly came closer, and Nate pulled Aaron's head down close so their foreheads rested together. Muscles relaxed that had been tense all goddamned day.

"I don't want you living with him."

"I'm not—"

"Living under the same roof as him." Aaron raised his hand. "Nathaniel, would you be comfortable if I had been with this man?"

Nate shook his head. "But I have to live somewhere."

"You will live with me."

Nate blinked. "Uh."

"I have a cabin. I have a washer and dryer. I have a TV, but it is not working now. You will live with me, sleep in… in my bed." Aaron swallowed.

"But Sam…."

Aaron took his hand, and Nate felt immediately claimed.

He didn't resist as Aaron tugged him from the barn.

"We will tell him tonight at dinner."

Chapter Nine

NATE CLEARED his throat. The cherry pie was damned good, but it might as well have been sawdust for all he cared. He'd been on edge all during dinner. Aaron wasn't helping. He said nothing, seeming calm and patient as he went about preparing the food while Sam laid out the dishes. It left Nate with nothing to do but fret.

When was Aaron going to tell Sam? *How* was he going to tell him? Shit. Nate pushed his hair off his face, thinking he'd have to get it cut soon since it was getting in his eyes again. It made him wonder how Aaron liked it. He'd told Aaron he liked his beard, hoped he'd keep it. Did Aaron like to wrap his fingers in Nate's hair? He ached to lie with him in the same bed, to get closer, to find out for himself.

But he also ached to make Sam smile, to see the kid more at ease. Sam was still so locked up inside himself.

"I liked your drawings," Nate told Sam. "I'm going to head into that neck of the woods tomorrow, have a look around for your horses."

Sam's face briefly glowed, and he pointed to his own chest.

"You want to come with me?" Nate asked, and the kid nodded. "Well, tell you what. School ends after tomorrow for the holidays, right? Why don't I take you there with me the day after tomorrow?"

Sam's face reflected a tiny bit of disappointment over the delay, but he finally nodded his agreement.

"I know, school's a drag sometimes," Nate said. He couldn't help thinking of Aaron's worries of what might lie ahead for Sam on that front. Sam nodded vehemently, and Nate laughed, deciding to push it from his mind for the moment. He still wanted to see if he could make some holiday magic work for Sam.

Nate said, "Aaron, thanks, the dinner was great."

At the same time, Aaron said, "Nathaniel is going to come live with us now, Samuel."

Nate's breath caught in his chest, and his gaze shot to Sam. The kid furrowed his brow, and he turned from Nate to Aaron, looking confused.

Nate waited, sure Aaron would add more to his lightning bolt, but he said nothing. Sam's face darkened, and he slid out of his chair.

"Wait! Damn it!" Nate reddened as he swore in front of Sam, but he still wasn't used to kids. He huffed out a breath and came to his feet. "Sam, your Papa and I...." Oh geez. "We really, uh—"

But Sam shoved aside another chair and ran for the door, tearing it open. Aaron shouted at him.

"Aaron, fuck!" Nate snatched his heavy jacket. "His world keeps getting rocked. It keeps getting rocked, so he hides inside himself."

Aaron swallowed, right beside Nate, his coat on. "He likes you so much, I can see that. I thought—" Nate saw the same distress reflected on the father's face that had been on the son's. He hated he was the cause of it. "Where has he gone?"

"The shed with the animals," Aaron said, nodding toward it, and Nate saw sure enough the light was on in the little lean-to. "He goes there when he is upset."

"And you leave him alone when he does that, don't you?" Nate asked, trying to get the lay of the land.

Aaron nodded. "I try to respect his thinking time."

"Well, we'll give him lots of time to think about this," Nate said. "But first I think we need to clear up the confusion. I'd like to talk to him. Please trust me?"

Aaron held his gaze. "I trust you. You said one day you would make me want to dance, but I want that for Samuel. I want that for my son."

Nate swallowed. "I know you do." Nate reached out and squeezed Aaron's arm. "You just had no clue how to tell him about us. You were afraid."

THE AIR in the shed had that warm, pleasant muskiness, welcome after the sting of the chill outdoors. Sam was sweeping, the broom a little taller than his slight figure. Nate and Aaron entered, but Aaron lingered near the door while Nate delved farther into the space. One of the banty hens made a soft sound from her shelf on the wall, annoyed at all the intruders after dark.

Nate pulled out the single armless chair in the space, sitting down. He watched Sam for a while. "Do you like me, Sam?"

Sam hesitated but continued sweeping, his face set.

Nate swallowed. "I hope so because I... well, I really like spending time with you. I think you have the makings of a first-class rider with your love of horses."

Sam still didn't look at him, but Nate had the impression he was listening.

Nate shoved his hair off his forehead. "I'm sorry you're confused." He cursed softly under his breath. "I'm sorry. I don't want that for you." He cleared his throat and looked back at Aaron. "What we said tonight at dinner was wrong."

Now Sam looked up, slightly disgruntled. Nate sighed. "We told you that someone else was coming to live in *your* house, without asking how you felt about it. That's just not right."

Nate looked to Aaron, and Aaron picked up his cue, saying, "Your papa made a mistake tonight, Samuel." He walked forward now and took the broom from his son. "Sam."

Nate couldn't resist anymore, so he reached out and ruffled Sam's hair. "So we still on for that day of looking for your wild horses?"

Sam carefully studied him and then his father. He nodded.

Aaron put his hands on his son's shoulders. "Come on. It is time to go to bed."

Still subdued, Sam went with Aaron. Nate left the shed, watching them. When Aaron reached the door of the cabin, he looked over his shoulder at Nate once before disappearing inside.

"JUST WHAT do you think you are doing?" Aaron's surprised voice roused Nate the next morning.

Nate sat up, groaning from his stiff back. "I *was* sleeping. What the hell time is it?"

"It is nearly five," Aaron said.

"That's at least half an hour earlier than I usually get up," Nate grumbled. "You get up really early, know that?"

Aaron widened his eyes. "It is a ranch. Why are you here in my shed, Nate?"

Nate shrugged. His throat tightened as Aaron knelt beside him, putting aside an empty wire egg basket. "Is Sam okay?"

"He was very quiet when he went to his room last night, but...." Aaron's eyes gleamed. "Before I turned out his light, he hugged me."

"Oh." Nate studied Aaron.

"He—" Aaron cleared his throat. "He has not done that in a long time."

"I'm glad he did," Nate said quietly.

Aaron's brow wrinkled. "Will you tell me why you are sleeping here?" His face darkened. "Sean did not do something?"

"No!" Nate gripped Aaron's hand. "No, but last night I was so… strung out, I guess." Nate looked around the small shed, sliding out from his sleeping bag. "All I could think was, you didn't want me staying in the bunkhouse anymore, and Sam isn't anywhere ready for, um…. So I hit on the idea of sleeping in the shed. It *seemed* logical last night at 2:00 a.m."

Aaron blinked. "You would do this? This is… crazy Happy Nathaniel stuff."

Nate pushed back hair he had no doubt stuck up at weird angles around his head. "Yeah, it is. But I'll do it."

Aaron shook his head. "No, you won't." Nate didn't resist as the larger man leaned his forehead against Nate's.

"But—"

"I will deal with my jealousy. I will trust you not to hurt me," Aaron said very simply.

Nate's shoulders sagged as he let out a sigh. "Okay. That dirt floor…. Yeah, I'd be okay with that."

"One day soon my son will want you to move in with us."

Nate's eyes widened at the certainty in Aaron's voice. "You really believe that?"

"You have made me believe." Aaron lifted one corner of his mouth. "Come to breakfast. I will make you pancakes with strawberries."

"My favorite!"

OVER BREAKFAST Nate saw Sam slowly relaxing as things remained the way they always were between the three of them. Aaron directed his son to put out plates for the hands, and Nate pitched in to put condiments on the table while teasing both his men. When the other cowboys came in, the usual joking around went on, and no one said anything about finding Nate helping out. He figured by now his interest in Aaron was probably pretty clear.

"Since I'm heading over to that old farm, you can ride with me to school if you want, Sam," he suggested a little later.

Sam hesitated, looking to Aaron.

"Go if you want," Aaron encouraged gently. Nate felt relieved he didn't make it an order and push his son.

Samuel gave a shy nod.

Nate finished scraping off his plate and looked up to meet Aaron's gaze. Aaron looked like he desperately wanted to kiss Nate this morning.

Nate swallowed, wanting the same thing. But one day…. Aaron said he believed it would happen, that they could become a family.

"Well, uh, see you in the horse barn, Sam. Ten minutes, okay?"

SOMEHOW HE wasn't surprised when Aaron saddled up the Belgian he was fond of and joined him and Sam on the ride to school. Sam chose to ride with him on his Morgan. Nate found himself relaxing and just enjoying the sunny late-December morning. He could feel in the brittleness of the air that soon they'd have snowfall, but the sun lit the remaining leaves a glowing amber as they fluttered down from the trees in slow, lazy circles.

As their horses clomped over gravel and frozen ground, Nate began to relax. He wasn't sure how things would work out, but seeing this change of season, he couldn't help but feel that maybe by spring… or summer… there was time for it all to happen.

"*Nate!*" Aaron's shout broke his reverie. He had ridden a little farther ahead, around the bend where the willows grew by the creek.

Worried, Nate urged Pete on, even as the big Morgan snorted, clearly unhappy about something.

He caught sight of the shape of a reddened rib cage, rigid feet sticking out…. He dismounted immediately, helping Sam down and blocking his view.

Nate squeezed Sam's shoulders. "The schoolhouse is close by. I want you to head over there now, all right?" The schoolhouse was on the other side of the rise, so Sam should be safe.

Sam shook his head vehemently.

"Sam, do it," Nate ordered. He waited until he saw the kid start down the familiar path before joining Aaron.

"One of the mustangs," Aaron said.

"Shit, maybe that cougar again. Looks like it," Nate said. "I can't tell if it's one of the horses from Sam's drawings. If it's the mare, there was a foal…."

Aaron shook his head, studying the disturbed ground around the carcass. "No sign of a foal."

"I'll call this in, get another hand to help me." Instinctively he didn't want Sam to get a closer look on his way back from school today, especially not after all the drawings he'd done.

Aaron nodded, leading the horses back into a grove of trees where he secured them. When he returned Nate had made his call and studied the ground farther out from the creek.

"Tracks near the trees, maybe from this morning. Might be the foal."

"The little one won't last out here alone," Aaron said.

"That's why I'm going to keep looking, Aaron," Nate vowed. "I had this idea—"

"*My fault.*"

The voice sounded rusty like a door that had gone unused.

Nate frowned, thinking the other hand he'd called up had arrived here damn quick. He looked up at Aaron and saw astonishment cross his face.

And then he saw him. Sam had returned. His book bag lay on the ground beside him as he stared at the remains of the wild horse.

"Sam, it's no one's fault," Nate said, as soft as he had ever made his voice. After all these months, all these many months, Sam had finally spoken. Sweat coated Nate's spine as he watched Aaron ball his hands into fists.

Sam's face was tight and pale as the coming snow. He looked a little spacey. "My mama fell down in our kitchen. S-s-she was…. She couldn't breathe. So I helped her sit up."

Nate's voice dried up.

"She t-told me to stay with her. She said…. But I went to get her medicine. Knew where she kept it, but I couldn't…. I tried, but the chair fell." Sam's voice thinned out to a breaking thread. "When I went back downstairs, she wasn't moving. I left her, and *she died.*"

Nate's heart cracked like fresh ice. He strode to Sam, kneeling beside him, hurting for Sam, oh God, Sam—he took the boy's cold hands, squeezing gently. Sam blinked, his face expressionless, a mask.

"It wasn't your fault."

Sam stared at him.

"Do you hear me, Samuel?" Nate felt the chill of the tears on his cheeks. Sam wasn't crying. Nate somehow had to do it for him.

And then Aaron was there, crushing Sam close. "My little boy. It could never be your fault. Don't you remember how your mama loved you? She would not want you to carry this, Sam."

Sam leaned against him with the sound of something breaking free. He clenched his fist in his papa's coat.

After a long time, Aaron or Sam, Nate wasn't sure, tugged him closer until the three made a circle.

Chapter Ten

THE SNOW fell like feathers from a torn eiderdown when Samuel went to the door and opened it for Luke, Nate's friend. He nodded to him, then immediately peered around behind him.

Where was Nate?

"Hey, kid. Cold night for Christmas Eve," Luke remarked, kicking the snow off his boots on the porch before he came inside the cabin.

Papa pulled a cake from the oven. They tasted better lately since Nate had bought him a cookbook called *Italian Country Baking.*

"H-hey," Sam replied. His voice still sounded strange to his ears. He barely said a word to strangers, but Luke was Nate's friend.

Luke raised his brows but then gave his attention to Samuel's papa. "I brought that referral Morgan wanted you to have, Aaron." He glanced again at Samuel.

His papa nodded. He put aside the cake and took off his oven mitts, coming over at Luke and took a piece of paper from him. "Thank you. Samuel and I will be going to counseling. I am a little nervous, but Nate has promised to try to make us both supper the first time we go."

Luke grinned. "If he cooks like I do, hope you have the number of a good takeout place."

The door thumped loudly, as if something had struck it. Samuel jumped.

Luke studied him with his warm blue eyes. "Maybe you want to get that?"

Samuel looked at his papa, a little anxious.

"Go on. It is something Nate wanted for us."

Encouraged when he heard Nate mentioned, Samuel retraced his steps to their front door and slowly twisted the knob. When it opened he saw the hands they'd been feeding, all of them except Nate. Two of them held a small potted pine tree with a simple paper star at the top. Samuel moved back, staring at it as they came inside.

"Nate said you'd want to be able to plant it in the spring, Aaron, near your vegetable garden," Albert said. He puffed out a breath, face red from the cold. "Gotta say it was really hard to dig it up this late in the year!"

Samuel reached out and touched one of the branches.

"I thought to decorate it with popcorn. Will you stay?" Aaron invited the other men and women, also including Luke in his invitation.

Luke shook his head. "Gotta get to the mission. Princess is in this year's Christmas pageant. Morgan'll kill me if I'm late again."

"Princess?" Samuel asked.

"Our daughter, Jessica." Luke's face softened. "That's what me and Morgan call her. Well, see you, Aaron, Sam… guys. Merry Christmas, Happy Hanukkah!"

Samuel watched Luke leave along with a few of the hands who had to be somewhere else. Most stayed, and Papa put milk on the stove for hot chocolate, but Samuel lingered near the window, watching more snow fall. He watched until his father called him to help string the popcorn. But there was no sign of Happy Nate.

"WHAT'S THE quilt doing on the couch, Papa?" Samuel asked Aaron. He was yawning since he'd been allowed to stay up late. The little tree stood near the sideboard in their great room, covered with popcorn and a few folded paper stars the hands had made. So far Samuel had gone over to it a few times, fingering the needles, excited about the wrapped gifts under the tree with the names of all their friends. Aaron had been doing a lot of baking, so Samuel had to have guessed some were special treats for the hands.

"The quilt is for Nate," Aaron said. "He is going to sleep on our couch tonight. We are going to be giving wagon rides to the children in town tomorrow, so we all have to get up early."

"Can I go on one?" Samuel asked, and Aaron relaxed a little. Time, Nate had told him. Give Samuel time. He didn't seem uptight about Nate spending the night on their couch.

"Yes, you may, Samuel, though there might be somewhere else you want to be," Aaron said.

Samuel's forehead creased, but before he could ask Aaron what he meant, there was another knock on their front door. Samuel sped to answer it, opening it for Nate, who was balancing a pile of brightly wrapped gifts.

Aaron came over, scolding, "That is too much, Nathaniel!"

"No, it could never be enough," Nate said as he looked first at Aaron, and then at Samuel.

He strode into the great room and dumped the gifts under the tree before turning to Aaron and giving him a faint nod.

"You have one more chore before bedtime," he told Samuel, who was clearly itching to go over to Nate's offerings.

Samuel groaned.

Nate winked at Aaron. Aaron could see in his mind his happy cowboy was dancing, dancing in the dust the way he used to on late-summer mornings.

"Come on, we'll help you," Nate said, folding his arms and waiting as Aaron and Samuel donned their coats, hats, and gloves.

THE CORRAL wasn't new, but it had recently been repaired and extended so it came up to where Aaron's vegetable patch would grow again next spring. Nate fell back, letting Aaron lead Sam closer with an arm around his shoulders.

The stars were like a thousand points of light overhead, so Nate let his head fall back, looking up as he settled near his two guys. He felt a touch on his arm, and it was Samuel.

"Hey, kid." He took in their quaint clothing, the suspenders, Aaron's beard, and the dark trousers under their muffling coats. Probably they still looked strange to some, but to Nate, now they were his.

"It's cold," Samuel said pointedly, obviously wanting to get back to the warm cabin and the intriguing gifts.

"So it is." Nate looked over toward the meadow, nodding so Samuel would look as well. In the moonlight the mustang mare walked from the trees, and the foal followed closely behind.

"But...!" Samuel clenched his small hands on the fence. "I thought the mare was dead."

"No," Nate said, shaking his head. "It was another wild horse. This is your father's gift, Samuel. When I managed to find them, round them up, he came up with the money to build a little shed for them and helped me repair and extend this corral."

"Can I go see them?"

Aaron put his hands on his son's shoulders. "No, not yet. Nate is going to gentle the mare for us. This spring he will teach you to ride. But your chore will be caring for them, Samuel, as you do our chickens and goat."

"I promise!"

The horses stayed at the far end of the corral, coats still shaggy. Nate couldn't wait to teach Samuel how to brush them. He watched them, a little sorry now they weren't free, but with a cougar hunting horses on the prowl, they'd been in danger.

They stayed a little longer until the snow picked up again. Heavy snowflakes turned wet against his cheeks.

On the way back to the cabin, Aaron walked very close to him so their shoulders brushed. Nate knocked Samuel's hat a little so it tilted at a funny angle, and the kid gave him a smile.

ON NEW Year's Eve, Nate still slept on the couch. More of his stuff had migrated to sit in neat piles around the den furniture. He'd fixed the TV, so sometimes he and Samuel watched it. It still seemed to make Aaron slightly uncomfortable, though he liked watching cooking and gardening shows.

Their closeness had not gone unnoticed on the ranch, but the special tolerance Nate enjoyed seemed to also apply to Aaron. Besides, he fed the men well, and they didn't want to upset the hand that made their favorite food, probably. Luke had also mentioned that though there were only two other gay couples in town, mostly they were left alone. In Sylvan, people preferred to mind their own business.

It was quiet except for the ticking of the cheap clock on the mantel, all the chores done for the night. He sat up when he heard a creak from the stairs going up to the loft, and Aaron stood there with his suspenders fallen beside his legs and his shirt half-unbuttoned. Seeing him in the light from the woodstove, Nate's heart started to pound.

"It is time you sleep with me, Nathaniel," Aaron said, holding out his hand.

"Sam...."

"He told me tonight that you need your own room if you're going to stay with us."

"My own room with you, you mean. Hopefully our thing won't bring him more hassling from the other kids." The quilt fell aside. The couch was lumpy, but sleeping there these past days had been heaven, even with the pain of want, of denial, and of hearing Aaron preparing for bed every night and wanting to be up there to see him, to touch him.

Aaron was waiting patiently. "He is already weird, yes? And to be different means you will be teased by those afraid of that. Samuel must learn to live with who he is, as I have. Finally."

Nate went to him. He meant to say something more, to take Aaron's hand, but Aaron crushed him against the wall and kissed him the way he had the first time. *Possessive.* Next thing he swung Nate up in his arms, and Nate grabbed hold of Aaron's neck with a surprised laugh.

"This is not how it's done?" Aaron asked him as he carried Nate up the stairs.

"I guess this is how we do it," Nate said. "I don't know, Aaron." He said the last softly because Nate didn't know where they were going. He knew what his body wanted, but that just came down to touch. But the rest....

Aaron lowered him to the floor in the shadowed loft, which had only one light on by the bed. Nate couldn't stop himself from putting his hands on Aaron's bare chest, sending out waves of energy, healing, so Aaron shuddered.

"I feel your electricity, Nate."

Nate put his lips against Aaron's nipple, openmouthed, sucking. "I feel yours," he whispered.

Clothing was tugged, his, Aaron's, until he revealed Aaron's wonderful body again. He pulled him down onto the bed, and they were kissing, their bodies lined up, heat, suction. Aaron's hand shook as he reached out and stroked Nate so Nate caught his breath and arched his head back.

"Nate...." Aaron pulled back, and Nate admired him, his dark eyes contrasting with his white-blond beard, the hair disheveled from Nate's hands. "My wife was my best friend."

Nate swallowed. "I know, Aaron. I know you loved her."

Aaron said, "But you are who I *choose*. You are the husband I want inside my body."

Oh.... Nate gulped more air. Aaron wanted him to—

"I trust you," Aaron said. "Make me want to dance again."

Aaron had lube and condoms arranged on his bedside table. Despite his background he obviously was a man who believed in being prepared, in embracing his new world. Sweat breaking out on his forehead, Nate took the lube and put it beside Aaron's body.

"Lie back," Nate said.

Innocence. Nate was so aware of it as he cupped Aaron's face, as he looked at the faint squint lines by his eyes, at the full lips he was hungry to kiss. He started with Aaron's face, touching it, learning it so if he were blind, he would remember the shine of skin in the lamp, the firm, round shoulder, the sudden bob of Aaron's Adam's apple as he kissed the little furry patch at the center of his chest. He curled his hand around one of Aaron's thighs, tugging it slightly higher as he put his open lips against Aaron's hip so his lover's big body shuddered.

It wasn't until more snow had covered their window, wet and cold and clinging, when the clock downstairs had ticked out a long space of time, that he licked Aaron's opening, holding on to Aaron's bucking hips firmly. Aaron didn't deny him any part of his body. He gave himself as if it were his wedding, and as Nate touched him, he became his bridegroom.

When he breached Aaron with his shaking fingers, Aaron sat up to watch, eyes wide, and Nate looked up to see the expressions wing past on his face. Aaron laughed. "That feels good now."

Nate shook his head. "You make this…." He didn't have the words, but he teased and fingered until sweat broke out between Aaron's nipples and his eyes begged for Nate.

Nate covered himself and came to Aaron, mounting him, cushioned in hard muscle, feeling the rough, callused hands on his lower back pulling him down. When he entered Aaron, they stared into each other's eyes. He died a little at the flicker of discomfort, and waited… and waited… and when Aaron clutched him with his broad hand on his back, he pushed gently.

Aaron groaned when Nate fully seated himself, shaking, his hair dripping sweat, his body a glowing furnace in the act of love. Give, give, give—he was all about giving to Aaron. Pleasure, healing, laughter.

You have the saddest eyes. He remembered thinking that when he first met Aaron.

His eyes were melting chocolate now. Aaron smiled and parted his lips, so Nate kissed him and tasted Aaron's pleasure. He rocked them gently, as gently as a boat out on the summer lake until, like a fork of lightning, Aaron broke him. Between one thrust and the next, his body tightened and he gave his come, and Aaron arched, and they were both wet and warm with Aaron's release as he pulled Nate down, safe.

"WHAT ARE you doing?" Aaron rasped in his ear a hundred years later.

Nate shivered. He put down the water he'd brought in a basin from downstairs.

"I was going to clean us both off," Nate said. "The water's warm…."

Aaron brought his arms around him. He was sticky and broad shoulders and serious eyes in the faint light of a new day, a new year. His body…. He was a muscled god, beautiful, like a bearded Zeus.

"Later, Nathaniel."

They took a turn around the room. It was cold so Nate knew they'd soon return to bed, snuggle warm, and Aaron didn't dance very well, leading, following, but he was dancing.

At last he danced as Nate danced, with joy in his heart.

Epilogue

AARON LOOKED up when a shadow fell over him where he was weeding on a warm late afternoon in May. He saw Nate so he lifted his head, and Nate kissed him. He felt a ball of secret sunshine in his stomach, thinking of the previous night and making love to Nate. Nate seemed to like him inside despite how at first Aaron was frightened and clumsy, and he knew he'd caused Nate some discomfort.

But Nate held him, kissing Aaron's bare shoulder, combing his fingers through his hair so all Aaron could do was arch up and make that little "*Ah!*" sound Nate said he loved to hear.

"The mission garden is going to be showy this year," Nate said, slouching against the railing that led into the church, his cowboy hat low over his eyes, his hair matted from the sweat of a working cowboy.

"Showy, no," Aaron said, uncomfortable with that idea. "The herbs will be useful, and the flowers can be pressed."

He'd done the work because Mrs. Henderson had asked him to try to do something with the weedy patch around the mission. Aaron still didn't attend the services, but he had more friends there as a result of his gardening. And he liked talking to the teacher, not only about Samuel's progress in school, but about their shared passion for romance novels. Nate teased him, but he didn't seem to mind when Aaron read to him in bed. Whenever the heroes in the book said, "I love you," Aaron's voice became deeper, throatier, and he knew Nate liked to hear it. But when he said the words just for Nate, his breath broke against his lover's skin, and he always added "husband."

Nate shook his head. "Okay. But I still think it's going to look really great. It's nice of you to do it."

Aaron shrugged. It was not nice. It was useful. Good soil shouldn't go to waste. Nate had strange ideas sometimes, even when he said the same of Aaron.

"Sam and I brought lunch," Nate said, nodding over to Samuel. Their horses were tied inside the crumbling parking lot, with tails swatting some early flies. Samuel wasn't yet riding the mare, as Nate still worked with her, but Aaron knew his magic, his touch. How could she long resist Happy Nathaniel? "Thought we'd all go for a swim after."

Aaron raised his brows, and Nate grinned, as if he remembered how they'd come here once and Nate had shucked down to nothing, skinny-dipping in the lake. "I bought a suit in town," he said. "It's still early so all they had was one with orchids on it." He grimaced.

Aaron quirked his lips. He looked forward to some teasing of his own, though it would be gentle because he knew Nate only wore the suit for the sake of Aaron's sense of modesty.

Samuel brought over the basket of food, and Aaron sat up, leaving his work. Nate untied his bandana and gave it to Aaron to wipe a streak of dirt from his face. "This is perfect. The sun is perfect, and it's perfect being here with you," Nate said lazily, lying back, cushioned by Aaron's legs.

Samuel threw a piece of apple at Nate, and he grinned, stealing a bit of Samuel's pie.

When they all finished and the sun still poured down on them, Nate stood up and began to shuffle around the broken asphalt. Aaron's heart lifted. He wanted to join Nate, and sometime soon, he knew he would, not just alone in their room. He reached out and ruffled Samuel's hair as they watched Happy Nathaniel dancing just for them.

Afterword

THE THREE stories—*Sylvan, Luke,* and *Nate*—were originally written a little bit apart as I worked on other stories. Reediting them now, it's neat to see how they all fit together. I think more and more there is something larger at work when I write, something that knows where the story is going when I don't.

I hope readers enjoyed three simple country stories of broken hearts finding love. I know that I felt healed writing them.

Luke's Baby

Part One

His Jessie was snared in a blackberry patch. A monstrous one with tubes and lights beeping and fluids going into her little broken arms. Her face was gray and black, bruised and scraped. She was so small she barely made a ripple under all that white sheeting.

Luke Walker sat by her bed, wanting to touch her just one last time when she felt warm, but where? She was covered in bandages, in tubes.

He settled for her fingers. They were swollen, so he stroked them as soft as a dove's belly.

The door shuffled open, and Doctor Morgan Gallagher, Luke's long-term beloved, walked in. His eyes were red. He'd gone out to consult with their daughter's surgeon and come back with red eyes.

"I don't want to hear it." Luke's voice was hard.

"Luke…." Morgan squeezed his eyes closed. "Oh God." Morgan took the seat on the other side of Jessica. Unlike Luke he wasn't afraid to touch Jessie. He stroked her hair, ignoring all the machinery, the life support that gave her breath, the drugs that kept her pain free. Oh Christ, Luke hoped she was pain free. But was she scared where she was?

She'd died twice already.

Once in Sylvan's tiny ambulance on the way there, into Black Deer, the nearest town with a bigger hospital. Only Morgan had been riding with the paramedics, and he'd brought her back.

She died again when they were trying to piece together her vital organs on the table. Morgan was there too, assisting since they were short on doctors.

Luke couldn't imagine how he did it. Doctors weren't supposed to ever operate on family. And Jessie, Jessie was Morgan's girl.

Eight years old now and smart as a whip. She deliberated between being an archeologist, a paleontologist, and a horse trainer and pediatrician daily. Oh, and she'd also run a sanctuary for horses and elephants. And maybe be a prima ballerina as well.

Thing was, their little fireball could do all of it. She was freaking brilliant, already two grades ahead in school with special tutors Morgan hired.

At first it bothered Luke a little how much Morgan could shower on Jessica. She was Luke's biological daughter. But he soon swallowed that stupid he-man thing. He was a simple cowboy. He made a good living with his little trail-riding company, had his own men. He lived in Morgan's house, but he'd made sure it was in writing it remained Morgan's.

It was one of the rare times he'd seen Morgan completely pissed off.

He didn't even sleep with Luke for months afterward, and Luke, miserable, didn't have the words to make it right, to bridge the awkwardness between them.

He always counted on Morgan for that.

Morgan thought it was about Luke's pride, about what had happened the first time some of Morgan's fancy friends visited the ranch and got a look at an undereducated ranch hand with a baby sharing a house with Morgan, the town's only doctor.

That's when Luke learned Morgan wasn't just an M.D., but he'd been head of fucking surgery in a big Boston hospital when he'd called it quits. He had driven a Ferrari. He'd had playmates galore. He'd traveled the world and could speak four languages.

Luke spoke English. And horse. He spoke really good horse, so some called him a whisperer.

But that didn't add up to Morgan's education, influence or, hell, his money.

Morgan had a lot of it. More than Luke ever knew when they first had fallen into becoming a family. Luke recognized now Morgan hadn't wanted Luke to know, had guessed Luke would feel like he had less to offer… was less.

Which he knew he was.

Luke hadn't liked Morgan's sophisticated friends calling him a gold digger, or the gay-for-you cowboy who found a soft touch in Morgan.

But he let it lie. He was patient, even as he smoldered while they visited.

They were Morgan's friends.

He was just his live-in lover.

Of course that didn't hold long. They had a lightning storm of a fight when Jessica was staying with Gena, Morgan's housekeeper.

And Morgan got on his knees, begging Luke not to leave him alone again. Christ, didn't Luke see how lonely he'd been?

That put paid to Luke's pride. He stayed, and he knew he loved Morgan. He loved him better than anyone could. But he insisted on a legal agreement, and Morgan signed it, but he insisted Luke's company was then

Luke's… and that had made for a chilly atmosphere for an entire fucking winter when Jessica was three.

They had gotten through it. Partly because Luke discovered Morgan had just made Jessica his beneficiary anyway, and fuck Luke. Since Luke had done that himself, he realized fighting over who had the money was fucking stupid.

Morgan would always have more. But Morgan chose to live there with him. Chose to love him.

That was before this spring. Everything was so good. Challenging, yeah, but good until this hellish spring.

Luke wiped his eyes. He was… crying? His face felt like a cold mask, squeezing around his bones, tighter and tighter while he, the essence of Luke, whatever that was, was trapped inside his skull, screaming.

My little girl.

Morgan put his arms around him.

He'd moved his chair next to Luke's, and Luke was so lost he hadn't noticed.

Morgan held him. Morgan the strong one, the comforting one. Except without Luke in his life, Morgan had told him he'd be a dead man walking, so Luke had better not leave.

"A specialist is flying in from Los Angeles," Morgan said, lips against Luke's tears because, hello, Luke had turned into a broken fire hydrant, and he was waterworking them both.

"Good thing your dear old dad left you those billions."

Morgan stiffened a little. That was something they'd fought about. Morgan's father had walked out on his family when Morgan came out years ago. Morgan knew then he had to take care of not only himself, but his mother and sister.

And he'd done it. He talked about his mother's sacrifices, but Morgan's schedule at the time was insane. And he was also a freaking genius, so he'd been an advanced student, graduating from medical school when he was still in his early twenties.

Then years later when Morgan's father passed, he left all his billions to his son.

People magazine called Morgan the "Billionaire Country Doc." It didn't help that Morgan gave a lot of it away to charity. It seemed the more he gave away, the more came to him.

But he didn't let all that money change their day-to-day life. He was careful of that and to shield Luke and Jessica as much as possible.

He had to hire some security, but they were part-time cowboys, so they didn't rankle too much, and anyway, Luke would do anything to keep Jessica safe because Morgan was brutally frank and showed Luke letters of people threatening them and their daughter. That had given Luke nightmares.

So the ranch was still home, but it had been beefed up, and Jessie had a bodyguard.

It hadn't helped the day of the botched kidnapping.

"I should have let you go," Morgan muttered now. "That someone would do this for *money."*

"I couldn't walk away from you," Luke said. "And you know she wouldn't let me, anyway."

That was true. Jessica couldn't be parted from either of her fathers. Early on when her mother disappeared and her maternal grandparents tried to win custody, Jessica made her preferences plain.

They could have lost, should have, but the whole town had stood for them. Reverend Doyle had spoken eloquently to the judge.

They'd fought and won the right to keep their daughter.

But some out-of-towners who visited Sylvan saw them as an abomination. They firebombed Luke's barn one Halloween for a joke. They found him alone once and beat him so badly he lost his spleen.

That almost broke Morgan, and angered Jessica. She wanted to find the bullies and karate them into the ground, even though she'd just been a little thing with a toy bunny dragging all over their wood floors at the time. He accepted that, as long as he and Morgan were together and determined to be a family in the spotlight, he would have to protect his family with his body. Morgan could use his smarts and his money. Luke would use his fists.

"I thought the letters were from a crackpot," Luke said now, referring to Joshua Spenser, a cult leader from another state. He'd come for Jessie, to force her to become his child bride. The thought sickened Luke. Of course, that was just Spenser's cover. It was money he was after, plain and simple.

He somehow got through all of Morgan's men, coming over land. Morgan had a lot of it, and he'd left most of it undeveloped as a sanctuary for wild horses.

Luke had meant to go riding with Jessie that morning after breakfast. He was held up last minute with business and told her he'd catch up with her.

"Hey, Dads," Jessie had called, already mounted on her horse, impatient to get going. She was wearing her Goodwill clothes, as Gena, their housekeeper, referred to them. A skirt made of an old lace tablecloth

hiked up over gray tights and a tank top with one of Luke's old shirts that would have buried her had she not cut it down.

Morgan held the reins of her horse. "Impetuosus," he said, the Latin word for "impetuous." It was a joke between them. Morgan knew Latin, and Jess was also studying it.

Luke snapped his gloves against his jeans, wanting to get on his gelding, Sable, and join his daughter. Morgan had a patient recovering from surgery, so he had to stay behind. "Stay put, Jess," Luke told her.

She raised a sandy eyebrow, her eyes, the exact labradorite color of her father's, full of a combination of rebellion and laughter.

"You'll be forever," she lamented, and there was the eight-year-old under the genius.

Luke grinned, recognizing himself. Morgan rarely got impatient.

"Likely." He had to go in the barn and check on one of his horses. Morgan was already walking back to the house, phone out, texting about his patient...

And Luke had thought Jessie would wait for him. She always did, but for some reason she chose not to that morning....

That moment was gone, shattered like fragile glass against pavement.

Over and over he relived it, did everything differently. But it didn't matter a damn. Jessie was still in that hospital bed.

Jessica was alone when the cult leader rode after her, shot her beloved horse, which fell on her, crushing her.

Then the man tried to drag her away.

Luke closed his eyes, making an animal sound of denial. No, he didn't want to think of it again. Didn't want to see it. Just be that morning again, Morgan with his boring healthy cereal and Jessie with cocoa puffs and Luke with eggs and bacon. Just another morning for them. Nothing special, oh Jesus.

Luke put a little egg on Jessie's plate, and Morgan took away the sugar bowl before she could spill more into the coffee she'd insisted on drinking since she was six. "Sugar's a stimulant, and you don't need that," Morgan had told her.

"I'm already sweet enough, right? That's what Samuel says, anyway." She'd grinned, not looking up to see Morgan and Luke looking at each other, that slightly befuzzled feeling Luke still experienced now and then welling inside him, that he had a daughter, that he had Morgan. Like he'd time traveled into the perfect life or something.

He looked down at his hands now, tanned against Jessie's hospital bedding, saw they were scratched and bloody. His blood? Or Jessie's?

She was gasping for breath when Luke found her with Spenser. Her face like paper, her eyes dilated in silent pain, and with a knife at her throat. But her gaze kept going to her horse, her distress all about her animal. Just like Luke taught her, take care of your horse first.

Luke recognized Joshua Spenser from the file Morgan's security men had shown them both months ago. Pale gray eyes, face expressionless, hair military cut. A man who never laughed, who had various children with his many "wives" but didn't seem to give a damn about any of them. One son, who reportedly had been "different," had disappeared.

He had a knife at Jessie's throat.

"Gallagher, I'm takin' her—" Spenser began.

Luke shot him with the rifle he always carried. He didn't give him any warning. He didn't care about anything but doing what he had to do. If a rattlesnake had been about to strike Jessie, he'd have done the same.

Blood spattered Jessie's face like gory freckles.

Luke put down the rifle carefully, then flung himself at Jess, pushing the body away from her, cradling her face in his hands. "Jessie, baby, you're okay! Oh Christ, look at me." His hands ran over her, neck, arms, legs. Her lips skinned back from her teeth as she hissed in a breath.

Oh, yeah, Luke thought dully as Jessie's hospital machines chirped and whirred. He guessed that was where the blood still under his nails had come from. It was Spenser's.

Jessie breathed. Her heart beat.

And Luke counted. Every breath. Every second. Another tie. Another moment she was still there. Another moment made bearable by her presence.

He cradled Jessie while he fumbled his cell phone with hands shaking so hard he'd dropped it. Twice. When he reached Morgan, he screamed for help.

Holding her, aching to move her, he knew he couldn't. She muttered something, he leaned close, and caught her pleading for him to take care of her horse. Please. Then she passed out, her skin damp and chilly under his hand.

Waiting for Morgan, tears blurring his gaze, Luke retraced his steps to his rifle. He took Sable's reins and walked him into the trees, securing him on a branch.

Then he returned and shot Jessie's horse, raw, tearing sounds coming from his chest.

It was all he could do for his little girl.

She remained unconscious until Morgan arrived with the paramedics.

And Luke had had to stay with the town sheriff until Morgan's lawyers sprang him free.

By then his little girl had died twice.

MORGAN HELD on to Luke.

He felt like he'd been doing it for years now, and how futile was that? Luke was a firefly, something brilliant and burning and something you shouldn't try to hold down.

But he knew Luke loved him. Luke once joked he loved Morgan more than his spleen. A black joke. A black, fucking joke.

Morgan remembered the night Luke returned with one eye swollen shut, his shirt torn, his lips pulped.

Luke had tried to sneak into their shared bath and shower off the blood.

"Waaaaait a second!" Morgan caught him stripping, spotted the bruises dark as thunderclouds on Luke's lower body.

Luke couldn't hide a wince as he tried to pick up a towel and conceal his battered body.

"The hell? I'm a fucking doctor!" Morgan roared. He helped Luke sit down on the toilet and touched his face gently, checking out his pupils as best he could in the dim light.

"I don't want..." Luke hissed as Morgan began running his hands over Luke's torso.

"It hurts there? More when I press in or out?"

"Out..." Luke listed to the side, knocking over razors and shaving cream.

"This is about us, isn't it?" Morgan's rage built. He wanted to go into town and find whoever had beaten Luke. It hadn't been one man. He knew his Luke could handle himself. He'd helped enough cowhands to recognize when someone had been deliberately brutalized.

"They were out-of-towners," Luke said.

"And that makes it right? Stay there. Can you?"

Luke nodded. "It's just a few bruises, Doc."

Jessie chose that moment to walk into their bathroom. Morgan reached down and tossed Luke a towel.

"Whaa's wrong?" she asked in her lisp. Her bunny was in one hand, the pink gone gray with prairie dust. Her eyes were wide, focused on Luke.

Luke's gaze met Morgan's, and they were instantly united.

Morgan reached down and picked up their daughter, feeling her warm, solid body, taking comfort, yes, goddamn it, from holding her.

Luke wouldn't let him protect him. Some stupid macho cowboy thing, he guessed, but at least he could keep their daughter safe from worry.

"Your daddy hurt himself so we have to take him to the hospital."

"Like h—" Luke stopped himself, swallowed. He paled, and Morgan carried Jessie out before she could see her father retching.

When he returned from taking Jess to Gena, Luke was in no shape to argue going to the hospital.

They'd had to remove his spleen.

It had taken a few months before Morgan stopped wanting to punish himself.

On the outside people thought Luke had it good. All that money. A rich sugar daddy.

Luke made Morgan come to life. He hadn't known he could be so alive until Luke's fire warmed him. Deep inside there was a darkness in Morgan, a place that was afraid, afraid Luke would leave him one day. Be taken from him. Luke and Jessie both.

It was the black heartbeat that shadowed Morgan's life. He smiled, lived, made love to Luke, laughed, took care of his patients, and was so careful, so very careful his money didn't drive Luke away.

He often wished to take them all on vacation, but that would have been rubbing his wealth in Luke's face, so he never did it. Now he ached for not having tried. With his resources Jessie should have been to London, Paris.... Though knowing her, an archeological dig somewhere would have suited her better. Like Luke she loved the outdoors and not the flash of the city.

But Morgan could have done that for his family.

He'd held back from even trying, out of fear.

What a joke, because here they were—and Jessie's surgeon warned Morgan she would not live the night—and his money was for nothing.

He was going to lose them both. Because Luke was not coming back from this. If Jessie died, Luke would go into the mountains, and Morgan knew he wouldn't come back. He'd find a way to die.

How could he doubt it? Luke had killed for their daughter. Morgan remembered the carcass of the horse, Jessie's white face, the blood, the broken bones, and Luke being handcuffed as his gaze screamed for Morgan to save her.

Because Doctor Morgan Gallagher walked on fucking water.

Only he didn't. Luke should have known better because it was with Luke that Morgan cried when he couldn't save one of his patients.

A nurse entered the room, glanced at Luke and Morgan, then quickly away, probably because of their silent agony. Morgan understood. Once he'd had that distance until he felt it eating away at his soul. He'd come to Sylvan to find the healer in himself again. And for the forlorn hope he might find love.

What he found was a desperate cowboy with a baby.

He fell for both of them that day.

"Dr. Harris left these for you." The nurse indicated the green scrubs on the trolley table for Luke and Morgan.

Morgan realized then he was still wearing his surgical scrubs with his daughter's blood on them, and Luke had her blood and her horse's on his clothes. He'd come straight from the sheriff's office.

"Luke, I'll stay with her. Go shower quick."

"No." Luke shook his head, not looking away from Jessie.

"Luke…." And Morgan couldn't believe what he said, but it just fell out. "When she wakes up, she can't see us covered with blood. She's going to be scared. She won't be able to move—"

Luke jerked to his feet, stumbled, and grabbed the proffered clothes. He walked out like a zombie.

Morgan reached out and took Jessie's hand. "You know he's not coming back from this, Jessie. You have to stay with us." Morgan could feel her as he'd felt other patients, not quite in her body, not quite gone. He knew she'd want to go; her body was broken. Pain waited for her here.

But so did two men who would never be the same if she left them.

THE HOURS went by.

Somehow time was passing, but for Luke, each moment was a beat of his little girl's heart. His own heart felt leaden, like a thunderstorm cloud on the prairie. He didn't matter anymore; he was just a placeholder because everything he was was with his girl.

He felt, distantly, a kind of guilt when Morgan took care of everything. Talked to the specialist, stayed while the man examined Jess, and Luke wouldn't leave, even then. He didn't listen to them, anyway. He was willing every heartbeat to continue.

Morgan took care of the lawyers, the press, and their men from the ranch.

He told Luke that Leif and Mal were in the waiting room with Gena and Nate and Aaron King and their son, Sam, who was a new friend of Jessie's. In fact, most of the tiny town of Sylvan came by and held vigil as the night wore on. Sometimes when he got up and walked to the window, he saw a tiny huddle of kids from Jessie's school, standing in the dark with candles lit.

But Luke couldn't find it in him to care.

Her heart beat, another minute, another hour, it beat.

And so his kept beating.

And Morgan knew.

He tried not to think about it, to give it away, but Morgan knew what Luke would do if Jessie died. They'd taken his old rifle away for evidence, but he had another. If she didn't come back on her own, then her daddy would go up into the mountains and he wouldn't come back. He'd find his own way of being with Jessie again.

And he knew it would kill Morgan. And he loved Morgan. But he couldn't change who he was. He was a cowboy to the bone. A simple man.

"Back when we first met, I thought I could leave her in a church," he rasped. "Christ."

"Oh, that old story again," Morgan teased, but his eyes were strained. *Please don't, Luke,* Morgan's eyes were asking him. But he didn't make it real by speaking it aloud. Because he believed, had come to believe, as Luke had, that love had to be free.

That the essential nature of Luke could not be broken, could not be changed, and could not be pleaded with.

It was that iron inside him that made him accept Morgan as the love of his life, after so many one-night stands with girls he didn't care to remember. And that iron weathered the scorn and the ridicule and the interest of strangers. Luke had turned his back on his former life and gave himself to his new family. And to fuck with anyone else.

And so Jessie's heart kept beating, and Luke held on to that, and Morgan held on to Luke.

And they drifted as if they were alone on a raft in the ocean.

"LUKE." MORGAN shook him.

Luke's eyelids stuttered open. He raised his head from where he'd rested it against his daughter's hand.

"We made it through the night," Morgan said.

Morgan said "we," and that was truth.

He held Morgan's gaze. Did he look as shitty as his lover? Morgan had less color than a ghost. His eyes were now neon red. But he wouldn't leave and Luke wouldn't leave, and this was it, for however long it went on.

"If we get through today…." Morgan's voice cracked because hope was a terrible thing. It was terrifying to actually dare to hope, but unbearable not to. "And tomorrow and…. The specialist will have to operate again on her back."

Luke made a hurt sound, reaching for Jessie as if to protect her. "God no."

"Luke, she won't walk again if we don't stay strong."

And Morgan was strong. Christ, he was a tower because he could lay it out for Luke and believe it when Luke could barely walk himself. He felt as broken as his daughter.

"Does she need anything? A kidney? I never asked, but…."

Morgan shook his head, and then his eyes welled up again, and then the chair scraped and Luke was holding him, crushing so close that he felt they'd break bones, shuddering together, drunk with weariness, with the live-wire of fear coiled in their guts.

After a hundred years, Morgan pulled back, wiping his eyes. So far he only cried alone, and Luke knew it was his greatest gift to be strong for Luke and Jessie, no matter what it cost him.

"The sheriff said that man… he was wanted, Luke. He'd kidnapped other children."

"I'm not sorry I shot him," Luke said. "I know you're not like that, but—"

"I would have shot him myself if I knew how to use a gun," Morgan said. "Anyway, you'll have no trouble. The evidence is clear."

Luke shrugged because he was supposed to care if they threw his ass in jail? He laughed, a cracked thing. "It doesn't matter what happens to me."

"It does!" Morgan flashed, his rare temper showing. "Because we fucking need your ass out of jail."

We again. Morgan was pushing it as a theme. But Luke needed that, and he knew Morgan could see it. Morgan knew him better than anyone.

Morgan dragged in air, steadying himself while Jessie still breathed, her heart still beat, and so life could continue for Luke. And then Morgan explained her injuries again. Luke knew he'd done it before, and the other doctor, but hell, after more than one broken bone, one organ they had to sew up and hope it would self-repair, after learning she might not have children, that her left leg would need reconstruction, and her back….

"She'll just adopt a bunch of baby elephants if she can't have kids," Luke said. It was a pathetic attempt at a joke, but Morgan got him.

"She'd adopt, period. Jessica's too strong to be laid low by this." And it helped to know their daughter's strength because it was shining and bright and visible in her, still there, still fighting to come home to them.

"She's always been like this," Luke said. "When I first saw her on the bed, just glowing, I was so fucking scared, so inadequate. I bathed her in the shower with me. I used my old cowboy hat to prop her up on the mattress. She slept beside me that first night, and I was so overwhelmed, I couldn't sleep. Probably just as well, as I might have crushed her if I turned over or somethin'. I put her in a drawer in the nightstand the next night."

"You were a good daddy."

"I was a 'I'll do my best' daddy, but only after coming into that church and accepting, yeah, my life wasn't going to be what I thought it would be."

Morgan nodded. He was there for that fateful moment when more than Luke's life was transformed. "I was thinking of the word *transformation*. It's something that some of us want, but it comes with a cost. It hurts, Luke. And it feels like being lost for a long time before it ever feels like you've found your home."

Luke knew he felt that way in the early days of his forbidden love for his benefactor. And he knew Morgan felt that way, maybe more so, knowing what he was risking. Luke wasn't exactly the horse to pick to cross any finish lines.

MORGAN FELT a hand on his shoulder in the cafeteria lineup. He swung around to see Gena, his housekeeper and long-time friend. She was an advocate of Luke and Morgan getting together when they were on shaky legs.

"Morgan." She enveloped him in a hug. "You should be up with Jessie and Luke. I could get food for you."

He opened his mouth to tell her he needed a break. That to be strong, he needed a bit of time to shore up, but he saw her read his face, find her answer there.

"Everything is okay back home?"

"The hands will remove Jessie's…." Gena's voice got husky. "Horse. When they get the okay from the crime-scene crew."

Morgan felt grief move in his heart. Jessie had loved her delicate little Arabian. Luke didn't want that breed for her, but Jessie talked him into it, and he saw to working with the horse himself so he knew Jessie would be safe.

That a stranger killed Molly, Jessica's horse, and was instrumental in the overwhelming damage to Jessica's little body made him sick. He couldn't understand it. He couldn't even let himself think about it too long, or he'd throw up.

So he coped by thinking ahead. Surgeries—four, if they were lucky. Therapy. A live-in nurse. A walker, crutches. He visualized Jessie in all of those stages of recovery stubbornly while he waited another hour, listening to her heart beating and remembering when it hadn't.

God, he'd be wrecked if he thought about that again.

"Sit down." Gena left him to retrieve food for them both, taking the tray from his hands. He wasn't aware of what he'd even put on it. Coffee… some kind of fuel.

She returned. No coffee, which made him growl. "Peach tea? Really?"

"You're crashing, Morgan. You know it, and I know it. I used to see you do it a lot before Luke came in your life."

"So what? You think I didn't do that in residency? It's a way of life."

"It's a brutal way of life." But she went back, got him decaffeinated. He knew he'd have to be satisfied with that. She was a lioness with him and Luke, and both of them listened when she got tough.

Looking at her, he saw her hair was scraped back and a bit oily. She wore glasses and not her contacts. No makeup, which wasn't in character. She wore makeup to bed, for fuck's sake, not that he'd ever gone there with her—she told him. She was the ultimate girly girl.

And Jessica was hers as much as Luke and Morgan's. She helped take care of that baby for years. She sewed dresses for her, poured her love into Jess. And once confessed to Morgan she couldn't have children herself.

Jessica didn't just have two fathers in her unconventional family, but a mother too. And lots of extended family in the town, on the ranch, in the animals she loved and cared for.

He often thought despite Jessie's various ambitions that she'd make a great veterinarian.

"How's Luke?"

"He's begun talking in whole sentences."

Gena gave a weak smile. "Because he knows she won't leave us." Her eyes filled, and she grabbed a napkin. "Oh fuck. Sorry."

Morgan covered her hand. "Thank you for always being there for me. For all of us."

Gena hadn't married. She'd been engaged forever. Morgan had wanted to pry, but because he loved her, he didn't. He knew she was happy. Did it matter, getting married?

But he felt a faint burn in his gut.

The old argument. He wanted marriage with Luke.

Luke, full of his insecurities and his pride, refused the one time Morgan had asked.

So Morgan didn't ask again.

It was the price of keeping Luke.

And why was he thinking about this now? He wondered wearily. Except when something like this happened, it shattered the family and there were all these shards everywhere, and you could see the pieces and not the whole.

He rubbed his eyes again, seeing his plate was empty. He was refueled. Good. He got up, feeling as mechanical as Luke, and went to get his lover a tray and coffee. No way would Luke accept herb tea.

THE SPECIALIST talked to them midafternoon.

Luke didn't follow everything, though the guy tried to spell it out clearly. He showed them the X-rays, which Luke found hard to look at. He could see the damage. He stood there with his arms crossed, watching Morgan ask the questions, listening to Morgan's request to be there for the second surgery, and he thought, *He expects to do this. He expects her to live this long and to have this surgery.*

The talk of recovery nearly broke him again.

And he looked at Morgan and thought of the terrible burden he'd laid on him, couldn't help but do it because of who Luke was and because of who Morgan was…. And just like that, he could feel empathy again.

Morgan looked at him, and his face seemed to light up for a moment, the sun coming out from all those clouds.

They shared a look.

Their little girl was going to make it. It was their vow.

BUT JESSIE didn't seem to know about any vows her fathers had taken, or the people waiting to hear how she was. She floated, and Morgan could feel her still in that twilight place between her body and the place where he couldn't heal her.

Never had he been more frustrated as a doctor, as a father.

Now it was Luke who was the strong one.

Luke suddenly believed. Not knew, not had faith. He believed their daughter would come back to them.

He began to study the files on surgeries and therapies, and Morgan could see him working it out like how he'd help with abused horses sometimes, putting together broken pieces, building peace and happiness with his callused hands and his easy voice and his belief in himself.

When the medical facts got tangled with worry, when Jessie's doctor remained apprehensive, Morgan leaned on Luke.

A quiet knock on the door broke the spell of hours of more waiting.

Morgan looked up, automatically wiping his eyes, which were, yes, wet.

Reverend Doyle waited at the open door, looking at Luke, his own eyes bloodshot since he'd been one of the townsfolk holding a vigil for Jess.

Luke squeezed Jessica's fingers and climbed to his feet. "Gotta go for a moment, Princess."

Luke gave Morgan a weak grin, still a shadow of the one that was lightning and sunshine all in one punch. Then his face sobered. "I have things to make right with God."

And Morgan knew Luke would confide in Doyle, and it was right he do so. He had taken a life, and oh God, Morgan hated that his Luke should ever have had to do that.

He watched both men leave and went to sit next to Jessie in Luke's place, touching her fingers as he did. Luke had been reading her Harry Potter. He picked up the novel and resumed, knowing she could hear him. From time to time, he leaned over and stroked the hair from her face and rearranged the dingy bunny Gena had dug out of Jessie's old things, just as much to comfort Luke and Morgan, as Jessie, Morgan thought.

Since he had her attention and Luke was gone, Morgan told her again how they needed her, how she was the strong one.

He went back to the book, trying to bring some emotion to his reading.

And Jessie's fingers twitched under his.

"I DON'T know how she's come this far, Mr. Walker, but her vitals are improving," Jessie's doctor told Luke.

"Of course they are," Luke said, wiping his eyes. "Thanks."

As he and Morgan returned to Jessie's room, it wasn't clear who was leaning on whom.

"Did you make it okay with God?" Morgan was a believer who had luckily found a comfortable fit with the mission in Sylvan. Luke, he hadn't been too sure about. He observed holidays, but Morgan always thought his faith was reserved for his daughter.

"I don't like shooting coyotes," Luke said. "And I don't see the difference in what I had to do. The reverend made it right with me."

Morgan knew actually Luke only shot animals too injured in the wild to survive. He was too tenderhearted to ever hunt. "Okay."

JESSICA HAD a second surgery for her back two weeks later.

She didn't remember what happened to her, which Luke was relieved over. They hired a therapist nevertheless so she'd have someone to talk through her ongoing ordeal, though Jess told them both it was just an obstacle course, and she'd run it and be okay again.

That made Morgan go into the hallway so he could cry.

What was hardest for Luke was telling her he had to put down her beloved horse, Molly.

That really hurt Jessica. She cried so hard they had to sedate her.

Luke felt terrible. He went home that evening and worked on the old barn and managed to break his hand. He told Morgan it was an accident.

Morgan was swearing as he sat with Luke through it being x-rayed, told Luke he wasn't buying it.

Yeah, okay, he'd punched the wall.

It was hard, so hard, to watch Jess accept the pain, pain Luke would take himself, into his own stronger, larger, and adult body, if he could. To see his little girl suffer was the toughest shit he'd ever endured.

All through this her mother never got in touch, though they tried to leave word. Luke worked to forgive her. He knew she'd come if she heard. She was who she was, and she hadn't shaken the empty party life that led to Jessica's creation.

And that made Luke feel sorry for her, even with what they'd all been through the past weeks. Because love was life. It was risk. It was adventure. It was meaning.

Morgan began to work again, half shifts, coming back to the hospital for long nights and early mornings. Luke stayed at her side throughout. He put Gena in charge of his cowboys, which delighted her. She bought some cowgirl boots she carried into Jessie's room to show off to her.

And Luke looked for another horse for Jessica. It was his way of believing she'd be well enough to ride again when her leg was in a sling and her arms and her body slowly healed.

He was afraid to let her do that, but he knew he had to because she wanted it. Though he knew she wasn't ready to replace Molly.

Luke had buried the mare in the woods where they all liked to walk on summer evenings. He felt it was important the horse not be taken from Jessica. That one day she could walk there and leave wild flowers on the little stand of rocks.

A COUPLE of months later, Luke actually found himself in the cottage alone with Morgan. They met in the bathroom, Luke coming out of the shower, Morgan going in.

They hadn't had sex, or anything, in all the time Jessie was lying in that bed.

Luke looked at Morgan, and next thing he was grabbing him and Morgan grabbing him back, and they kissed wildly.

The water continued to run.

They came together on the bathroom floor. Morgan hit his head on the toilet. Luke sprained his wrist. Well used, well loved, they lay there.

"Someone needs to turn off the water," Morgan groaned.

"It's cold now, dear."

Morgan snickered, and then Luke did, and then they were laughing. The tears came, Luke felt like a frigging tap lately, but the sex was a storm, a reprieve, a thanksgiving, a coming together.

A hello?

The thought traced across his mind like animal tracks.

Where were he and Morgan?

He gazed at his lover, and Morgan looked back.

No one got up to switch off the water for a while.

Part Two

THE DAY they brought Jessica back home and bundled her up in blankets in the great room by a fire with Gena cooking dinner, was a big day for the little family.

Morgan couldn't help but remember another dinner he once made to help Luke, a straight man, feel more comfortable with him under the same roof. It didn't go over well.

Things had changed since then.

Luke had made the live-edge table with his own hands, and the hand-hewn chairs, Gena the quilted runner, which was covered with bowls of steaming food and vases of wildflowers to welcome Jessie home.

Half the town wanted to come by, but it was just family. Gena, Morgan, Luke, and Jessie.

Jessie had a walker, which she despised. They had to take up all the hand-coiled rugs so she wouldn't trip.

"How does it feel to defy all the doctor's ideas and get well much faster than predicted?" Gena asked.

"I still walk like a dork," Jessica sulked.

"You aren't a dork," Luke said.

"Sam said so." Morgan found that difficult to believe. Samuel was as shy and quiet as his father, Aaron. But he was utterly devoted to Jessie.

As Morgan watched, indulgent, feeling better than in months, Luke braided her hair. He had learned how to french braid it just for her. And her blonde hair, the same wheat color as Luke's, turning and twisting as Luke styled it, brought it home they truly had her back.

The house felt different. Not empty and haunted as it was without her.

He wondered, if Luke and he made it long enough, how they'd get through empty-nest syndrome, because he had a feeling it would be an issue for them both.

Of course Luke always said sex was the solution to everything.

He met Luke's eyes over Jessie's head, seeing the shared amusement there. Luke knew what he was thinking. He always knew, blast him.

But then later they'd see under their quilt together.

When Luke carried Jessie to the table, she looked at Morgan and then Luke. "Can I see Sam?"

Luke sighed. "Soon."

She looked disgruntled. "I'm going to miss the wedding."

Aaron and Nate were set to marry in a week in a quiet ceremony in a meadow. Jessie had been excited about it for weeks since they'd asked her to be their flower girl. She and Samuel had endured teasing about their families from time to time, but Jessie was impatient with it and Luke had had to rescue a kid she'd once given a black eye.

"I can't even hobble," she grumped.

"So I'll carry you," Luke said. "And you can carry the fu—uh, frigging flowers."

"So when are you two finally going to get married?" Jessie asked.

JESSIE FELL asleep halfway through dinner, so Luke carried her up to the loft. She'd had the nerve to make her announcement, stir up both her dads, and then eat and fall asleep just like she had when she was a baby.

Luke figured she'd be tying gunpowder to his ass the rest of his life.

He looked forward to it.

He didn't look forward to talking to Morgan.

But they needed to.

Too much went unsaid during their ordeal. Too much was ripped away, their sense of security, for one thing, although Morgan brought in some really tough men to protect them now. If Luke let him, he'd have his own frigging bodyguard.

"I know what happened was my fault," Morgan said as Luke sat beside him on the couch by the fire.

"Oh, you do?" Luke heard the silky menace in his own tone. Morgan snapped his head toward him.

"Be reasonable."

"I will when you will."

Morgan sighed. "If I had just given all that money away…."

"You did that already!" Luke shouted. Then he flushed, looking to Jessie's loft upstairs. Remembering when he first came to live there and he shared the space with her up there.

"Sorry," he said, giving his own sigh. "You gave away a lot of it to charity. Your father's company just made more. This is your life, Morgan. And we agreed to keep the machinery going for all the charities."

Morgan nodded. He knew Luke was right. The money was mostly tied up in trusts. Their hope was their daughter would one day take over all those charities. Something they both knew she would be amazing doing.

Luke looked at his big hands, wishing he had Morgan's gift of words. "What happened, just happened, Morgan. It was bad luck." Somehow it sat ugly in Luke's stomach, putting it that way, but he breathed in and out, finally letting it go. "The man was sick."

"Yes," Morgan agreed. "I was thinking maybe you and I could use some therapy?"

"What for?" Luke knew his tone wasn't exactly reasonable now. "Oh, you mean for me? Sorry, Doc, I made it right with God. That was enough."

Morgan relaxed. "I see it is. I've worried…."

"Too much." Luke had to look away, take a deep breath. "About what Jessie said."

But Morgan stiffened. "You are *not* marrying me because your daughter asked you to!"

Luke reddened. "It's not like that!"

"From where I'm sitting, it is!"

They were both breathing roughly. Luke foresaw sleeping in the barn, and it pissed him off. "I can't talk to you right now," he said, getting to his feet.

Morgan turned away, studying the fire.

And Luke headed outdoors, resigned to a night in a lonely bed. Well, he'd fucked that up, so what did he expect? Morgan had pride too.

If Luke wanted to find his way back to him after all they'd been through, he'd have to swallow some of his own.

THEY DIDN'T talk again about all those things between them for a few months after that, though sometimes they both lay awake, and Luke felt everything unsaid burning in his heart.

But Jessica required all their free time. It wasn't easy learning to walk again. She had to do that on legs as shaky as wet pasta.

And she was still afraid to go outside.

It wasn't an issue at first because she wasn't exactly mobile. Luke knew she wanted to go to Molly's grave, make her pilgrimage, but she had nightmares, and then she made excuses.

Morgan insisted she take baby steps to regaining her confidence. Hence dance class.

They both went with her the first day, leaning against the wall, watching her in the beginner's class. She'd once taught it. Now she had to rediscover her mobility one faltering step at a time.

"I hate that she's here," Luke said.

Morgan looked at him.

"No, I mean that she has to start again."

But then Luke thought maybe she wasn't the only one. The crack between him and Morgan was growing and growing.

"I was afraid to go riding on my own," Morgan admitted. "Even knowing all the new security, the cameras and fences and guards. We're a glass window, and it feels like anyone with a rock can just… break us."

Luke scowled. "They didn't manage it before, did they?"

Morgan let out a breath. "No, you're right. We made it."

"Life hurts sometimes. But she's alive." Luke swallowed and then said it, out there in public where they couldn't be overheard, but they also couldn't make a scene. "I would have killed myself if she'd died."

Morgan closed his eyes. "I know."

"We haven't talked about it."

"*Christ!* You think I can calmly talk about that?"

"It wouldn't be because I don't love you. That's all."

Morgan held his gaze. "I know it. It's just… I live with a caveman. And sometimes I forget." He tried to make a joke of it, but Luke knew he was right.

"That's a cowboy."

"There's a difference? I haven't noticed. Especially when we're—" He leaned close to Luke, whispered in his ear.

Luke reddened. Damn Morgan.

POLISHING A saddle gave a man time to think, and Luke needed that. So much about the barn, the old cottage, and the fully restored outbuildings tugged at his heart as he looked outside, moving his hands absently.

When he first came here, the place was falling apart, and he felt needed.

More, he felt grounded in the work. He didn't know then about Morgan's wealth, and neither of them knew that would only increase beyond what Luke ever imagined. Luke had owned a horse, his truck, and a trailer. He never put a down payment on a house. He'd never really been anywhere, except once he went to Boston with Morgan—but that was a nightmare, and he'd returned early.

Morgan had traveled before they got together. He once joked to Luke he'd done so much he didn't need to do any more now.

But was that true?

Wasn't it an aspect of Morgan's personality, liking to travel? He certainly spent a lot of time over the dinner table telling their daughter about places he'd visited. Last night it was Santorini, a tiny white village topping brown cliffs in Greece. Morgan brought out his old albums to show Jessica pictures, including a comical one of Morgan riding a donkey.

Luke enjoyed teasing him about that one.

A knock on the barn door caught Luke's attention. Morgan stood watching him, looking like his ordinary Morgan, work shirt, boots, and jeans. He used to dress a little better, as Luke recalled. But now he basically dressed... like Luke.

No, he dressed like their lifestyle, which was camping under the stairs, bonfires, and horses, the town they both loved, and Jessica.

But somehow seeing him with fresh eyes now, it bothered Luke. Morgan had once liked to dress up too. To go out for dinner, until Luke's discomfort anywhere but the town diner had put paid to that.

"Where's our daughter?" Luke asked. He always needed to know now. He hoped to hell he'd get over that, or he'd be one of those helicopter parents, and Jessie wouldn't stand for that.

"Doing her homework with her tutor at the house. Luke, I was thinking…. Maybe she should get away for a while."

Luke felt his back muscles stiffen. Jesus, he knew this was something new coming, and he hated change. He took a deep breath, though, and let it go. Yes, change. But looking at Morgan, he could see a lot of the silent compromise in their relationship was on his part.

It was time for Luke to do his.

"I think I should take her on a holiday."

"But she's my daughter." And he hadn't just said that. Nope, he had.

Morgan's face darkened, but his gaze remained steady. "Yes. So either you have to man up and come with us, or we'll have to arrange for Gena to come with your permission since I'm not legally anything to Jessica."

"You're not—"

"When I brought her into the hospital, the only reason I was permitted to stay with her and to assist was because I was a physician from a nearby town. They did not acknowledge me as her family."

"That's fucked!" Luke tossed the saddle, the thump it made loud between them.

"It is, but it's the way it is, Luke. I have no rights but what you share with me."

And Luke didn't share any more than living in the same house. Of course Morgan was her father in all but name. He nursed her through colds. He was there in a hundred extraordinary ways Luke couldn't even count.

And Luke…. Luke was just waiting to see if things would work out.

Eight years in it was pretty clear he was the one holding them back now, clinging to a safety net that could never exist between two free souls.

"Oh God, Morg. I didn't think."

Morgan sighed, rubbing the back of his neck. "I know you didn't. I was afraid to push, to rock the boat with you. I always knew I had more to lose."

"What do you mean?"

"I mean if you left me, Luke, I'd lose not only you, but I'd lose the only child I'll ever have."

Morgan's words hit Luke right in the solar plexus. God, how could he have been so blind, so selfish? He'd worried so much about the world, thinking he was using Morgan for his money, but he'd instead been using him in an insidious and personal way.

He cleared his throat. "How do we fix it?"

Morgan's eyes sharpened. "Excuse me?"

"I mean… how do *I* fix it? I let my pride, my fear, rule us."

"I gave you the rope."

Luke twisted his lips. "And now I'm hanging. Morgan, she's yours as much as mine. You have to know that."

"Do I? You refer to her as your daughter sometimes in public, and it sounds true, yet when I do, I always feel self-conscious, like it's not."

"We can do something. We have to."

Morgan sat on a stack of hay, and Luke sat next to him. Now Luke felt like old, golden times with his love. He tangled their hands together. "We never christened this barn, you know."

Morgan laughed. "Au contraire, we did, and often. In the sun shower the first time, and the loft, and the—"

Luke laughed. "No, not what I meant." He pulled out his knife and stood.

"Luke, if this is some kind of western blood-brother ceremony, I'll pass."

Luke just shook his head and put the blade to the wood pillar in front of him, carving his initials in. He handed the blade to Morgan, who did the same. Luke added a plus symbol between them.

Then in the dust and sunlight pooling in, Luke sank to one knee in front of Morgan. "Morgan Gallagher, will you marry up with me?"

MORGAN FELT tears prick, but he had to laugh at Luke's exaggerated hick drawl. "Marry up? Is that related to gittyup?"

"Yes, sir."

Morgan got down next to Luke.

"I'll make it right," Luke whispered, reaching out to cup Morgan's face.

And Morgan thought, *I'm not getting over him. So why not take the final dare?*

"See that you do, cowboy," he muttered before kissing Luke. "And if you think we'll do this without the town...."

Luke groaned. "Set a date."

"When our daughter is well. I want her to walk us both up the aisle, Luke."

"You know she'll want a killer pink dress for that. Pink, Morgan. It will find its way onto our clothing for sure."

Morgan smiled, thinking of it. Now that was a visualization he hadn't held amongst all the others that kept him going when she was in the hospital.

But if the others had all come true, why not this one?

Epilogue

JULY CAME fast and hot, more days of dust and sweat. But this July day, Sylvan dressed itself in Jessica Walker-Gallagher's favorite color, pink.

There were balloons in the town, some rocking in the hands of youngsters. There were ribbons on the local library, which Morgan had pitched in to renovate. And the church was decorated in pink sweetheart roses by Aaron King, from flowers he grew himself.

Morgan, Luke, and Jessica parked in Morgan's sleek Tesla just outside town. Then both men, dressed up in Italian handmade suits, but with pink roses as boutonnieres, walked Jessica down Main Street. Since in Sylvan that was also the only street, it was a quick walk.

Morgan had a list of gratitude a mile long running through his head. He was grateful Jessica had finally visited Molly's grave a month ago and made peace. Grateful he and Luke found a new horse for her she was warming up to. Grateful he finally—finally!—after all these years, had his real family.

He'd be married to the man of his heart.

As they approached the mission where they first met almost nine years ago, all Morgan could think was it was fate that brought them together.

But love would keep them that way.

LUKE LEANED back in his chair high up in the white artificial hills of Oia, perched above the dark void of ocean below. Morgan was sipping his coffee, watching Luke. "Santorini to your liking?"

"It's an alien world. I never imagined…." Luke hadn't liked the long flights because he needed to move, to walk, but finally he'd been able to sleep. They brought Jessica and Gena since it was their honeymoon, and why not? Neither of them wanted their daughter to stay at home, although they'd put their foot down on inviting Sam too. Jessie could spend the rest of the summer with her beloved friend when they returned. "And a pool in our bedroom!"

Luke smiled. Personally he was hard-pressed not to put a pool in their room back home. Watching Morgan swim naked and come out of the water, wet and dripping and hard bodied while Luke waited on the bed….

It wasn't so bad.

"I still can't get over spending an actual month away from the ranch."

That was Morgan's request. And Luke agreed without hesitation. He wanted to show Morgan how much he mattered.

"So I've got a deal for you," Luke drawled.

"Oh yeah?" Morgan leaned forward, shoving aside the remains of their baklava.

"I've got a baby in my truck, and I don't know what I'm doing, how to take care of her. I'm going out of my mind tryin'."

"And I've got a home that's so empty it echoes at night."

Luke rubbed Morgan's gold ring. "It seems we can help each other."

"No," Morgan said, absolutely serious now. "I think we saved each other."

JAN IRVING has worked in all kinds of creative fields, from painting silk to making porcelain ceramics to interior design, but her award-winning writing is always her touchstone.

She feels you can't fully understand characters until you follow their journey through a story world. Many kinds of worlds interest her—fantasy, historical, science fiction, and suspense—but all have one thing in common: people finding a way to live together and accept themselves—in the most emotional and satisfying fashion possible, of course!

Visit Jan at her website at janirvingwrites.com.

Mastering Toby

Jan Irving

Jared Asche has secretly loved Toby Rafferty from the moment he grabbed Toby's bare ass and had pretend sex with him for the cameras on the soap *Mission Bay*. But Jared knows Toby is straight and just needs a friend, so he lives with the pain of unrequited love… until Toby impulsively kisses him, crossing the line between friends and lovers.

Despite his fears about being with another man, Toby pursues him, and Jared is helpless to refuse as their passion explodes during a sexy game. Confused, Jared decides to take a trip to see a longtime friend for advice, leaving an insecure Toby vulnerable to the advances of his ex-girlfriend.

Jared's hopes for life and love with Toby are crushed—but Toby's not willing to give up. He'll have to convince Jared that his intentions are serious if they're going to weather this and other threats to their newborn relationship.

www.dreamspinnerpress.com

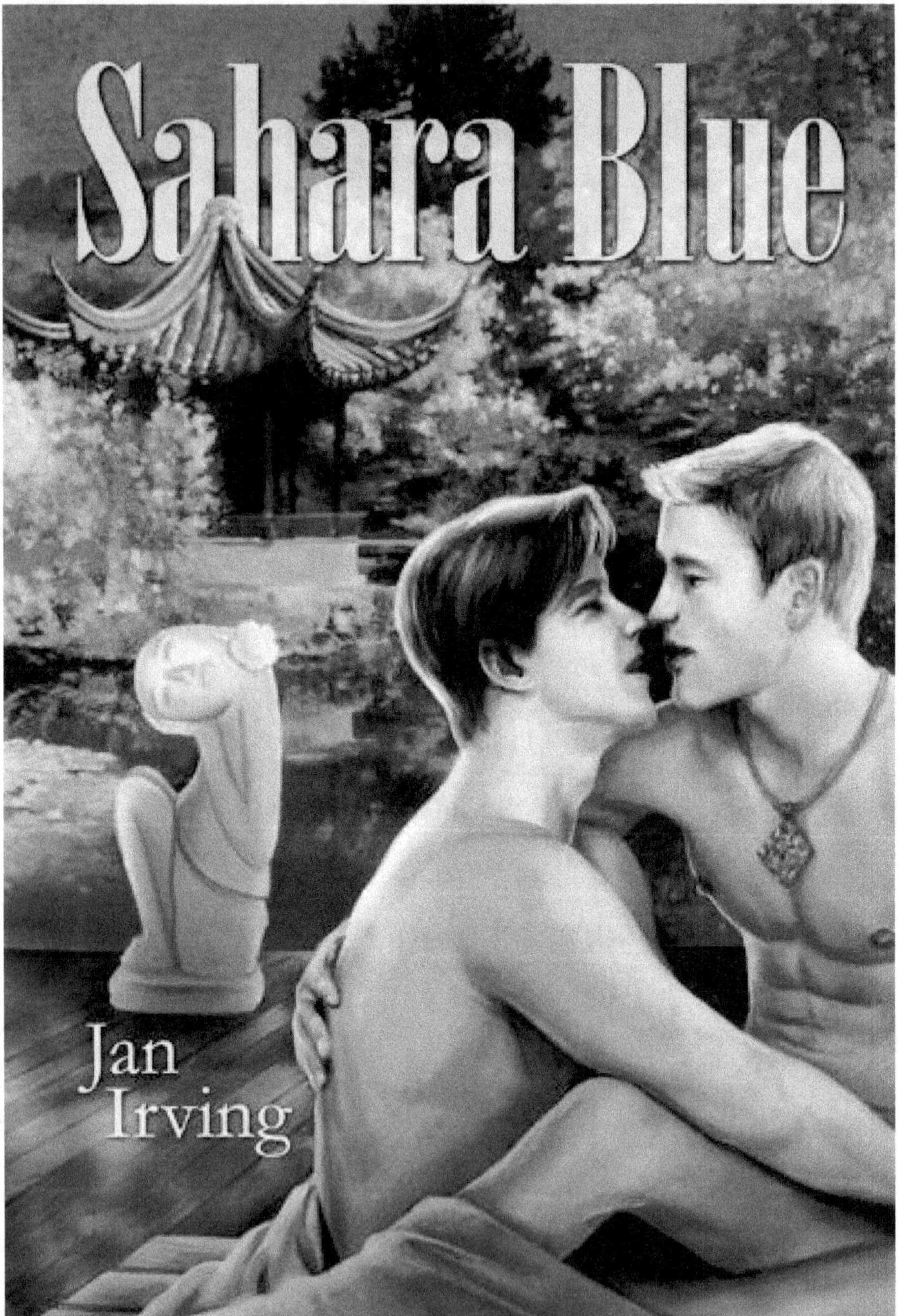
Sahara Blue
Jan Irving

A spin-off of *Mastering Toby*

Seth Hollis lives his passions online under the pseudonym "Lotus" and attracts ex-Navy SEAL Sahara Blue, who avidly follows the erotic tales of passionate submission Seth posts. While they forge a powerful connection, it's increasingly frustrating, because both men yearn for something real. Seth's writings have also attracted an unwanted and dangerous admirer, and when the glass window of Seth's shop is shattered one night, fate sends Sahara Blue to his rescue.

Unaware he has actually met Lotus, Sahara takes Seth under his wing, and that same mysterious and deep attraction flares to life. But Seth's deranged stalker won't let up, and Seth and Sahara will have to give up their secrets and learn to trust if they're going to keep each other safe.

www.dreamspinnerpress.com

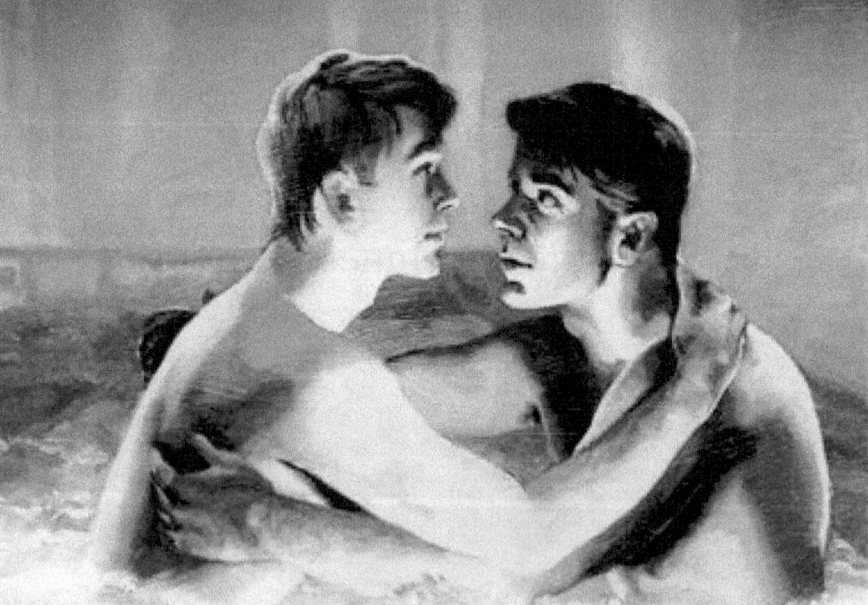

Wylde

Jan Irving

Noah Matthews brought his son Josh to the pristine woods of Washington State to make a fresh start. The first night in their new home, Noah meets Kell Farraday when the laconic police chief shows up on his doorstep searching for two people lost in the forest. It's the start of a sexy new friendship when Kell decides to pursue the shy but flirtatious Noah.

But a new beginning won't be so easy. Noah's former boyfriend shows up to try to reclaim a place in his life, and worse, Josh is drawn to the growing mystery in the forest. People disappear and then one turns up dead. There's something haunting the forest. Something watching. And soft-spoken and confident Kell's reassurances can't ease Noah's fear when Josh goes into the woods alone.

www.dreamspinnerpress.com

BORN TO BE Wylde

JAN IRVING

A spin-off of *Wylde*

Deputy Ken Ito wakes up from a nightmare in a strange place: a cave in the woods, cared for by a beautiful young man with long hair that smells of cedar. Ken falls under Wylde's spell, feeling like he's lost in one of those captive-captor romances: Wylde found him, saved him… and now he considers Ken his.

But Ken has to get back to his life and find out who beat him and left him for dead, suspecting it must have something to do with his investigation of disappearances on the remote stretch of road he patrols. Protective Wylde follows him and they begin a fledgling affair, but the danger to them—and their hearts—is following close behind.

www.dreamspinnerpress.com